P9-DDC-882

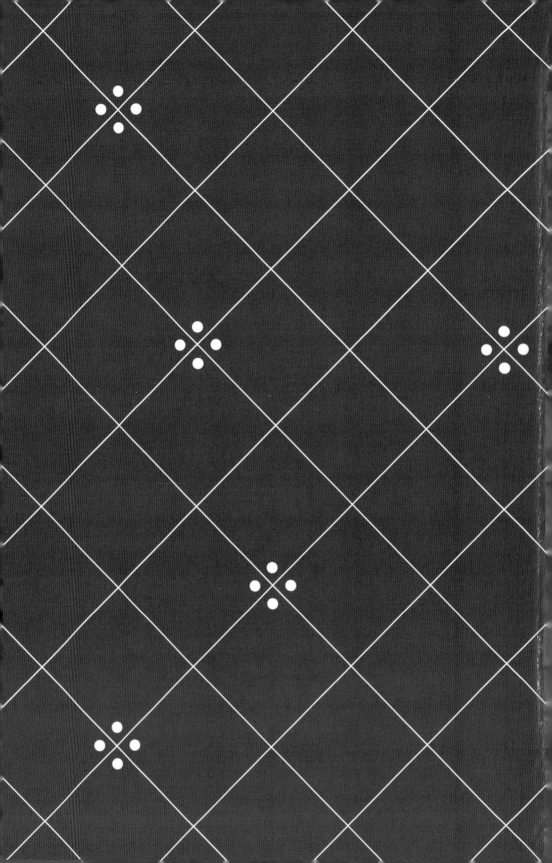

DRAGON KINGDOM
of Wrenly

THE COLDFIRE CURSE

By Jordan Quinn
Illustrated by Ornella Greco at Glass House Graphics

LITTLE SIMON

New York   London   Toronto   Sydney   New Delhi

This book is a work of fiction. Any references to historical events, real people, or real places are used fictitiously. Other names, characters, places, and events are products of the author's imagination, and any resemblance to actual events or places or persons, living or dead, is entirely coincidental.

LITTLE SIMON
An imprint of Simon & Schuster Children's Publishing Division
1230 Avenue of the Americas, New York, New York 10020
First Little Simon edition February 2021
Copyright © 2021 by Simon & Schuster, Inc.
All rights reserved, including the right of reproduction in whole or in part in any form.
LITTLE SIMON is a registered trademark of Simon & Schuster, Inc., and associated colophon is a trademark of Simon & Schuster, Inc. For information about special discounts for bulk purchases, please contact Simon & Schuster Special Sales at 1-866-506-1949 or business@simonandschuster.com. The Simon & Schuster Speakers Bureau can bring authors to your live event. For more information or to book an event, contact the Simon & Schuster Speakers Bureau at 1-866-248-3049 or visit our website at www.simonspeakers.com.
Designed by Kayla Wasil
Text by Matthew J. Gilbert
GLASS HOUSE GRAPHICS Creative Services
Art and cover by ORNELLA GRECO
Colors by ORNELLA GRECO and GABRIELE CRACOLICI
Lettering by GIOVANNI SPATARO/Grafimated Cartoon
Supervision by SALVATORE DI MARCO/Grafimated Cartoon
Manufactured in China 0222 SCP
6 8 10 9 7 5
Library of Congress Cataloging-in-Publication Data
Names: Quinn, Jordan, author. | Glass House Graphics, illustrator.
Title: The coldfire curse / by Jordan Quinn ; illustrated by Glass House Graphics.
Description: First Little Simon edition. | New York : Little Simon, 2021. | Series: Dragon kingdom of Wrenly ; book 1 | Audience: Ages 6–9 | Audience: Grades 2–3 | Summary: "Ruskin, the pet dragon of the royal family of Wrenly, forms new friendships with the dragons of Crestwood and goes on exciting adventures"–Provided by publisher.
Identifiers: LCCN 2020024829 (print) | LCCN 2020024830 (eBook) | ISBN 9781534475007 (paperback) ISBN 9781534475014 (hardcover) | ISBN 9781534475021 (eBook)
Subjects: LCSH: Graphic novels. | CYAC: Graphic novels. | Dragons–Fiction. | Fantasy.
Classification: LCC PZ7.7.Q55 Co 2021 (print) | LCC PZ7.7.Q55 (eBook) | DDC 741.5/973–dc23
LC record available at https://lccn.loc.gov/2020024829

Contents

Chapter 1

All was quiet on the island of Crestwood in the kingdom of Wrenly. Until...
FWOOOOOM
Looks like Ember's coming in *hot.*
Ummm... hot?

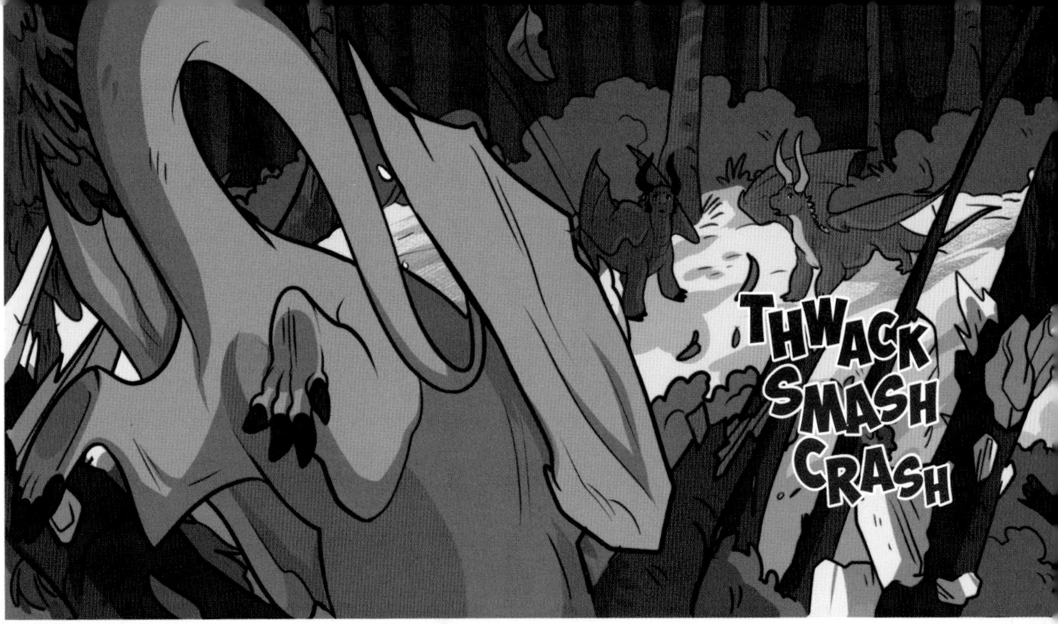
THWACK
SMASH
CRASH

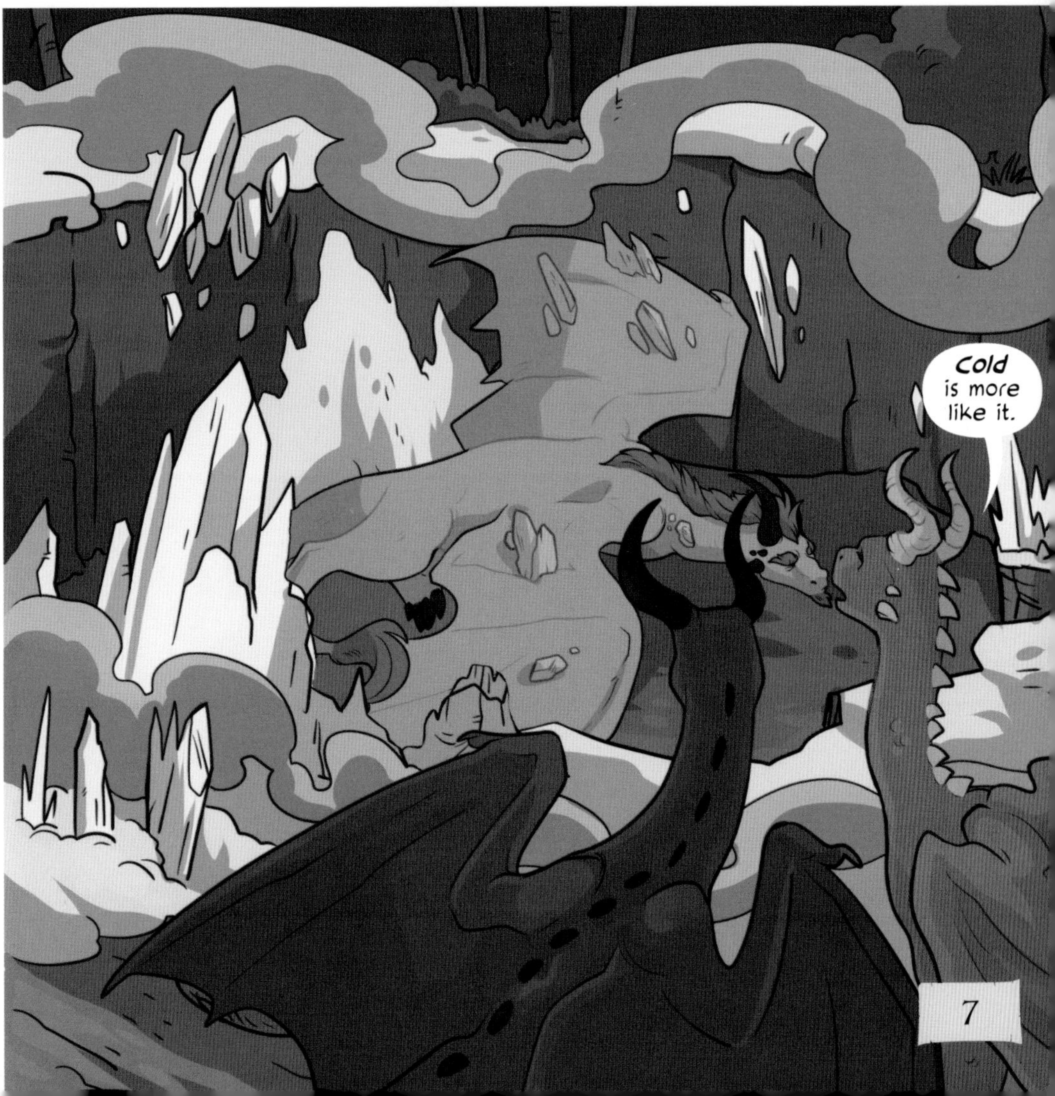
Cold is more like it.

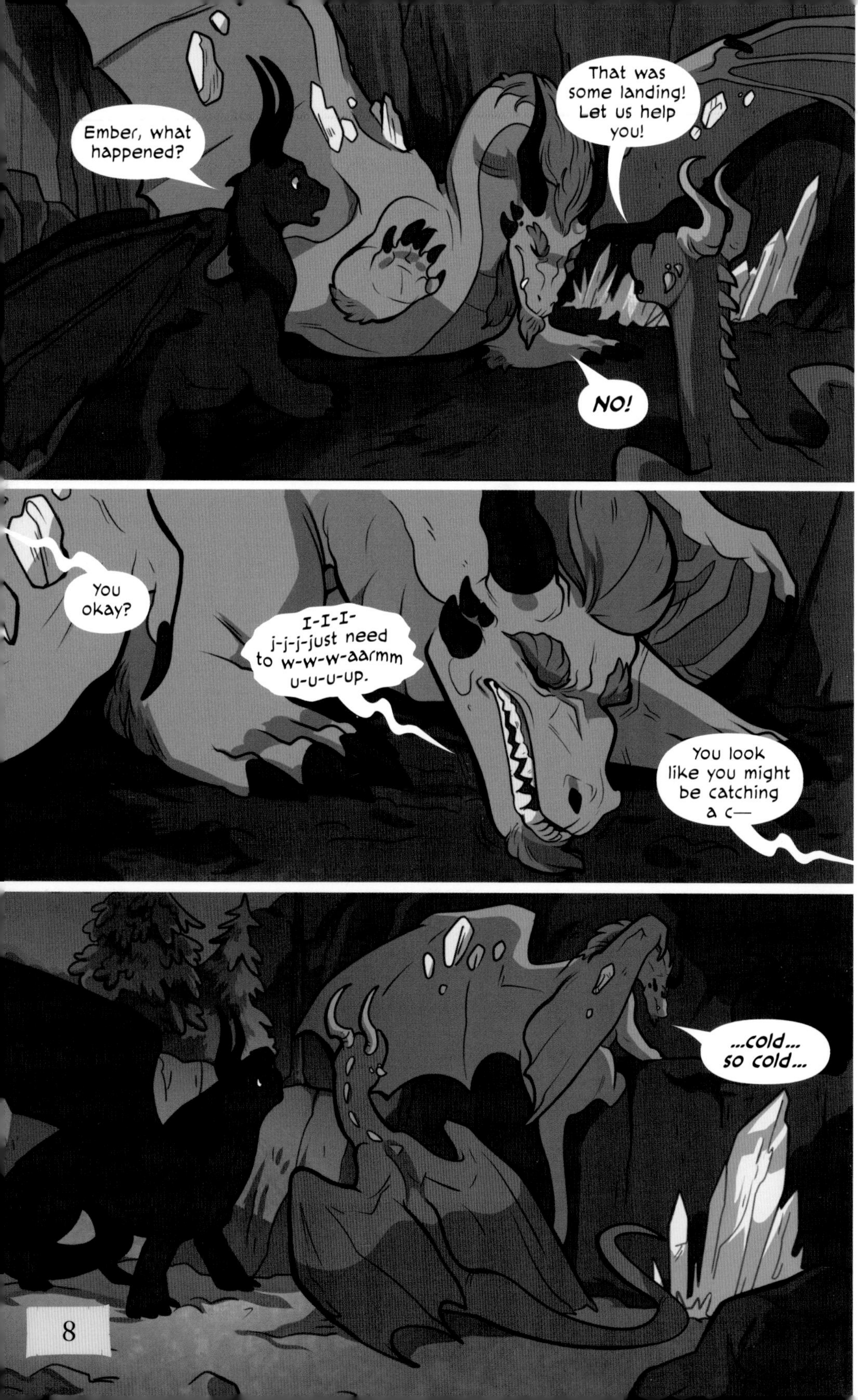
Ember, what happened?
That was some landing! Let us help you!
NO!
You okay?
I-I-I-j-j-j-just need to w-w-w-aarmm u-u-u-up.
You look like you might be catching a c—
...cold... so cold...

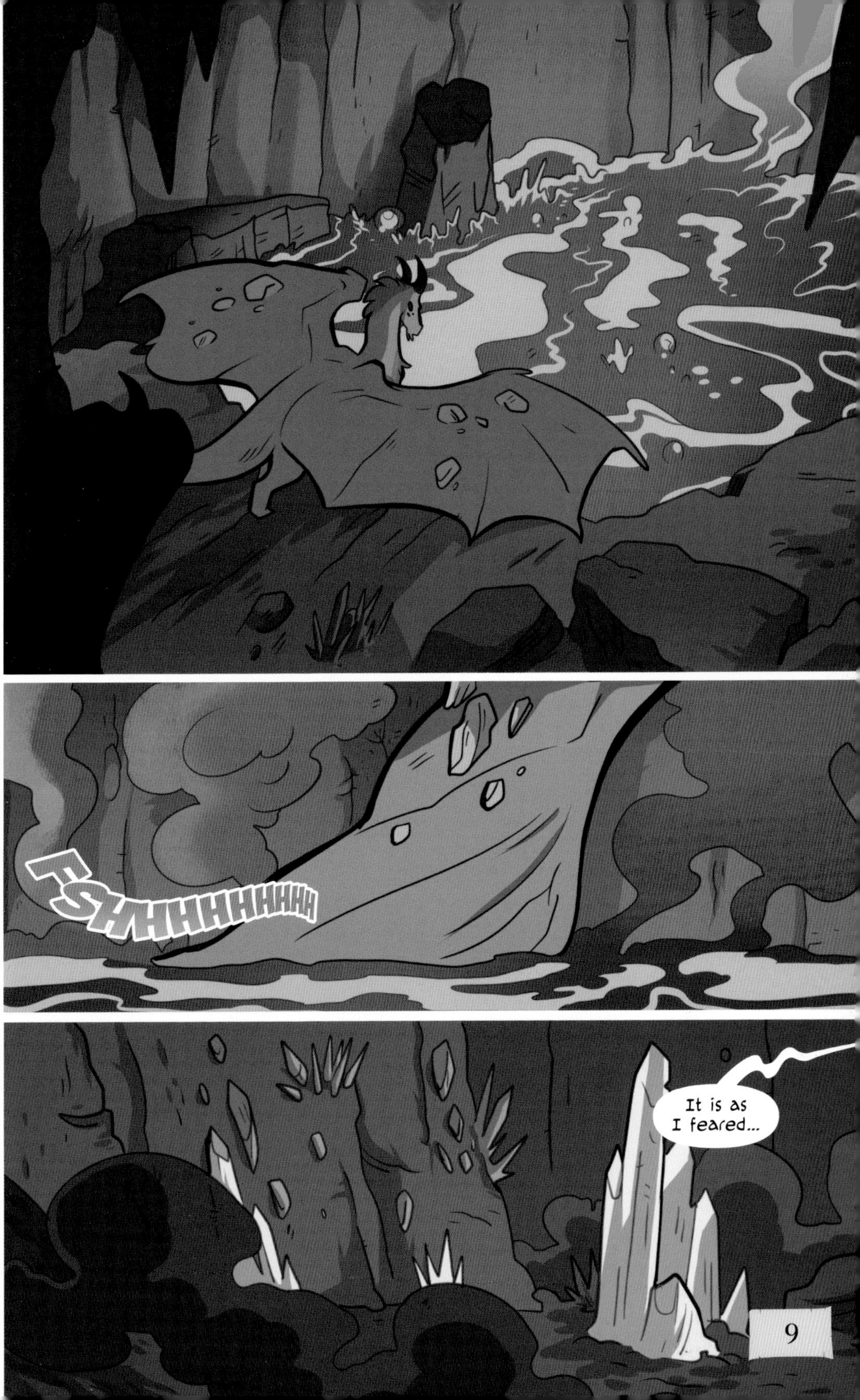
FSHHHHHHHHH
It is as I feared...

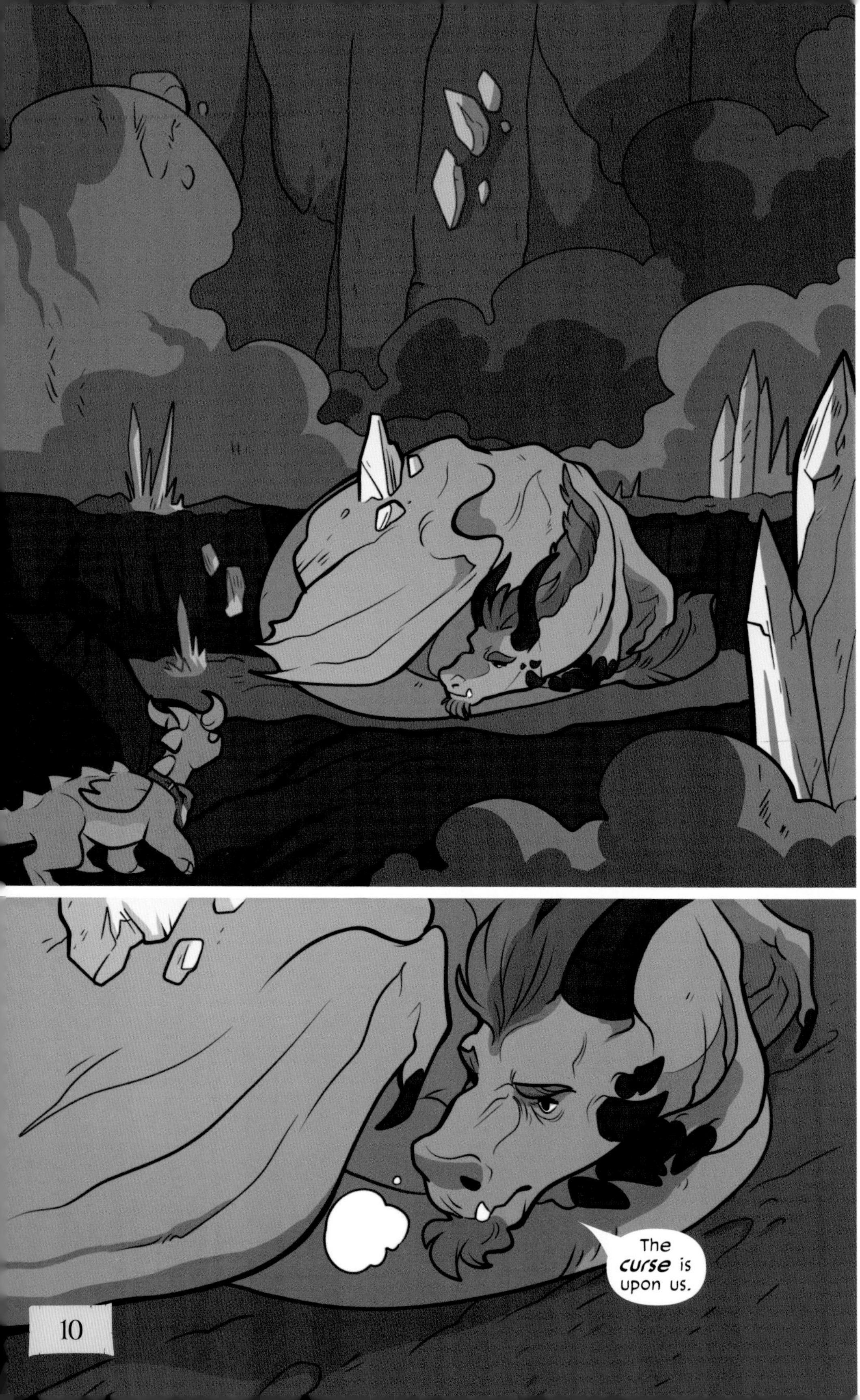
The curse is upon us.

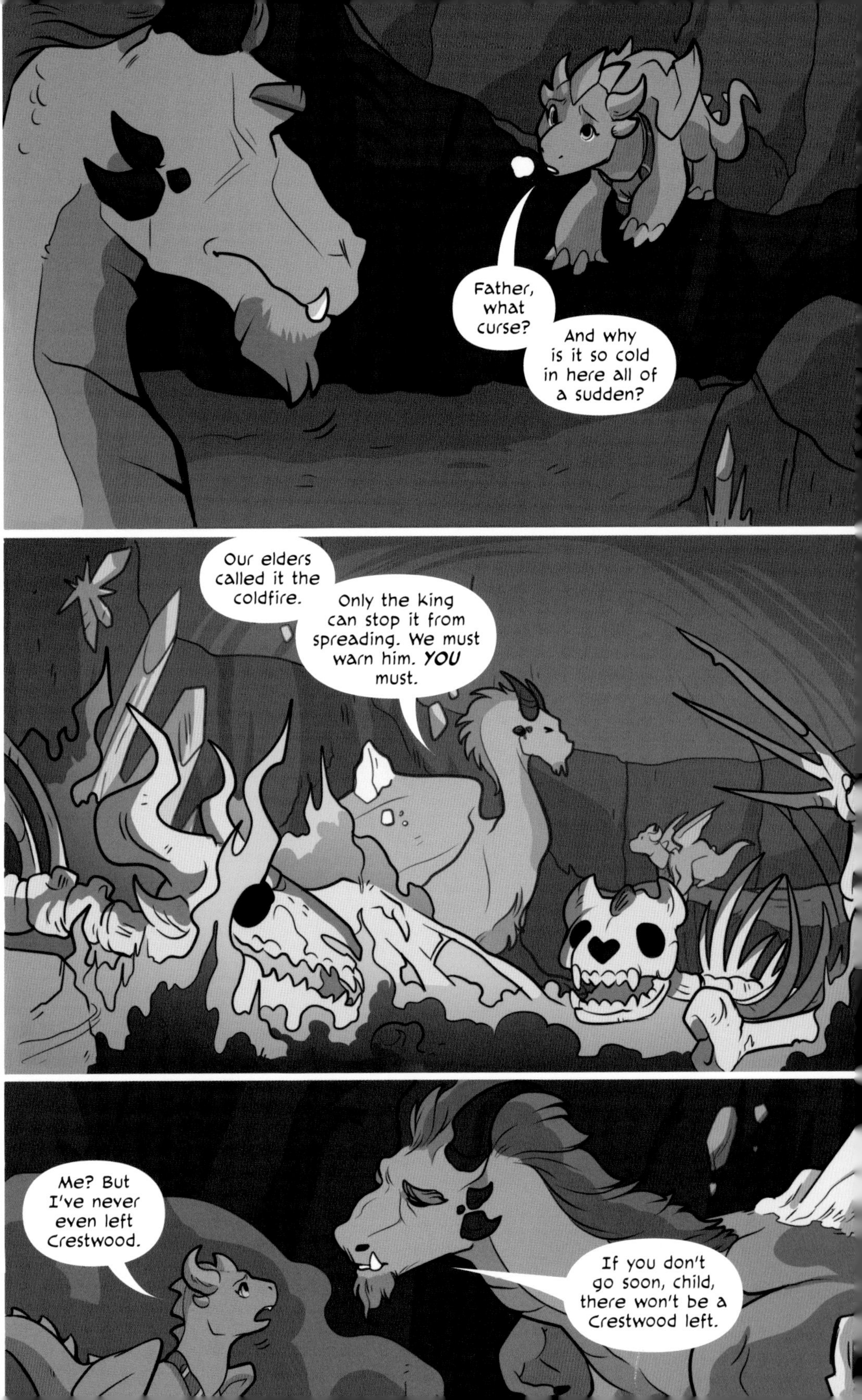
Father, what curse?
And why is it so cold in here all of a sudden?
Our elders called it the coldfire.
Only the king can stop it from spreading. We must warn him. ***YOU*** must.
Me? But I've never even left Crestwood.
If you don't go soon, child, there won't be a Crestwood left.

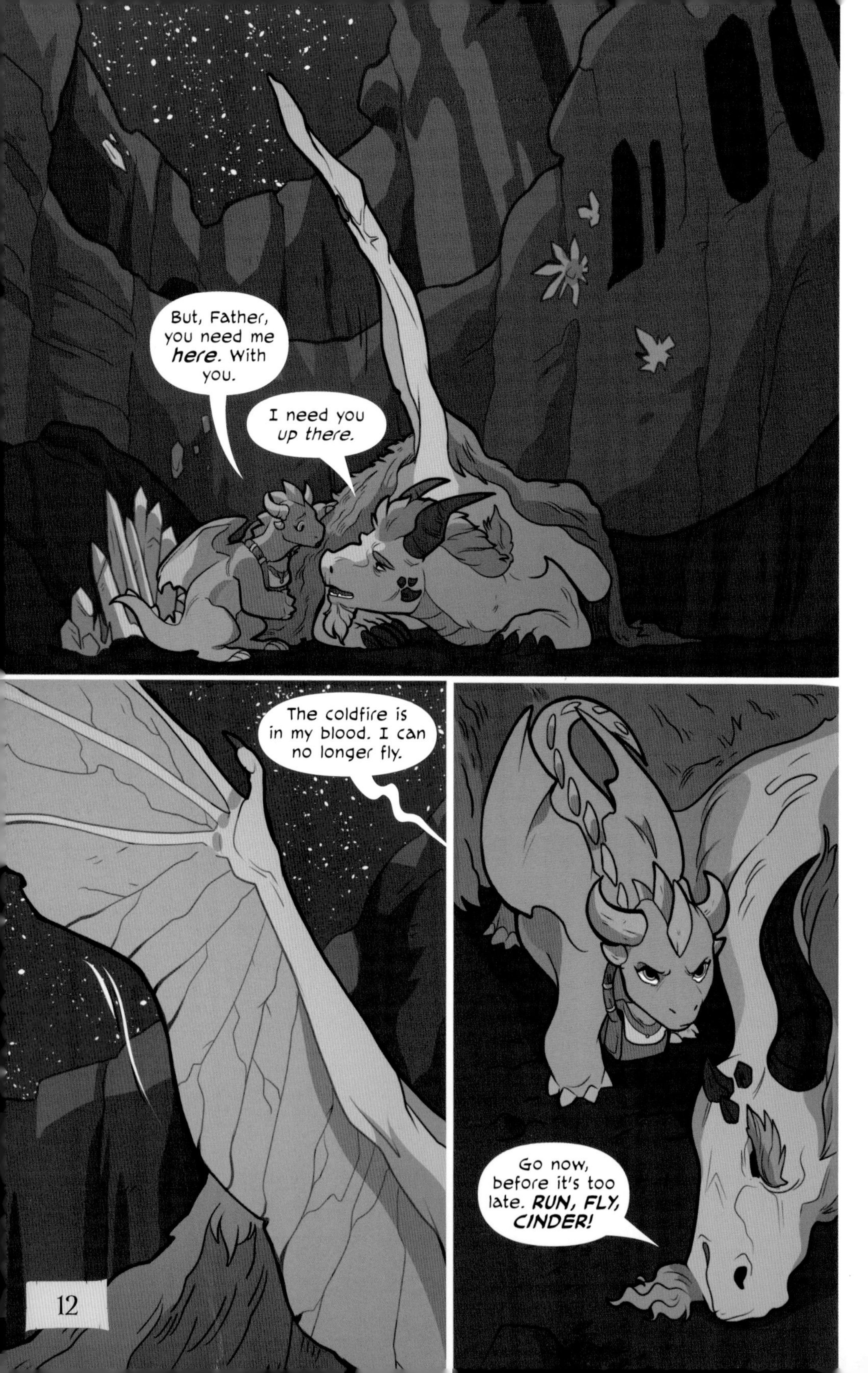
But, Father, you need me **here.** With you.
I need you *up there.*
The coldfire is in my blood. I can no longer fly.
Go now, before it's too late. ***RUN, FLY, CINDER!***

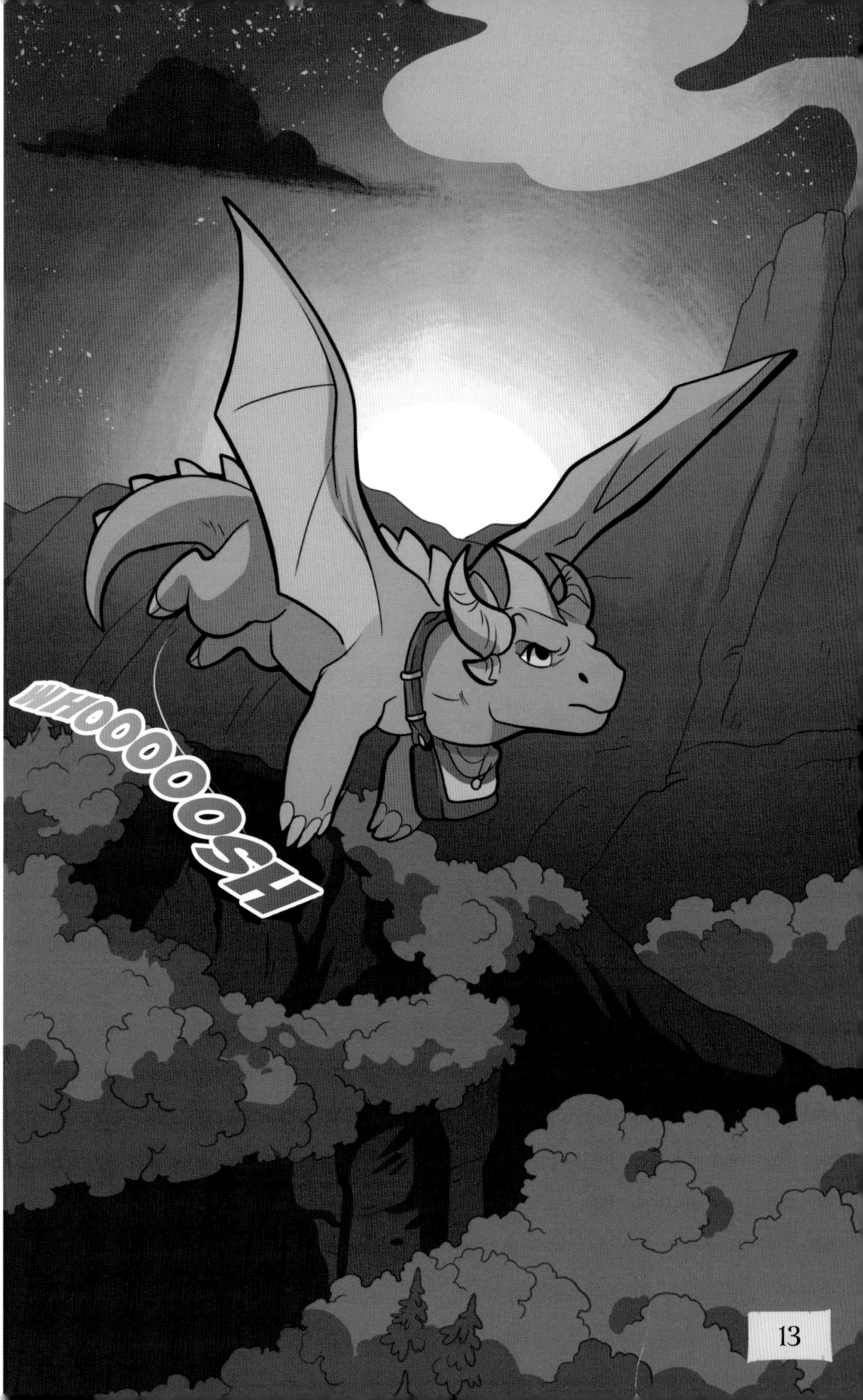
WHOOOOOSH

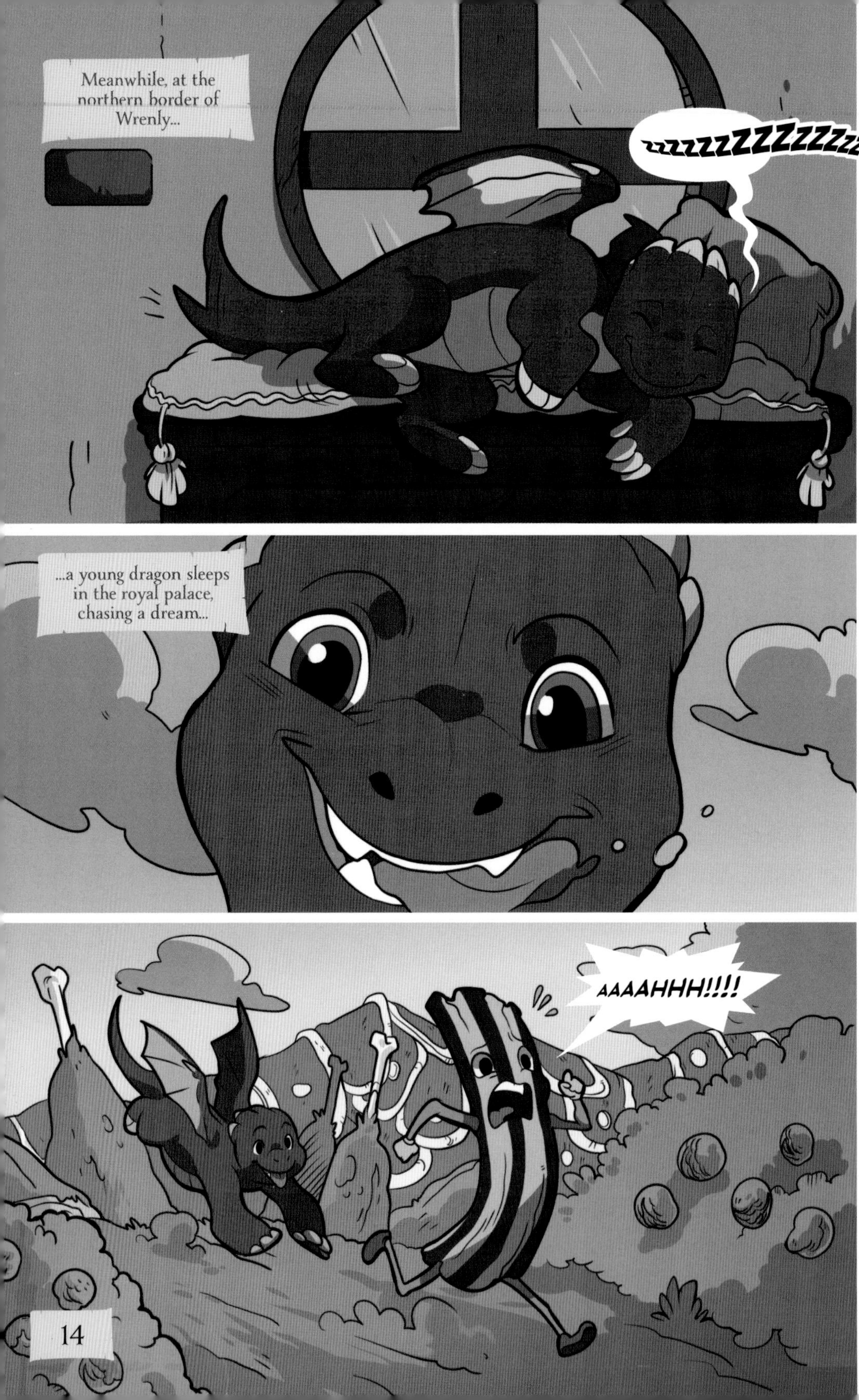

Meanwhile, at the northern border of Wrenly...
zzzzzzZZZZzzzzz
...a young dragon sleeps in the royal palace, chasing a dream...
AAAAHHH!!!!

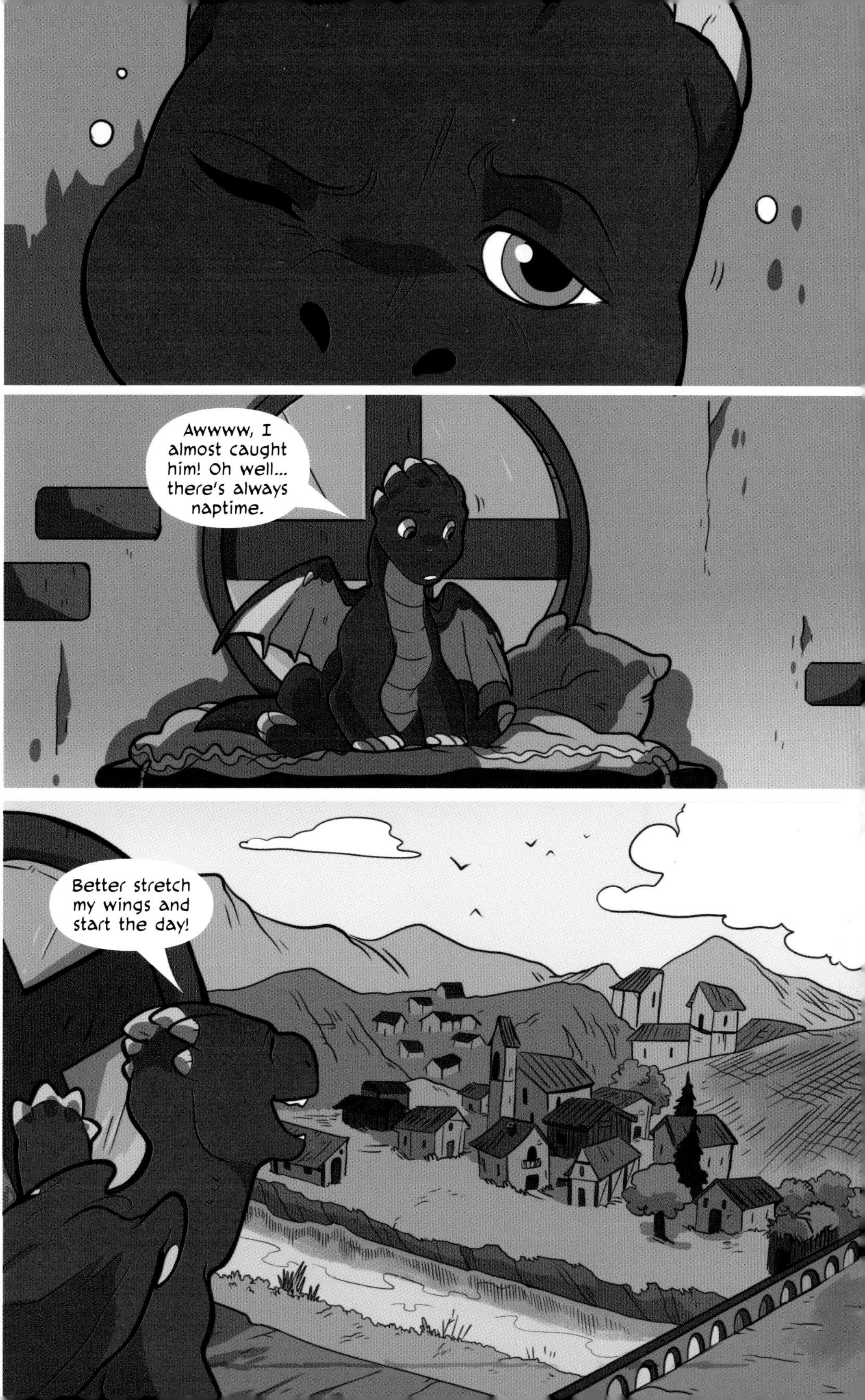
Awwww, I almost caught him! Oh well... there's always naptime.
Better stretch my wings and start the day!

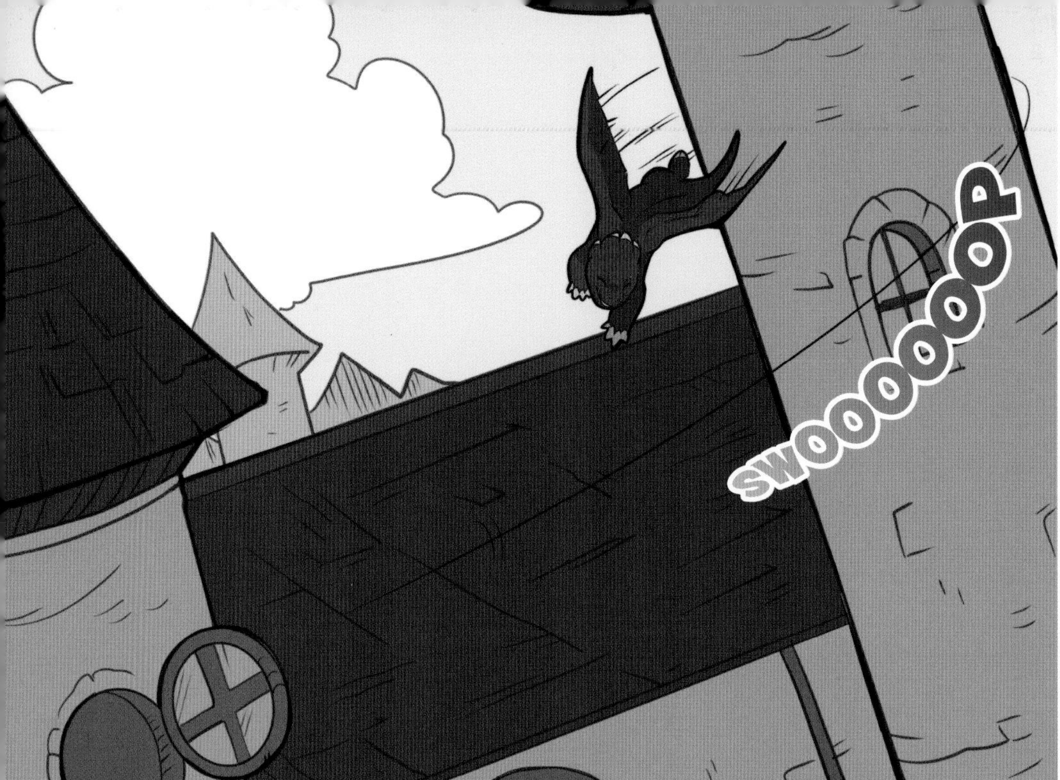
SWOOOOOOP

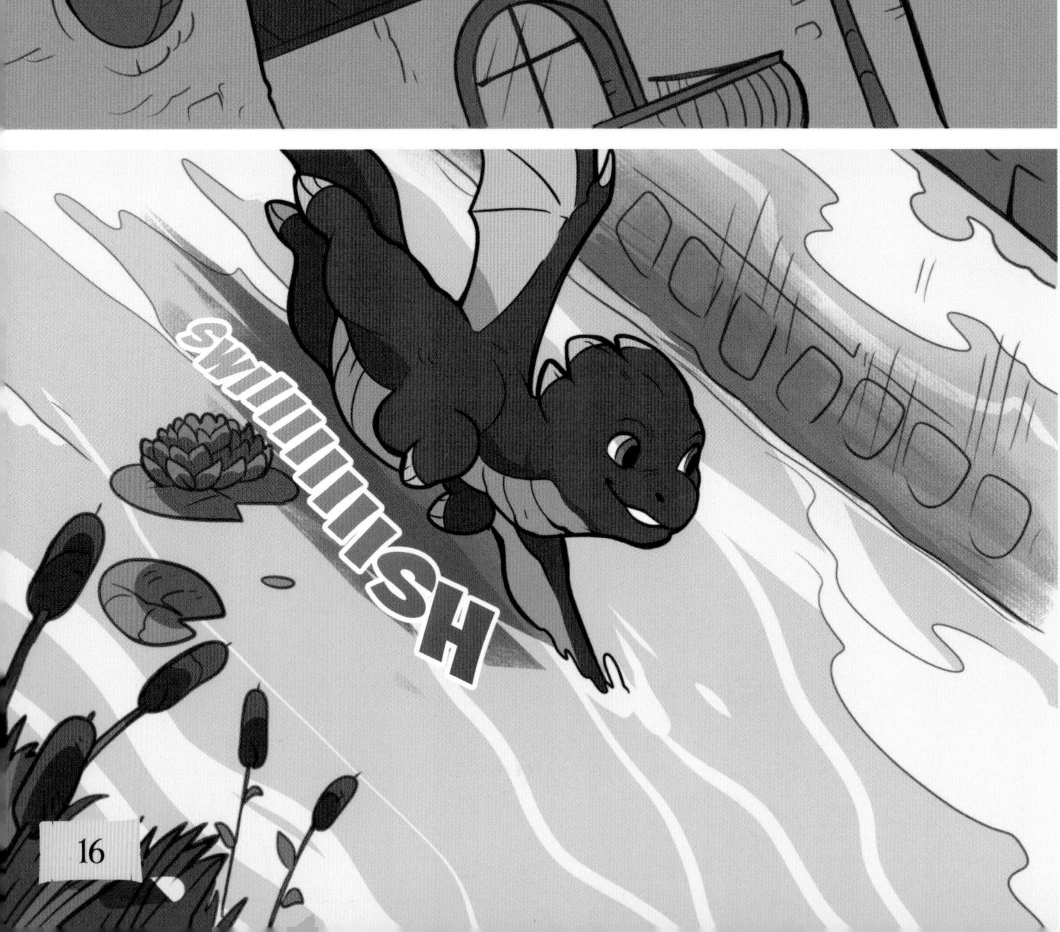
SWIIIIIIIIISH

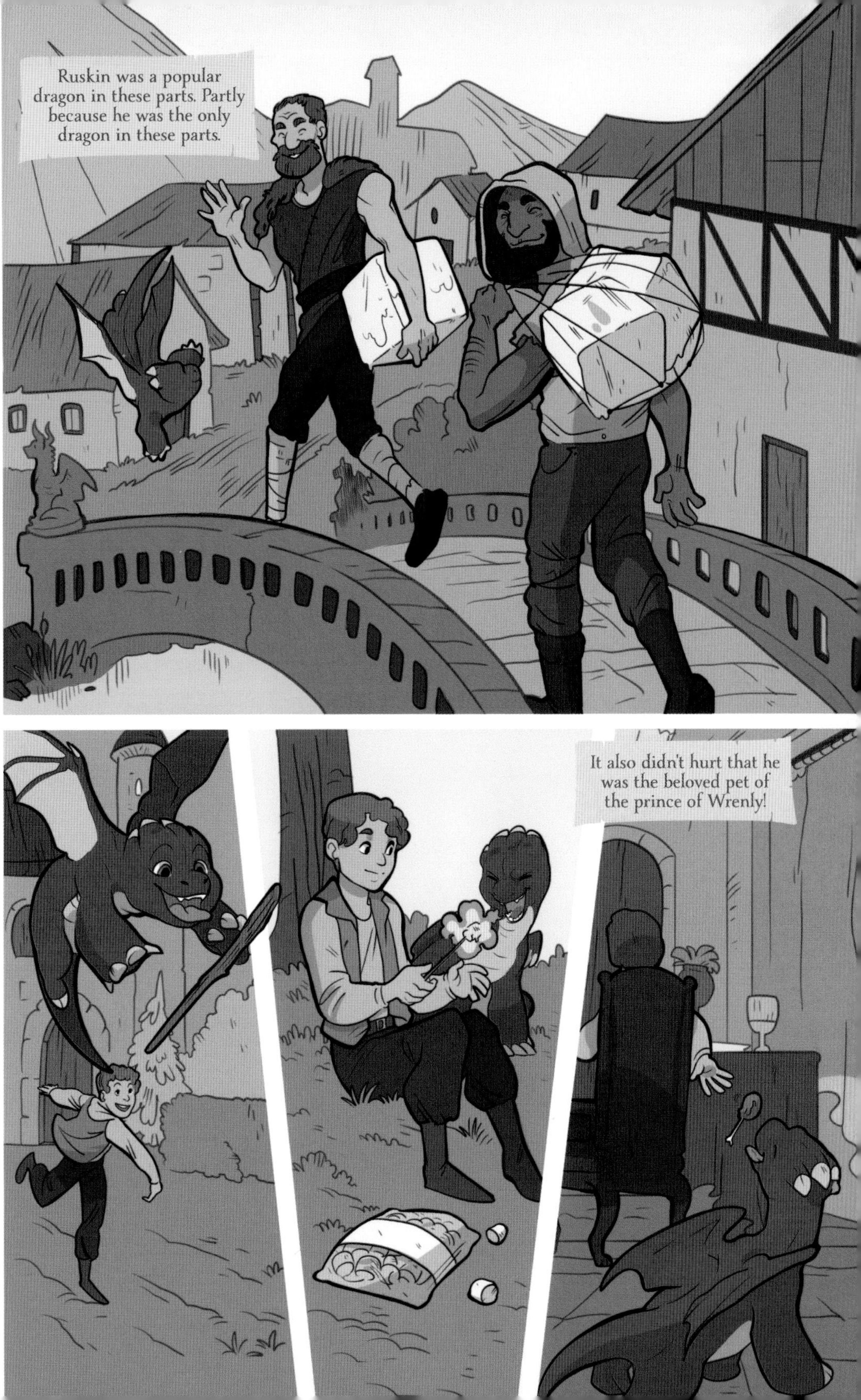
Ruskin was a popular dragon in these parts. Partly because he was the only dragon in these parts.
It also didn't hurt that he was the beloved pet of the prince of Wrenly!

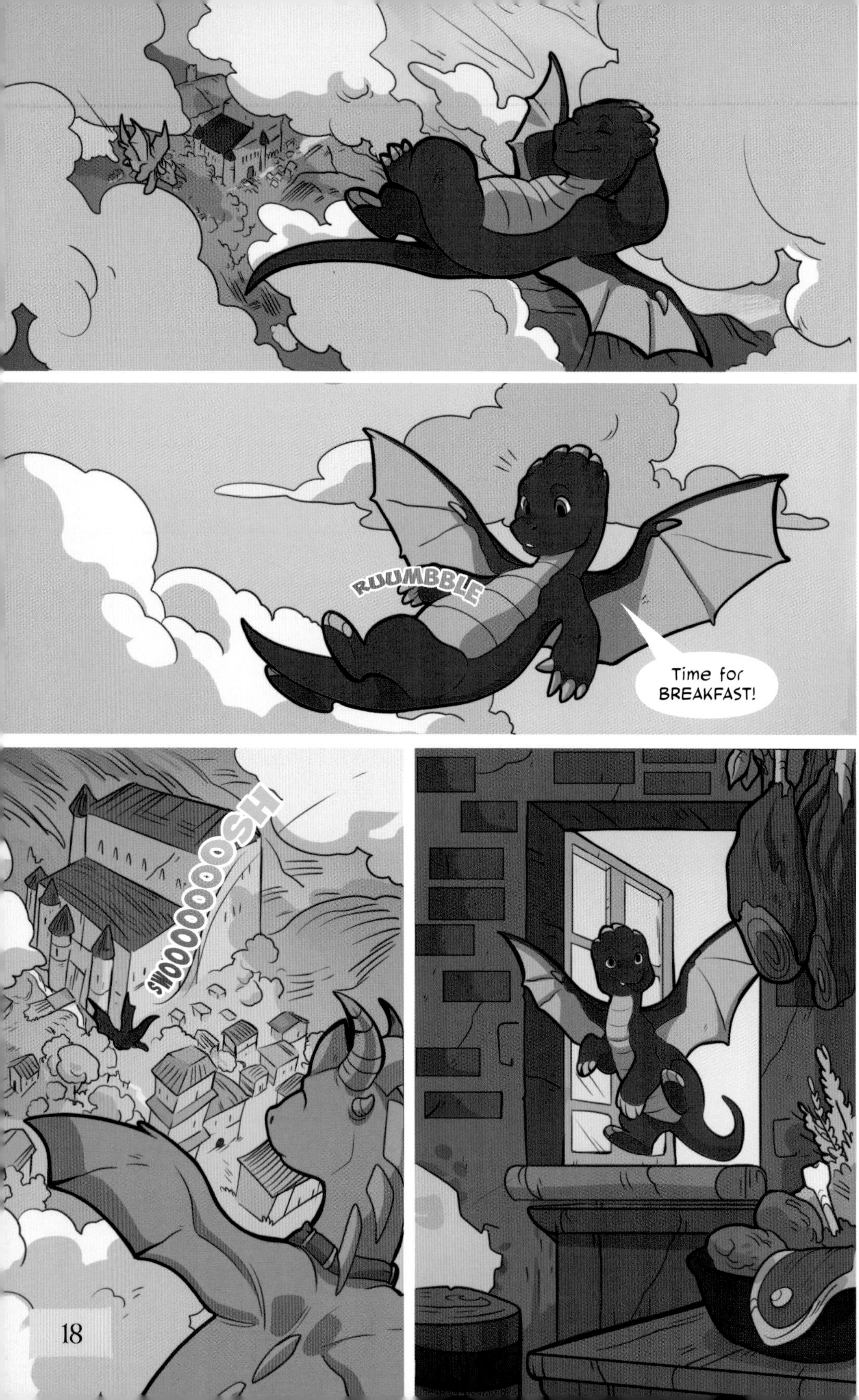
RUUMBBLE
Time for BREAKFAST!
SWOOOOOOOSH

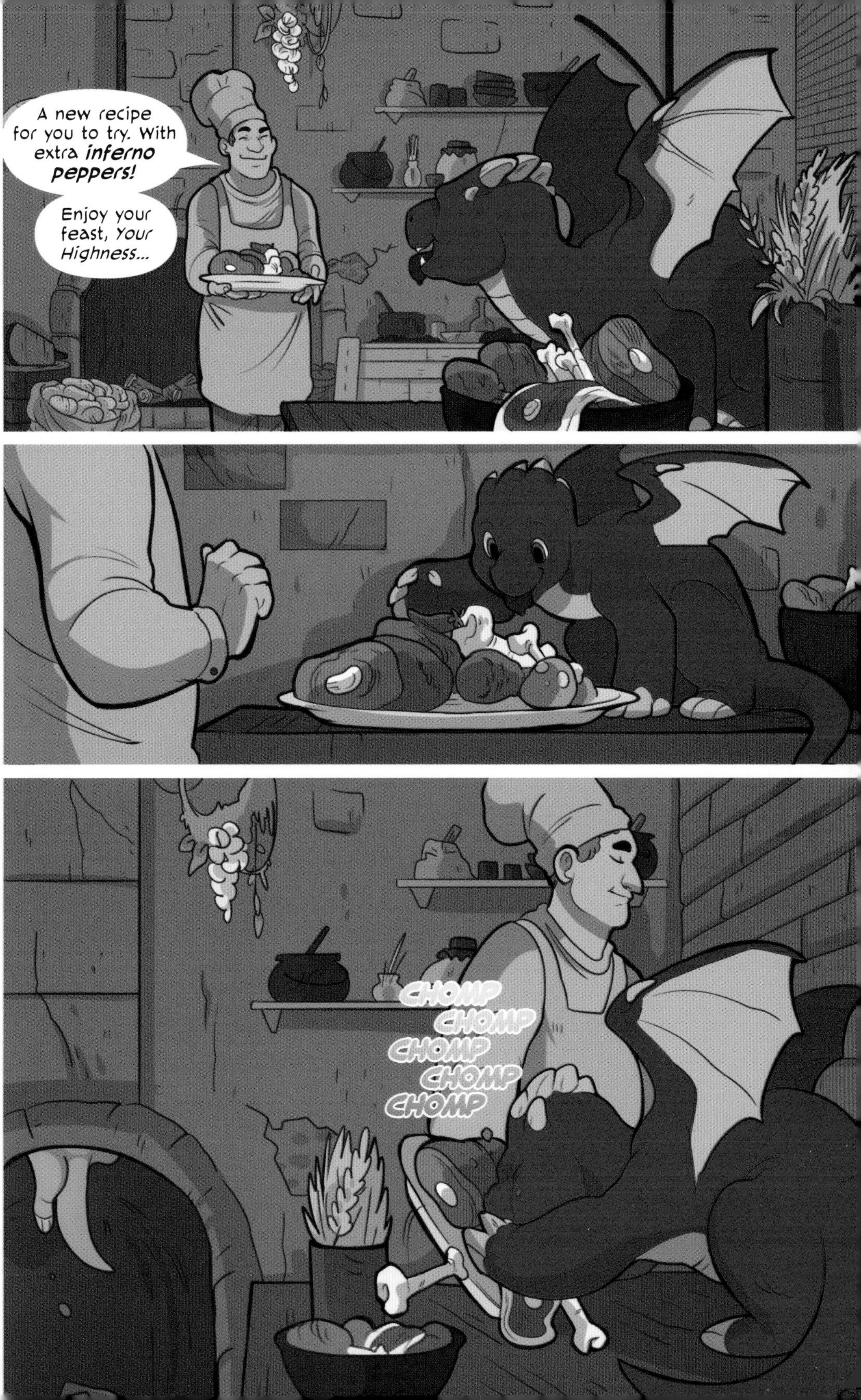
A new recipe for you to try. With extra *inferno peppers!*
Enjoy your feast, *Your Highness...*
CHOMP
CHOMP
CHOMP
CHOMP
CHOMP

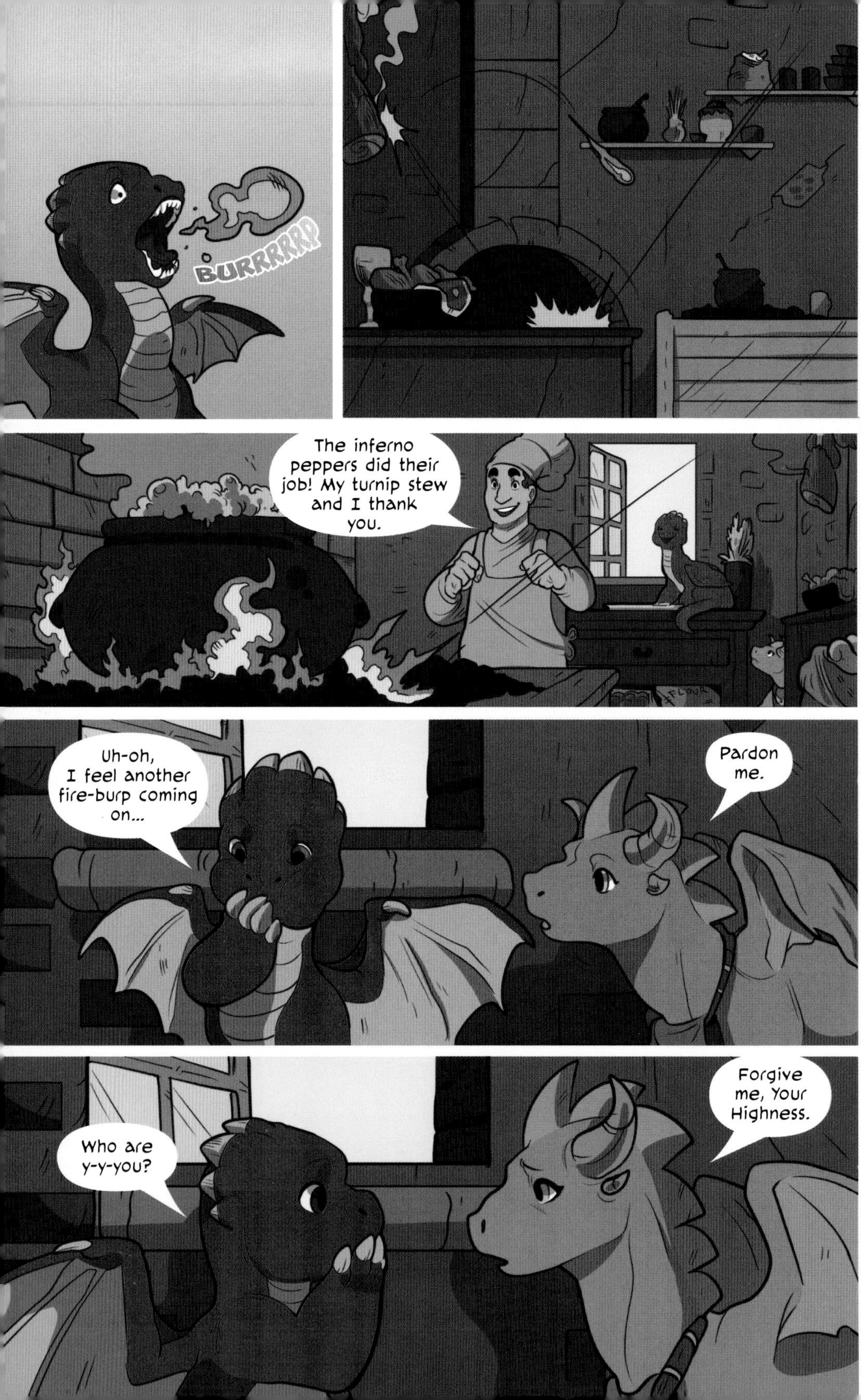
BURRRRRP
The inferno peppers did their job! My turnip stew and I thank you.
FLOUR
Uh-oh, I feel another fire-burp coming on...
Pardon me.
Who are y-y-you?
Forgive me, Your Highness.

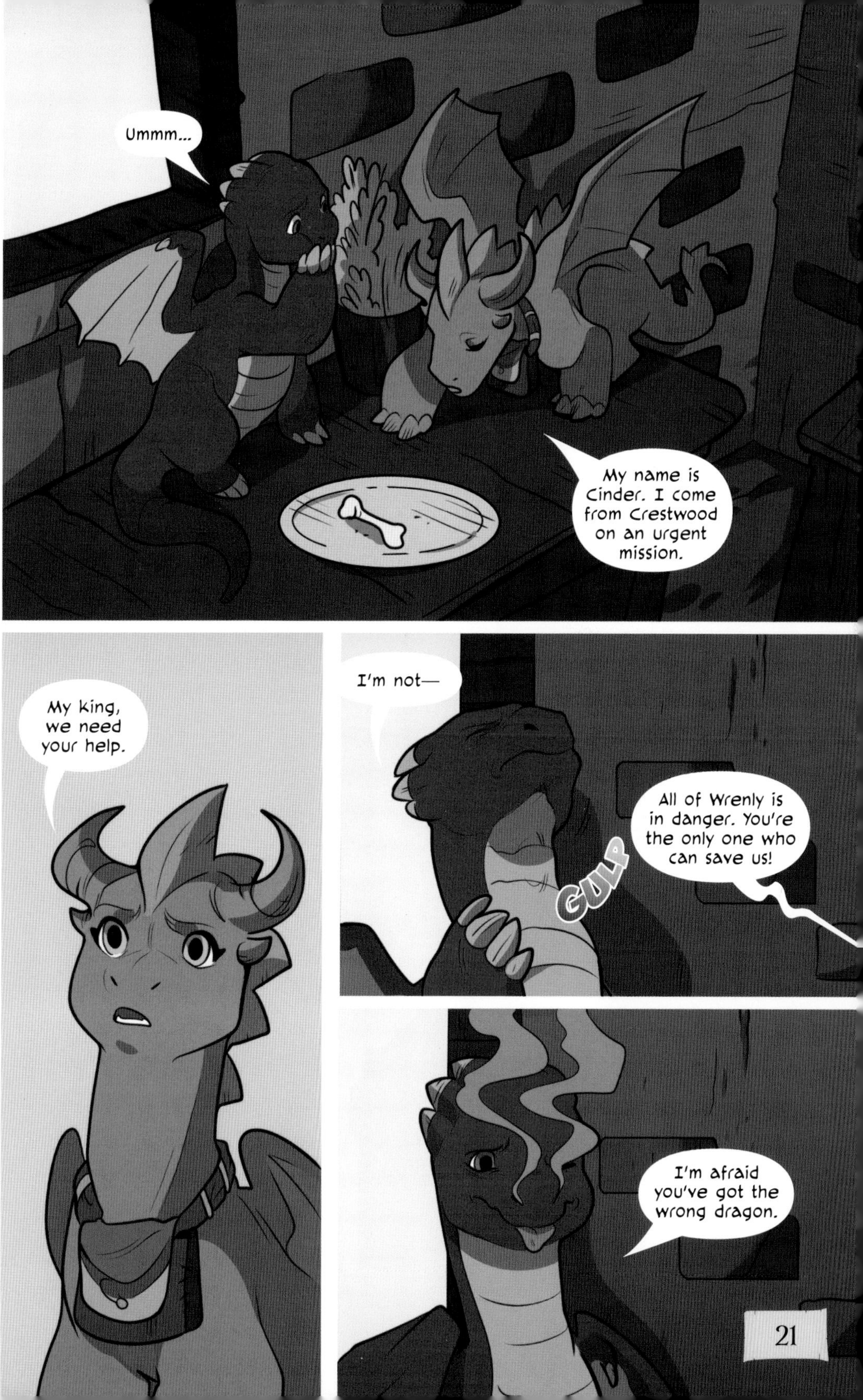
Ummm...
My name is Cinder. I come from Crestwood on an urgent mission.
My king, we need your help.
I'm not—
GULP
All of Wrenly is in danger. You're the only one who can save us!
I'm afraid you've got the wrong dragon.

Chapter 2

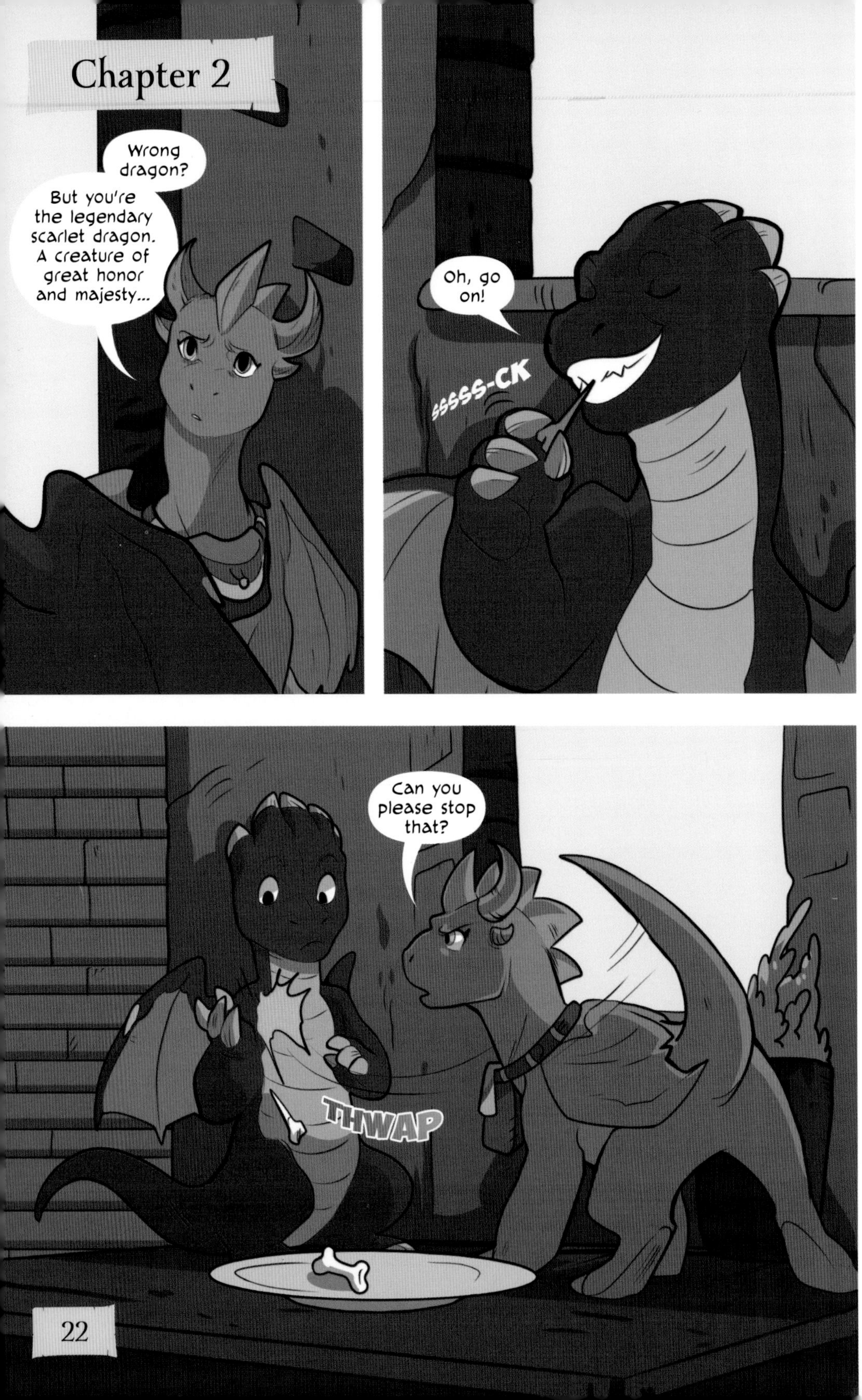

Wrong dragon?
But you're the legendary scarlet dragon. A creature of great honor and majesty...
Oh, go on!
SSSSS-CK
Can you please stop that?
THWAP

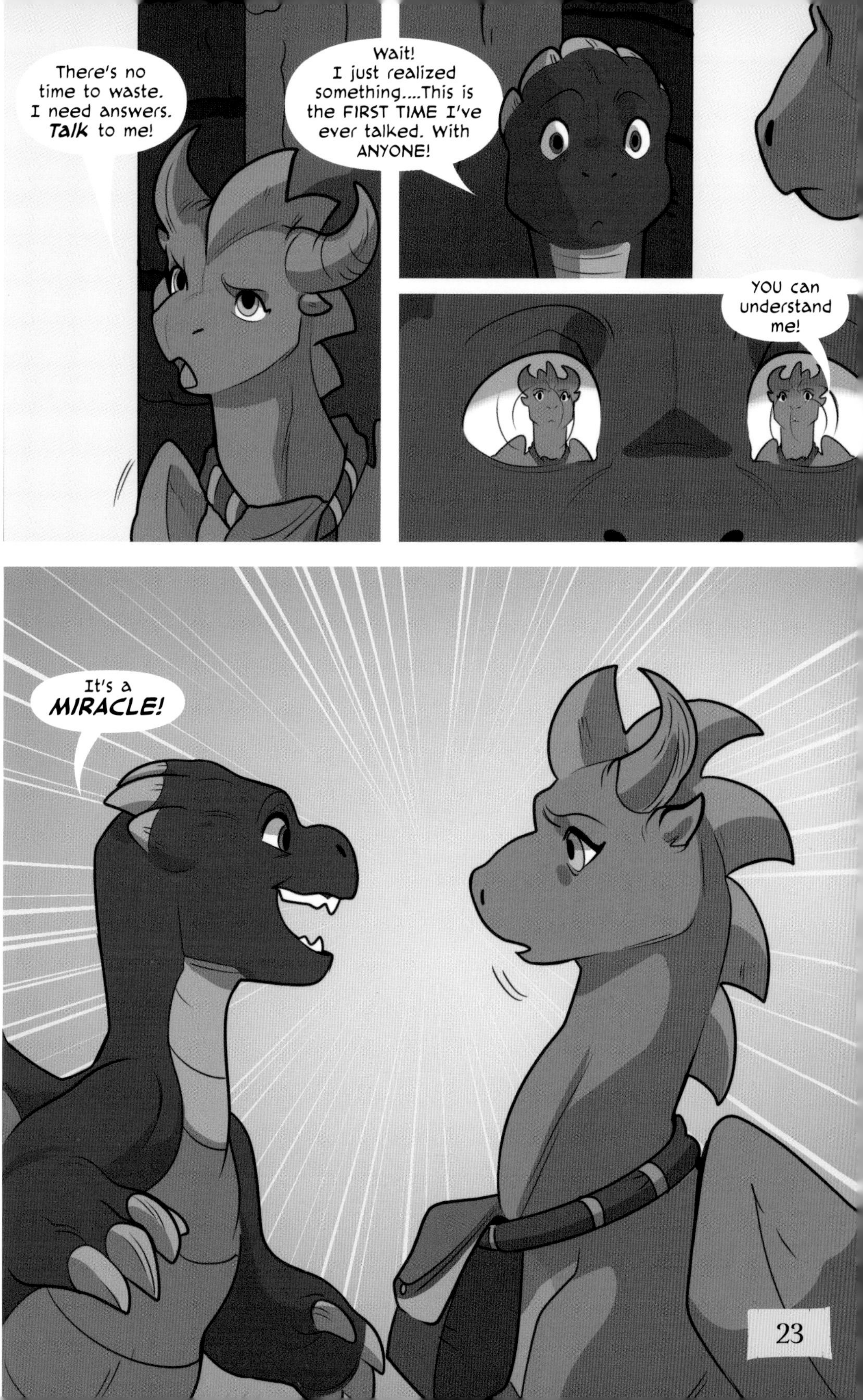
There's no time to waste. I need answers. *Talk* to me!
Wait! I just realized something....This is the FIRST TIME I've ever talked. With ANYONE!
YOU can understand me!
It's a *MIRACLE!*

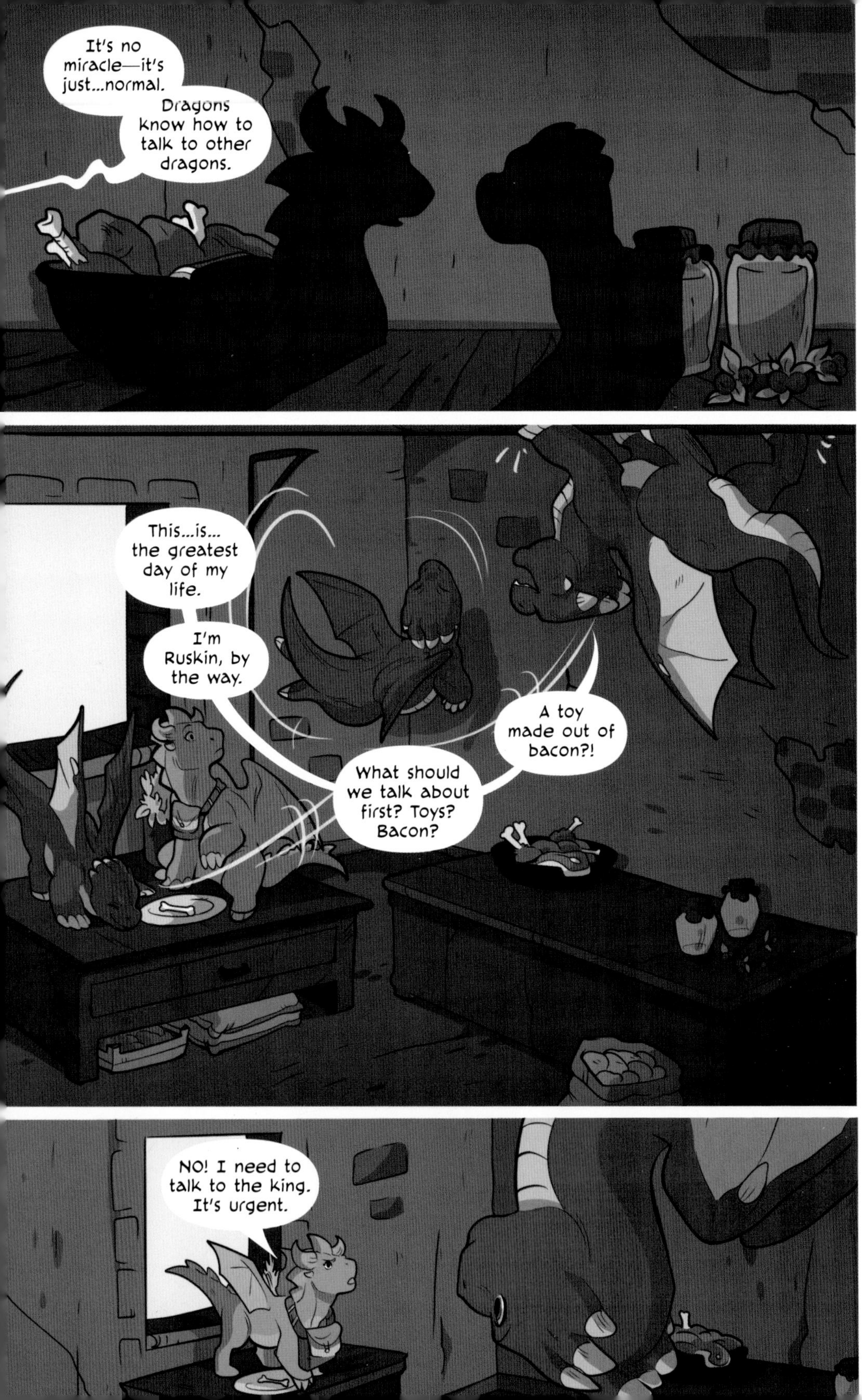
It's no miracle—it's just...normal.
Dragons know how to talk to other dragons.
This...is... the greatest day of my life.
I'm Ruskin, by the way.
What should we talk about first? Toys? Bacon?
A toy made out of bacon?!
NO! I need to talk to the king. It's urgent.

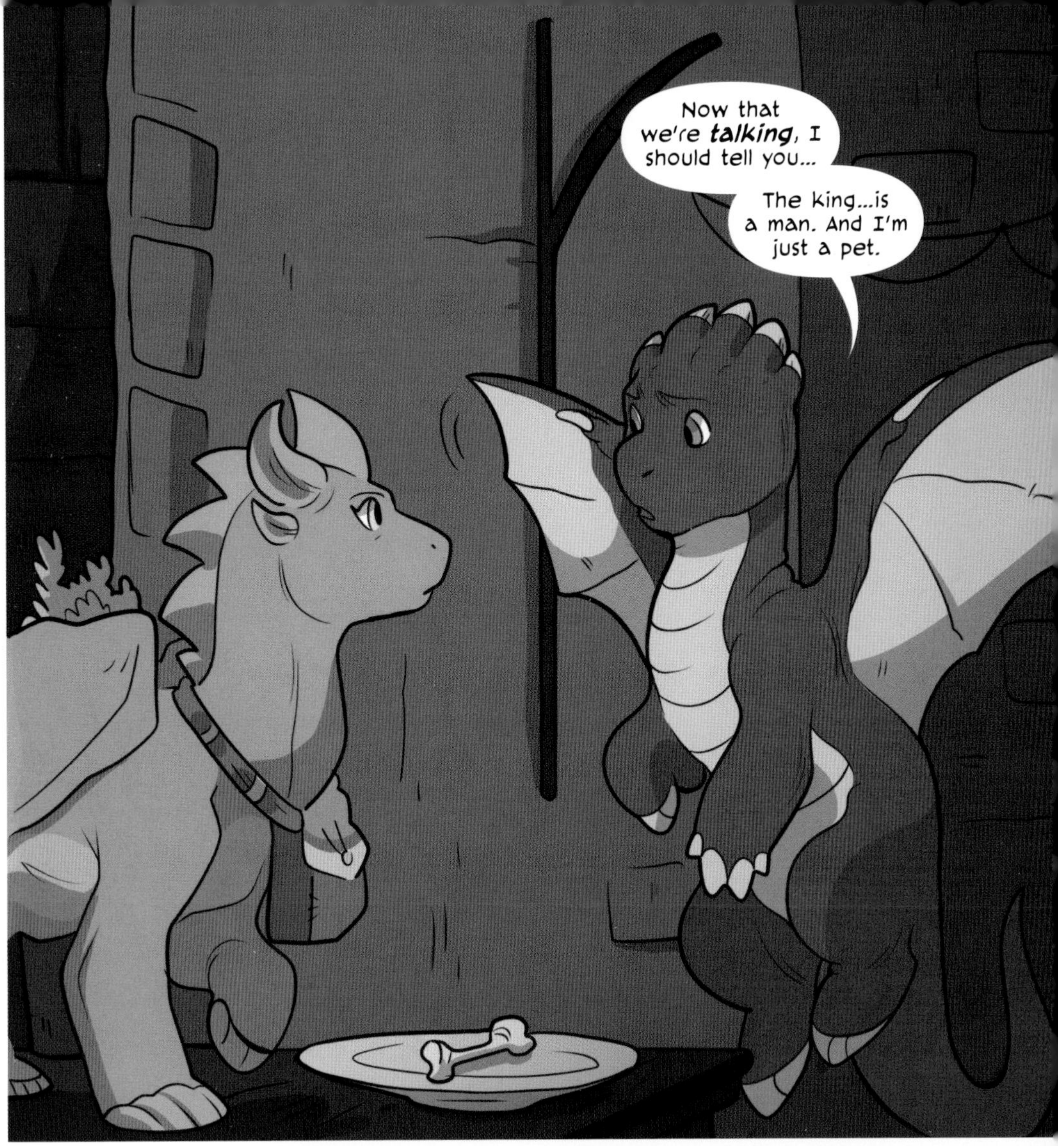
Now that we're ***talking***, I should tell you...
The king...is a man. And I'm just a pet.

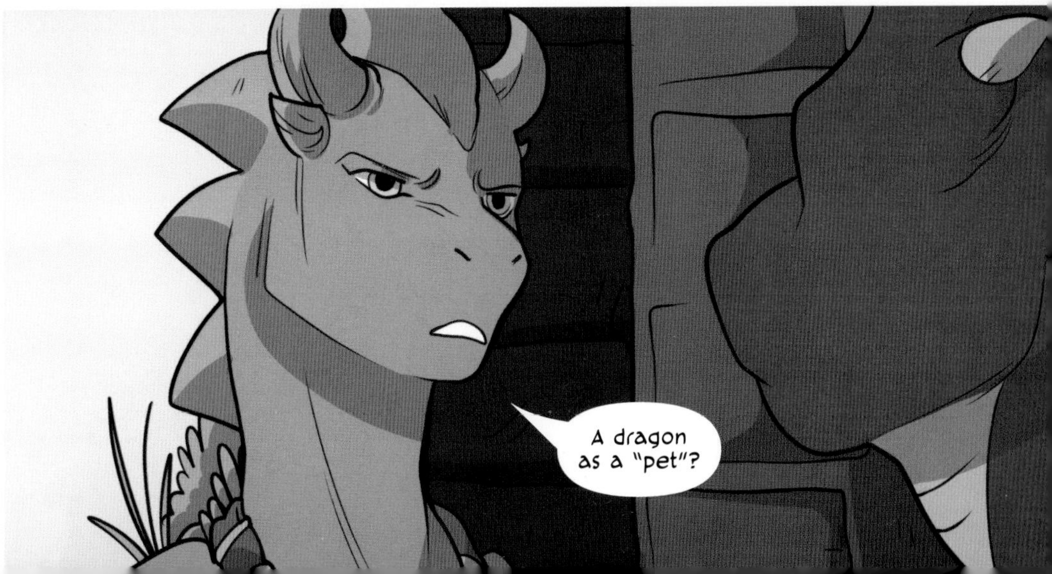
A dragon as a "pet"?

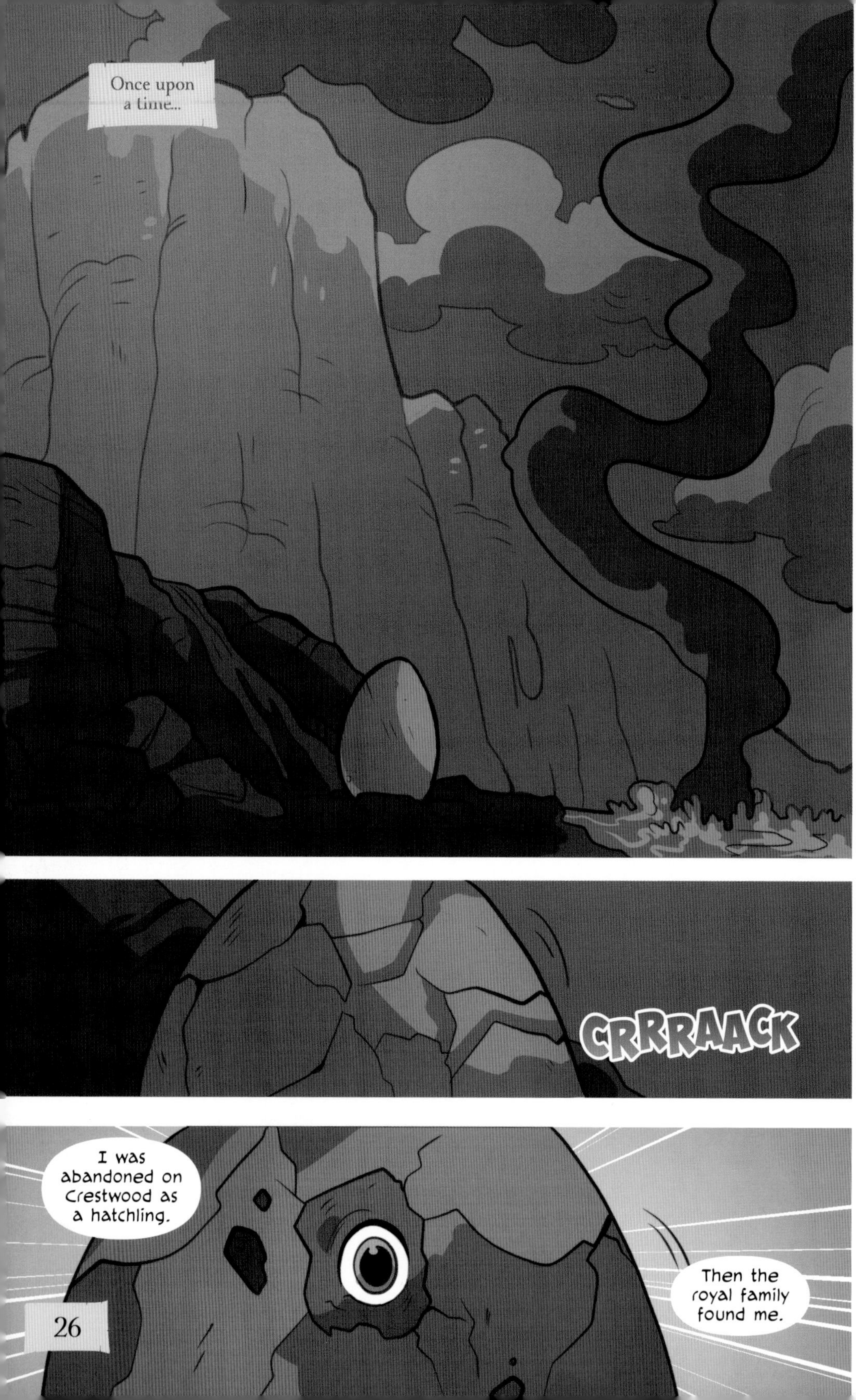
Once upon a time...
CRRRAACK
I was abandoned on Crestwood as a hatchling.
Then the royal family found me.

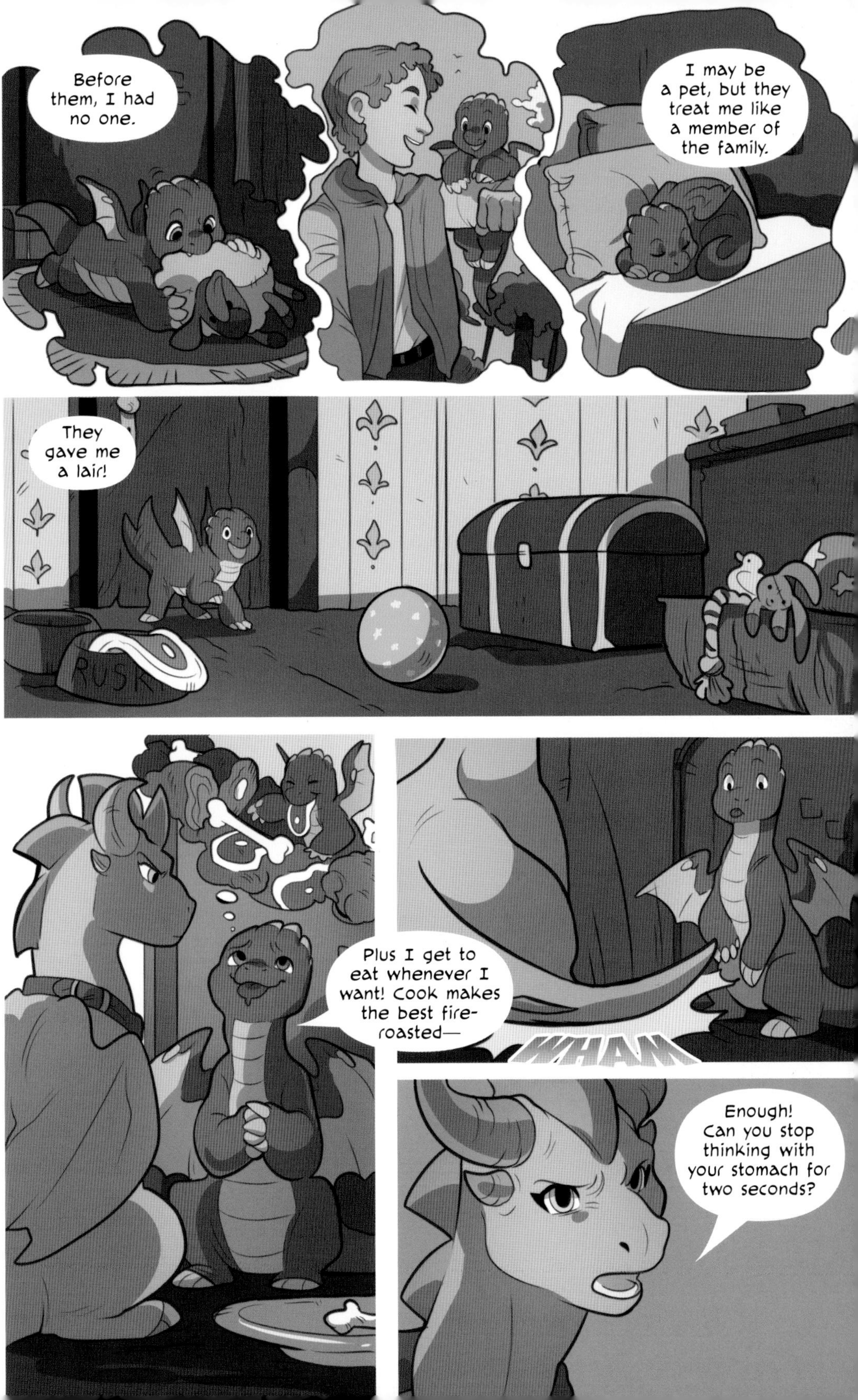
Before them, I had no one.
I may be a pet, but they treat me like a member of the family.
They gave me a lair!
RUSK
Plus I get to eat whenever I want! Cook makes the best fire-roasted—
WHAM
Enough! Can you stop thinking with your stomach for two seconds?

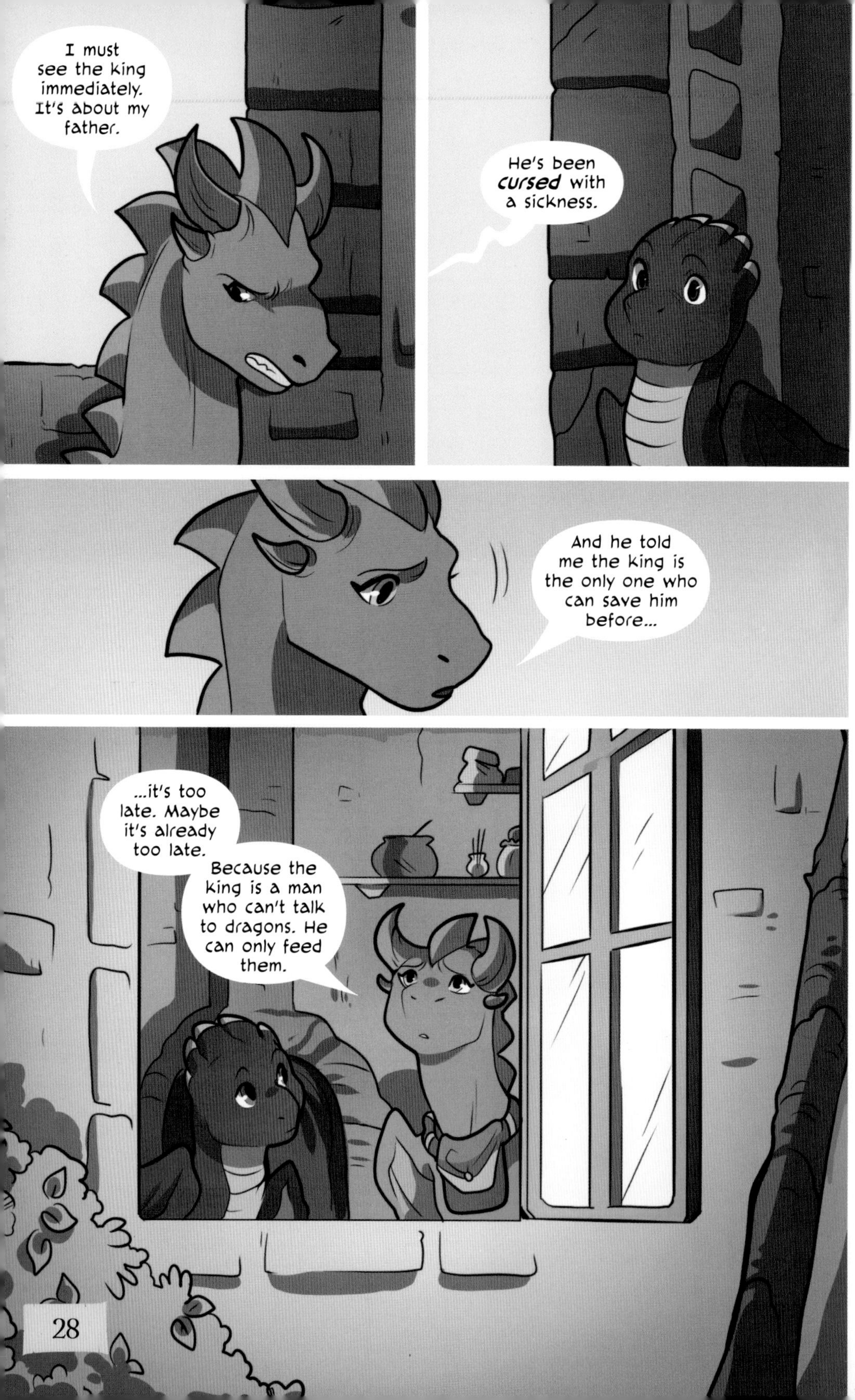
I must see the king immediately. It's about my father.
He's been *cursed* with a sickness.
And he told me the king is the only one who can save him before...
...it's too late. Maybe it's already too late.
Because the king is a man who can't talk to dragons. He can only feed them.

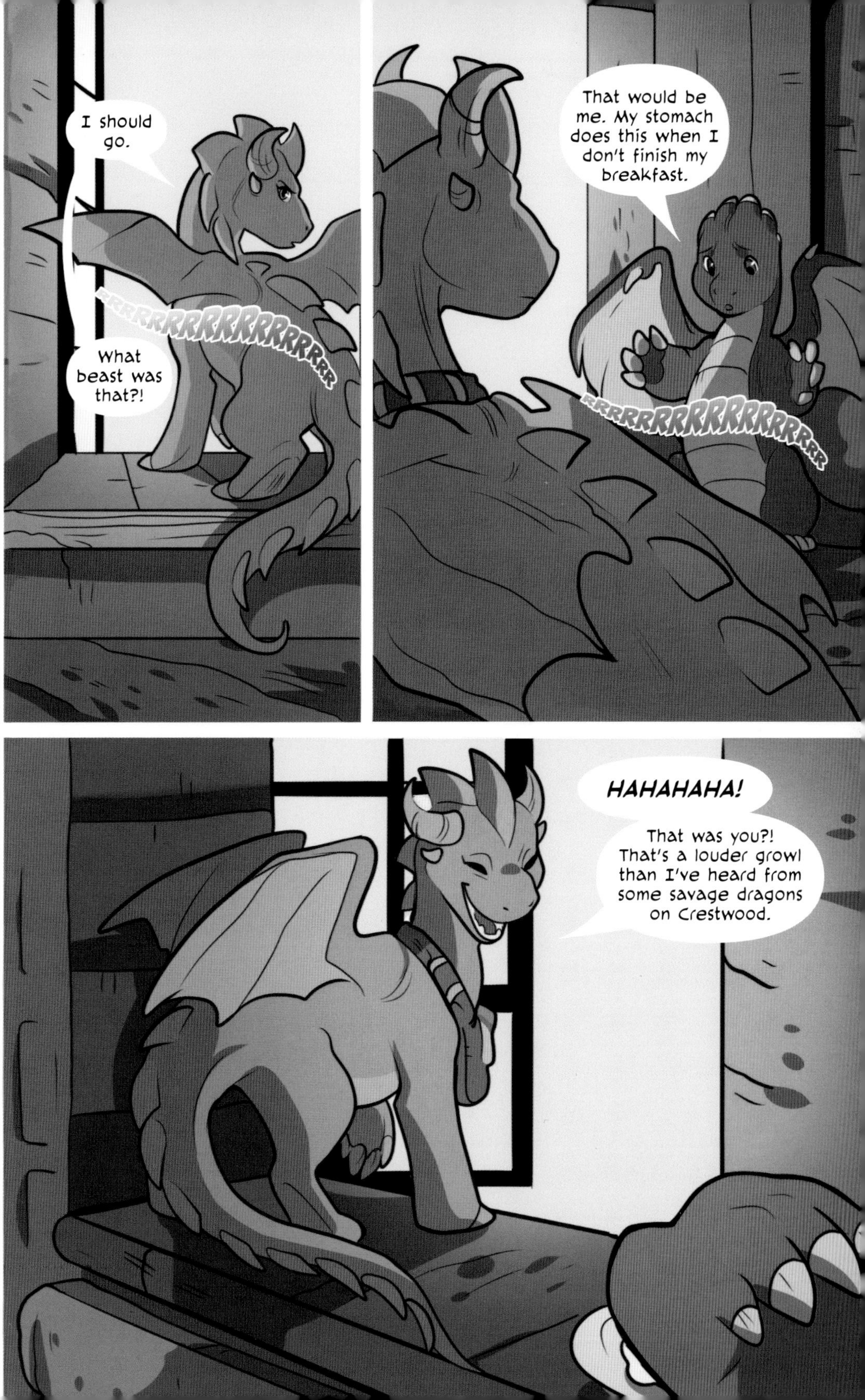
I should go.
RRRRRRRRRRRRRRRRRRRR
What beast was that?!
That would be me. My stomach does this when I don't finish my breakfast.
RRRRRRRRRRRRRRRRRRRR
HAHAHAHA!
That was you?! That's a louder growl than I've heard from some savage dragons on Crestwood.

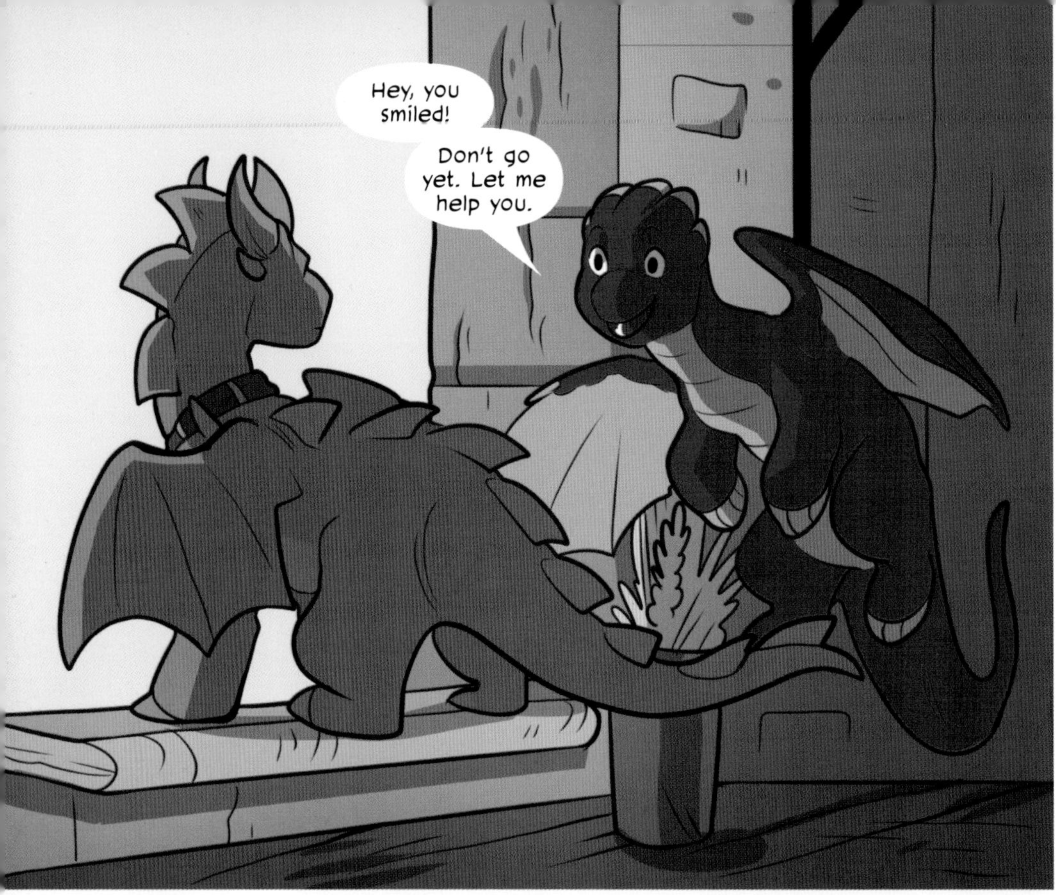
Hey, you smiled!
Don't go yet. Let me help you.

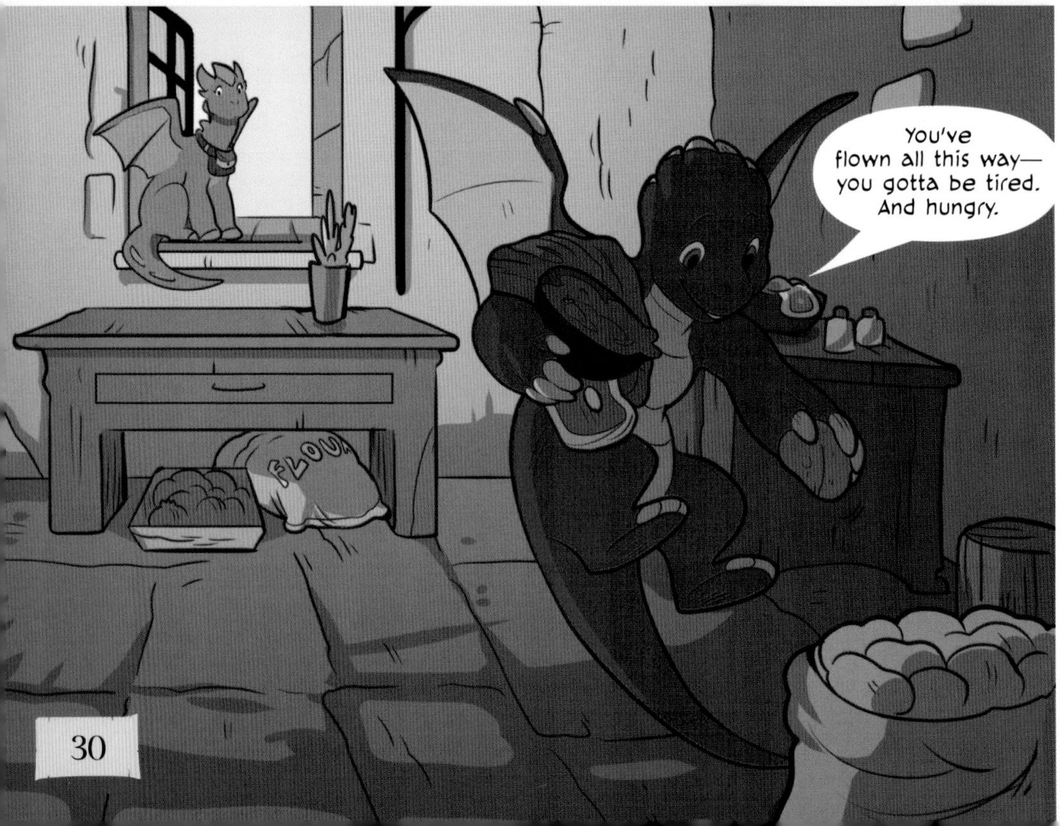
You've flown all this way—you gotta be tired. And hungry.

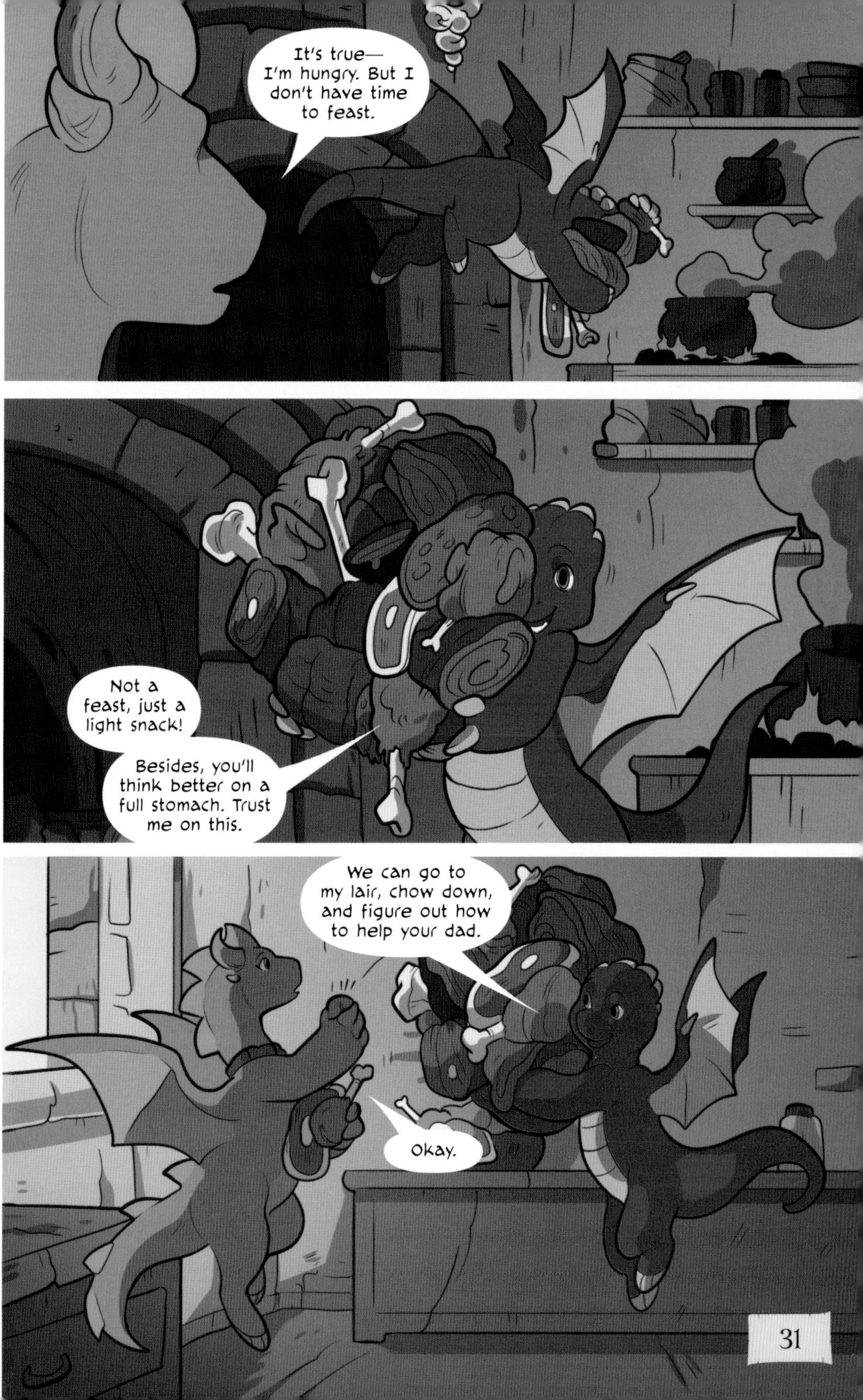
It's true— I'm hungry. But I don't have time to feast.
Not a feast, just a light snack!
Besides, you'll think better on a full stomach. Trust me on this.
We can go to my lair, chow down, and figure out how to help your dad.
Okay.

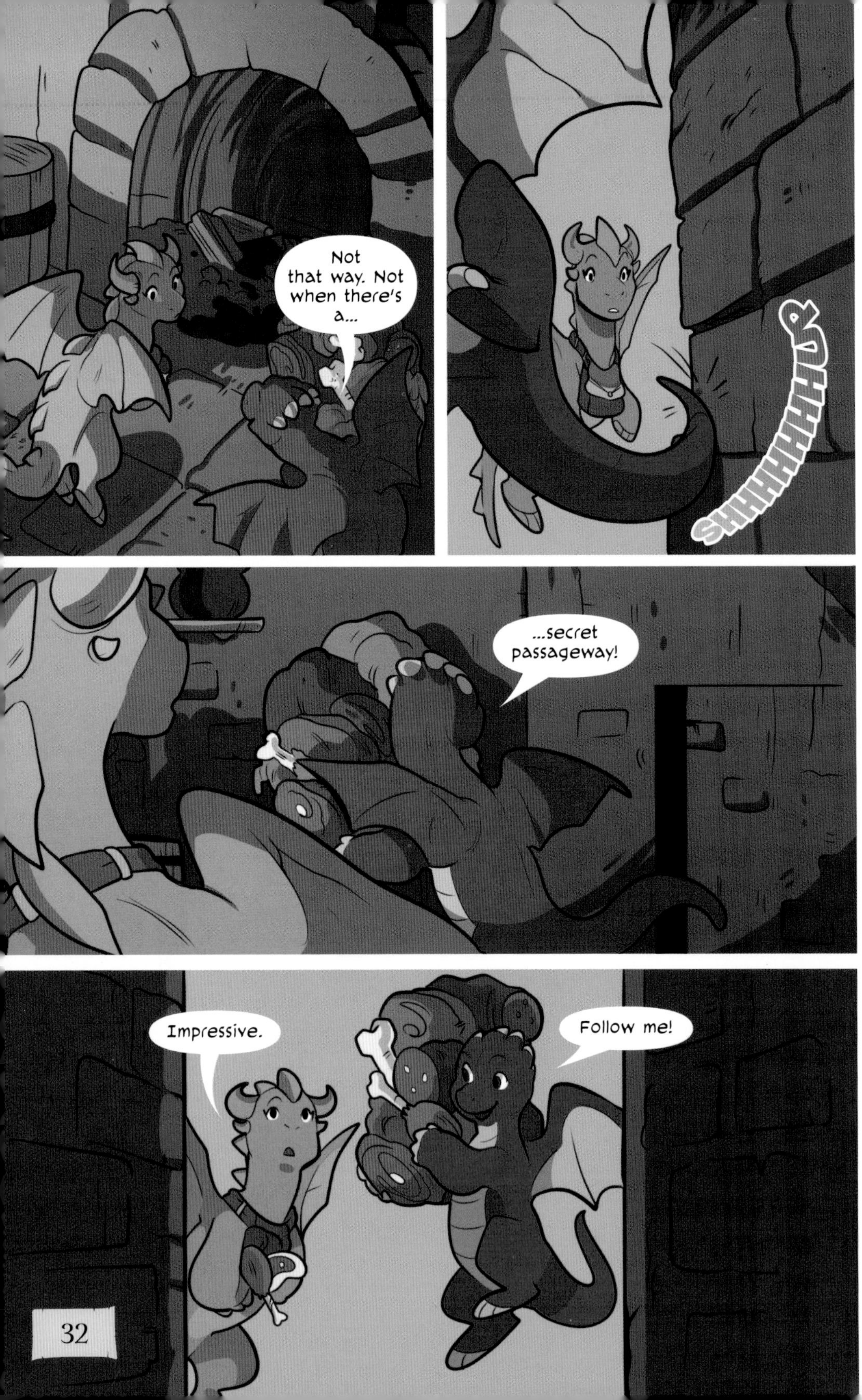

Not that way. Not when there's a...
SHHHHHHHHH&
...secret passageway!
Impressive.
Follow me!

Chapter 3

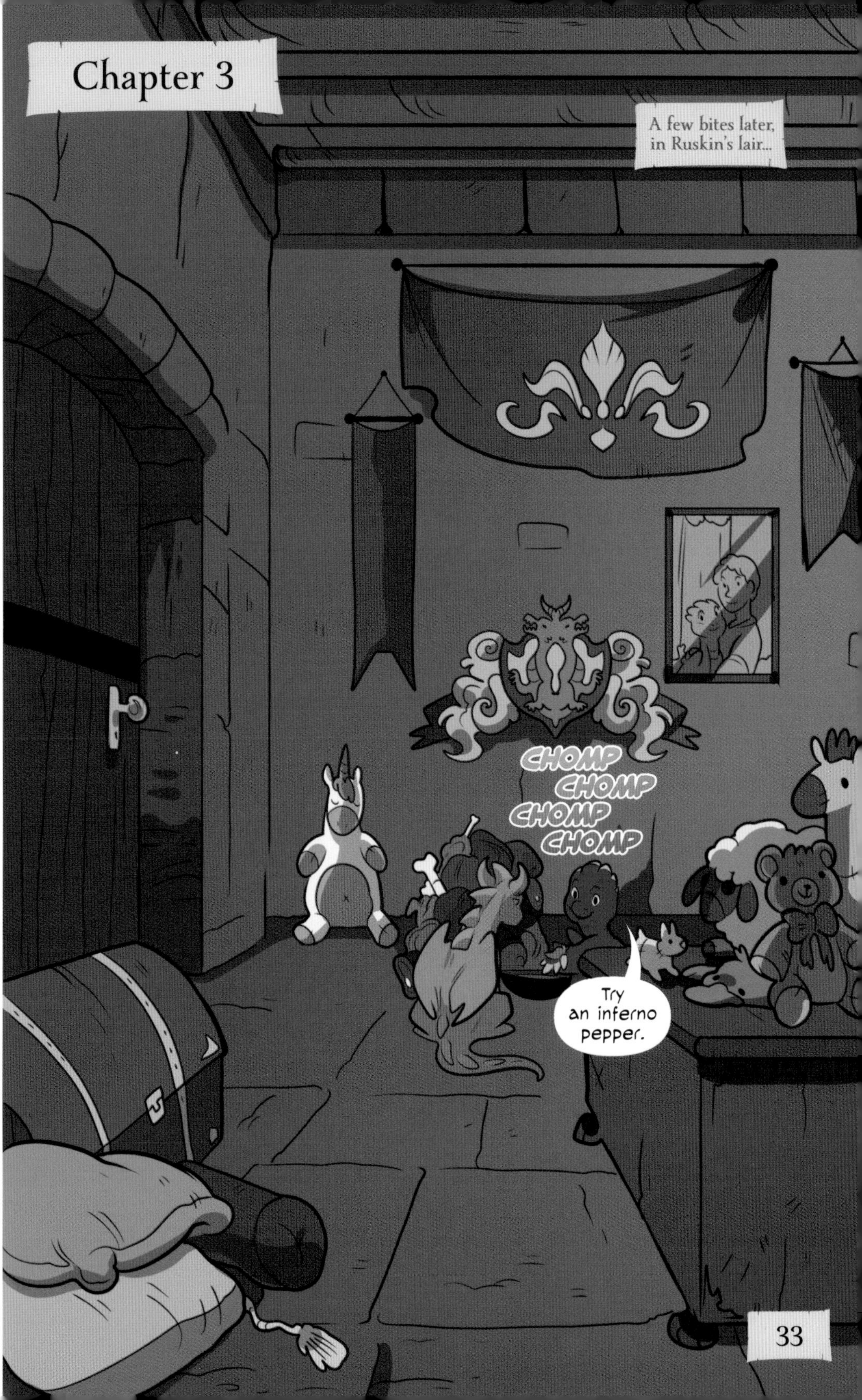
A few bites later, in Ruskin's lair...
CHOMP
CHOMP
CHOMP
CHOMP
Try an inferno pepper.

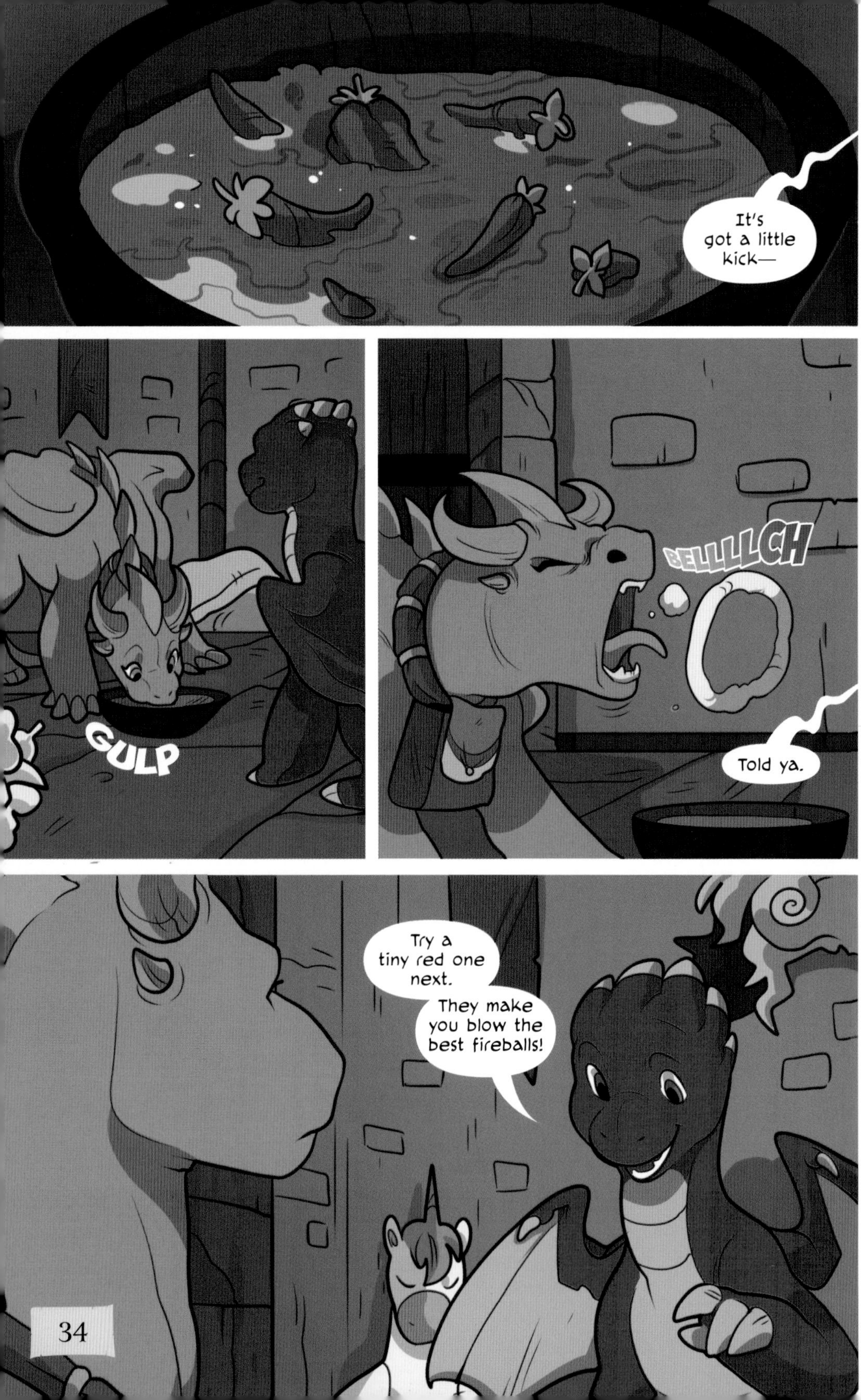
It's got a little kick—
GULP
BELLLLCH
Told ya.
Try a tiny red one next.
They make you blow the best fireballs!

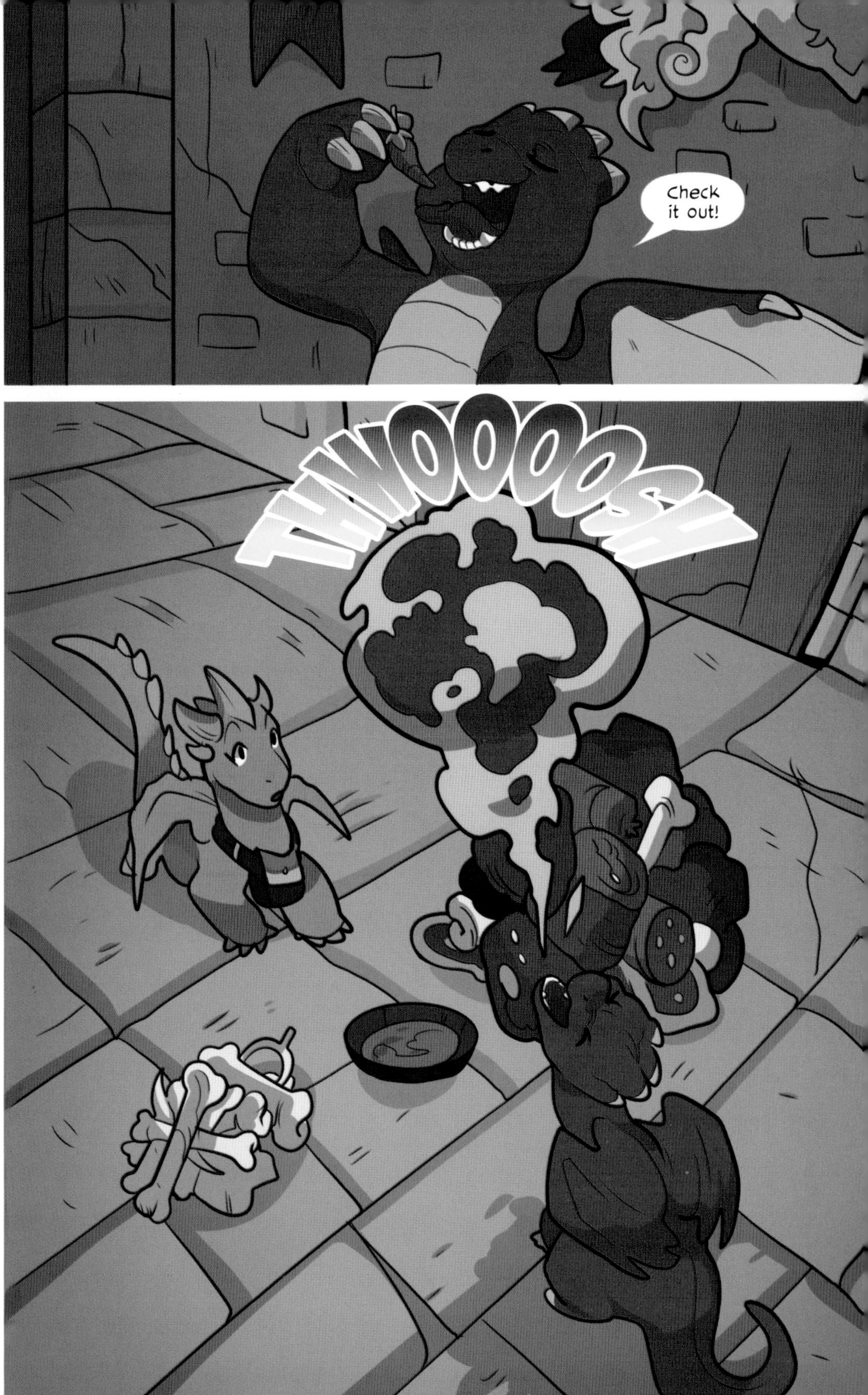
Check it out!
THWOOOOSH

36

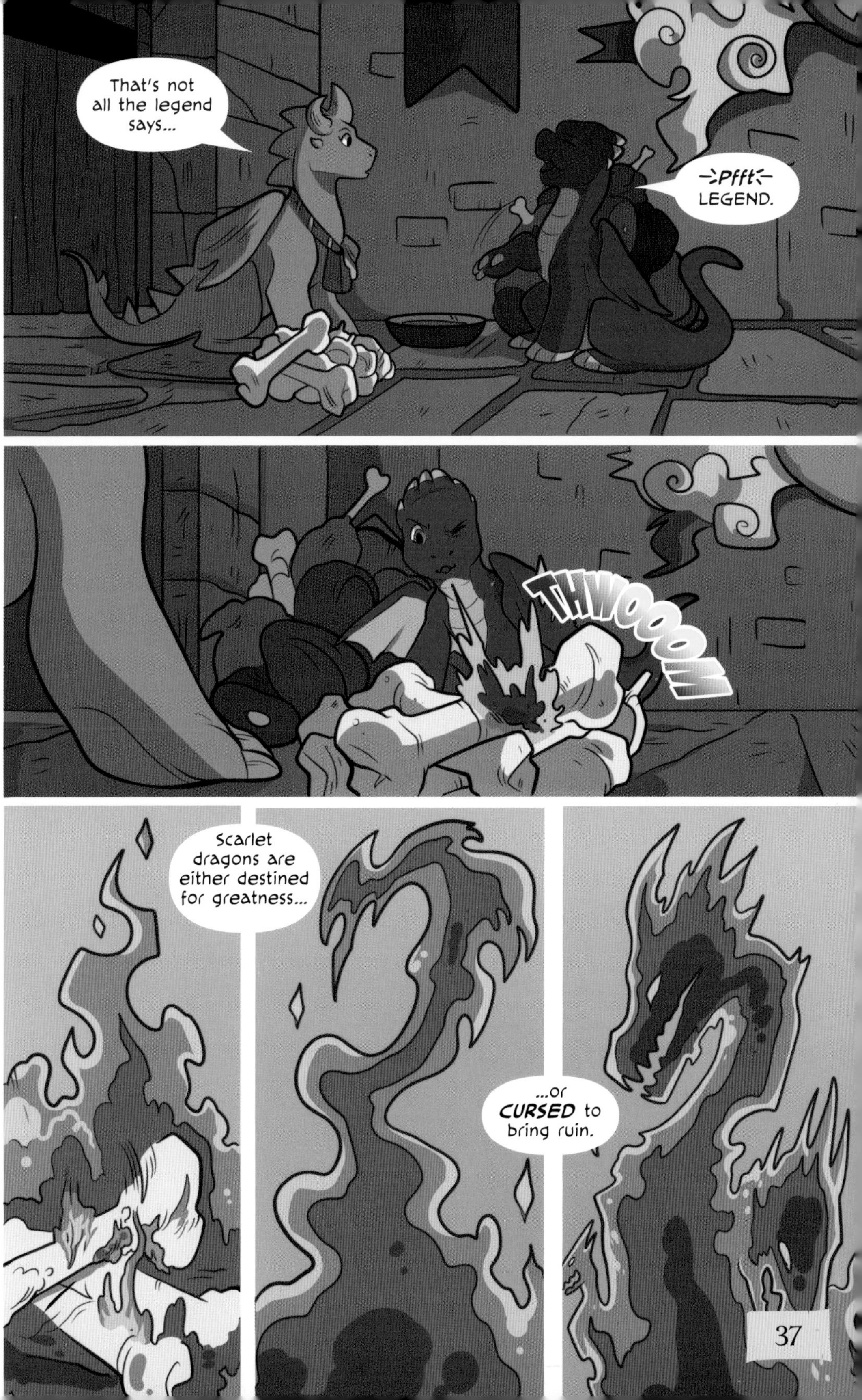
That's not all the legend says...
Pfft LEGEND.
THWOOOM
Scarlet dragons are either destined for greatness...
...or CURSED to bring ruin.

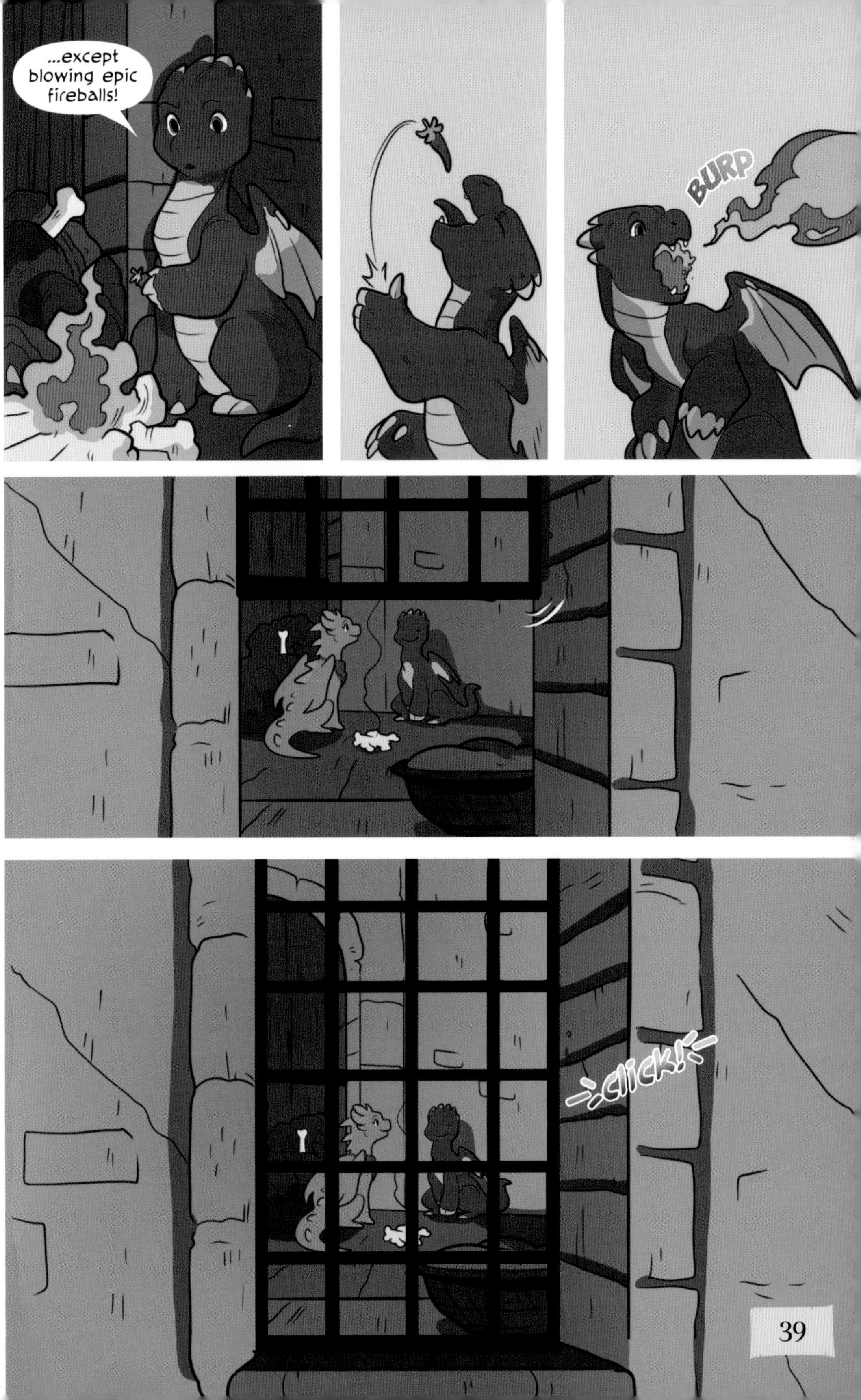
...except blowing epic fireballs!
BURP
CLICK!

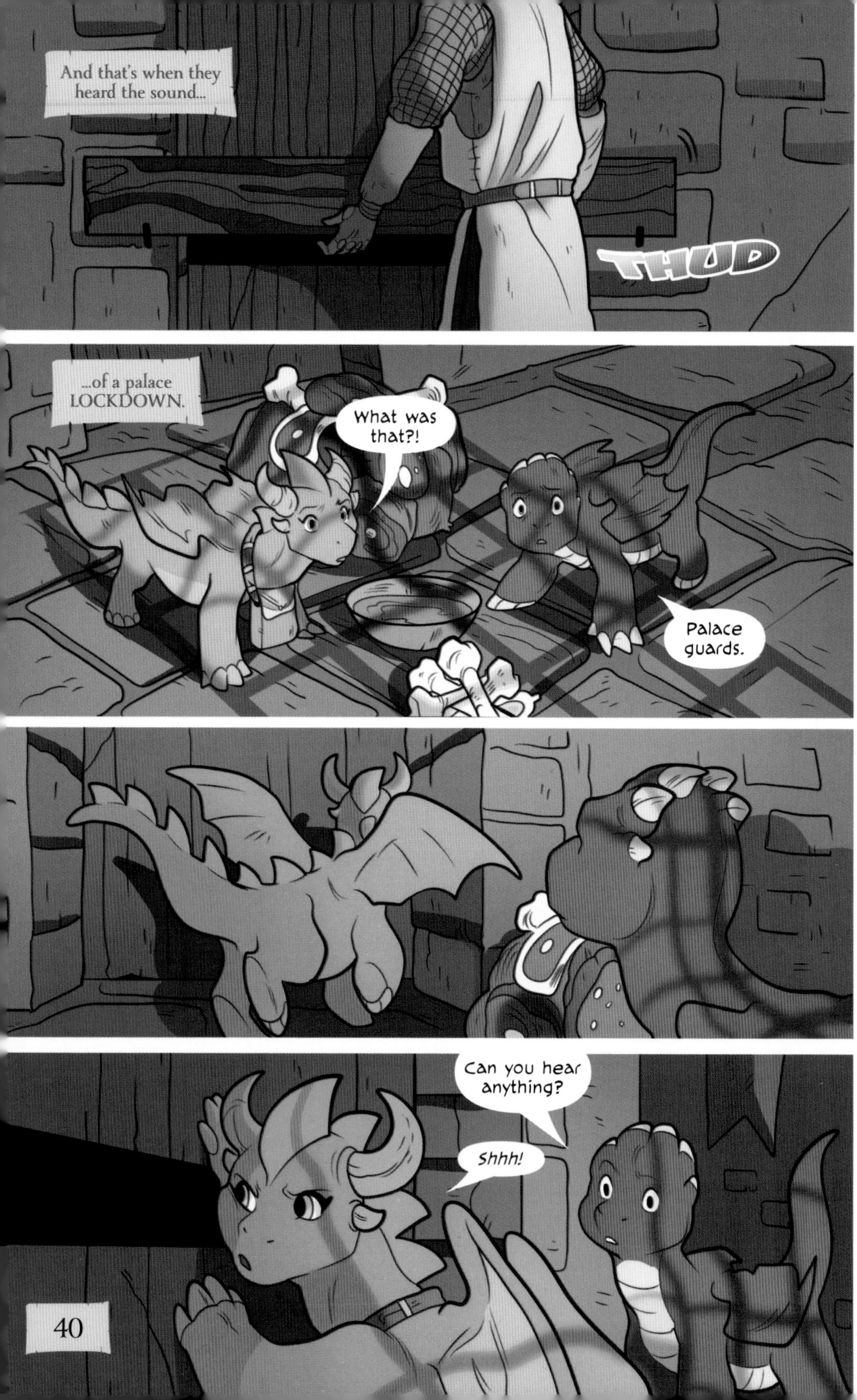
And that's when they heard the sound...
THUD
...of a palace LOCKDOWN.
What was that?!
Palace guards.
Can you hear anything?
Shhh!

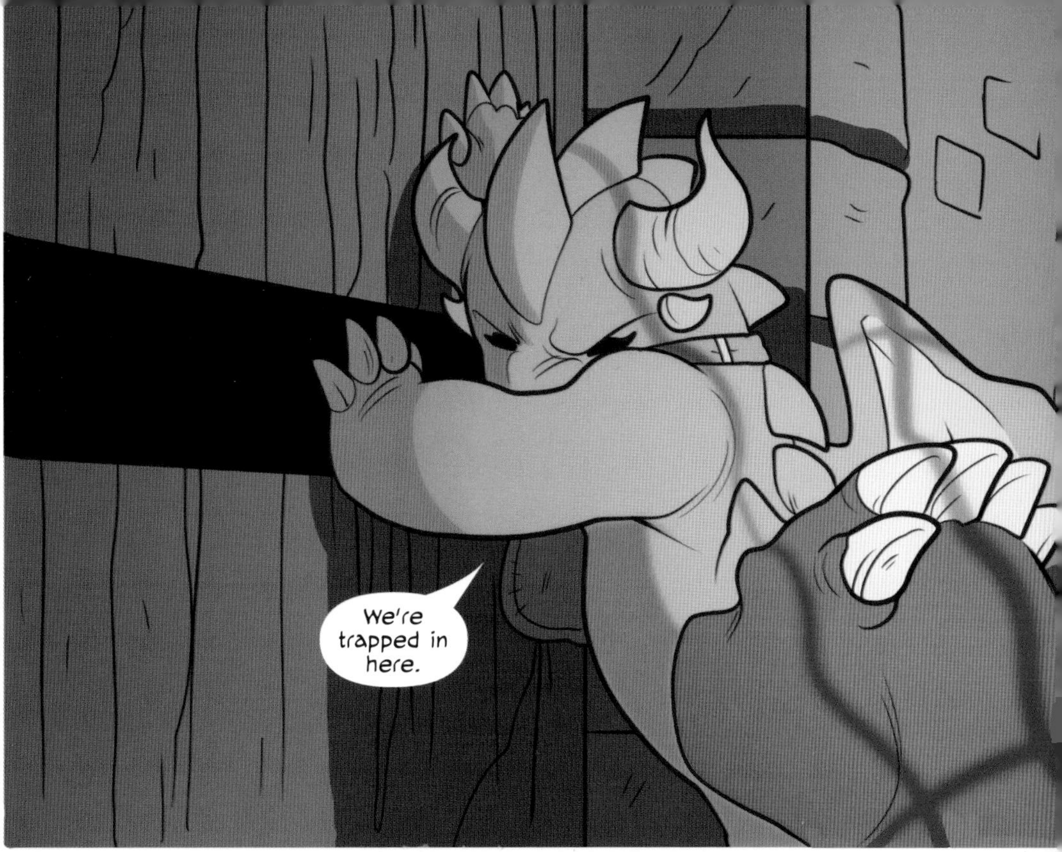
We're trapped in here.

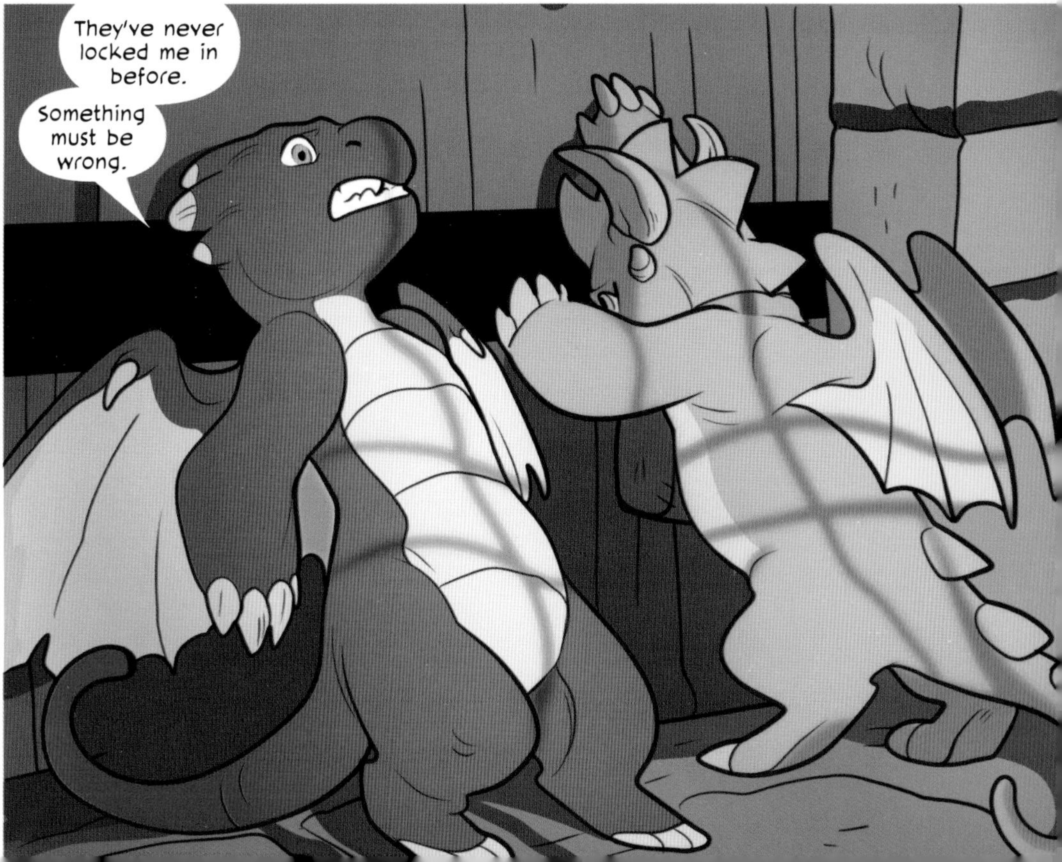
They've never locked me in before.
Something must be wrong.

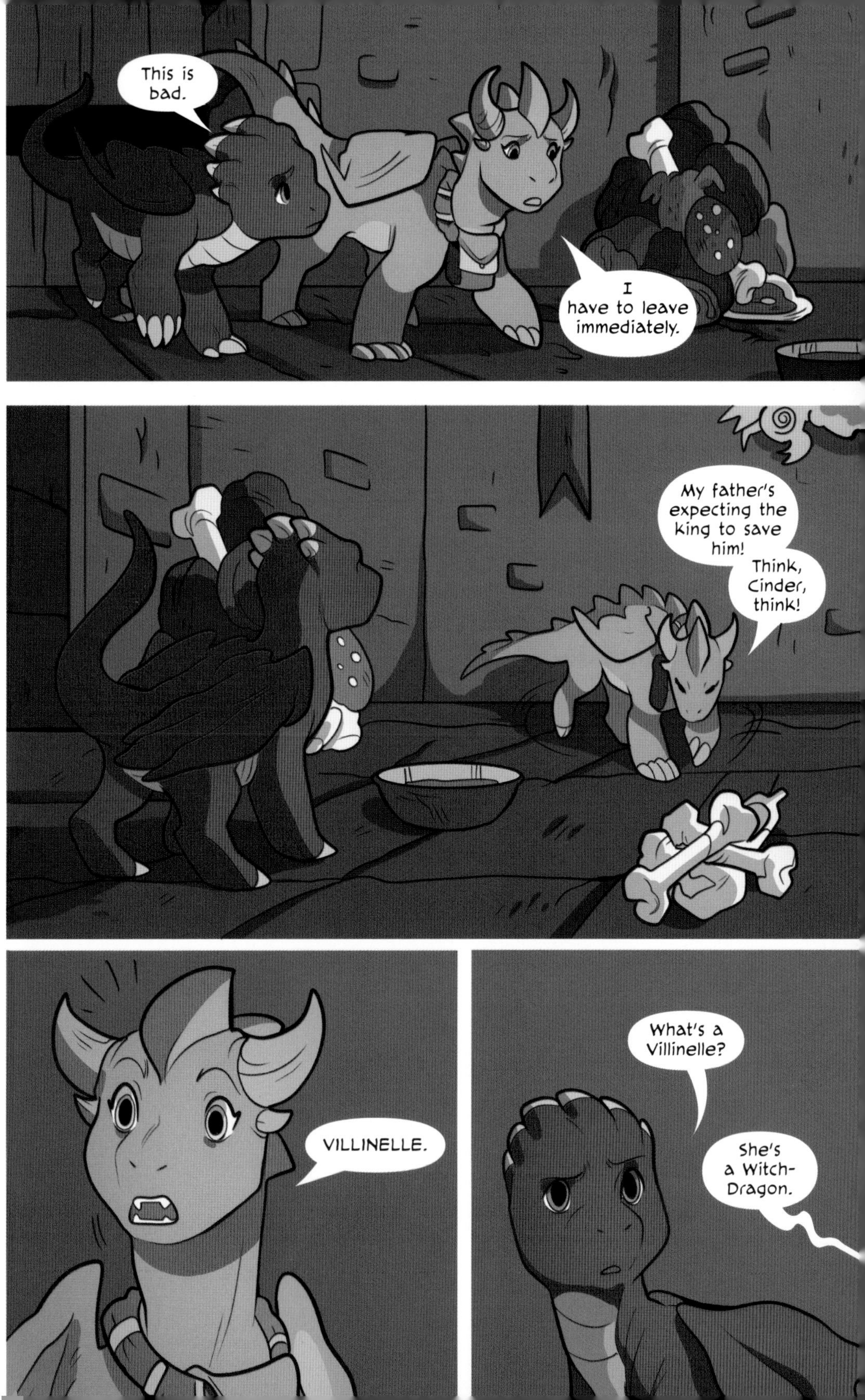
This is bad.
I have to leave immediately.
My father's expecting the king to save him!
Think, Cinder, think!
VILLINELLE.
What's a Villinelle?
She's a Witch-Dragon.

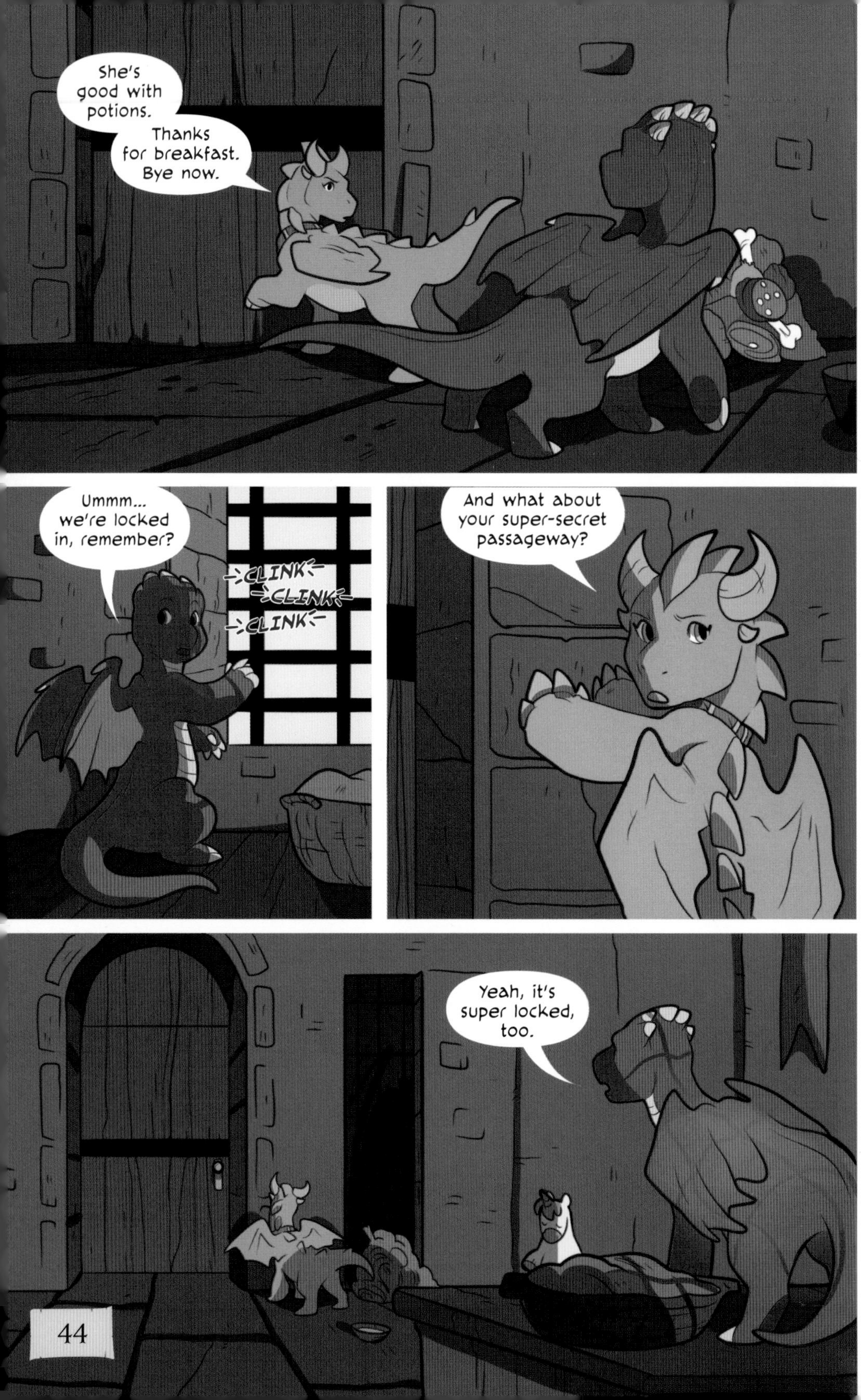
She's good with potions.
Thanks for breakfast. Bye now.
Ummm... we're locked in, remember?
CLINK
CLINK
CLINK
And what about your super-secret passageway?
Yeah, it's super locked, too.

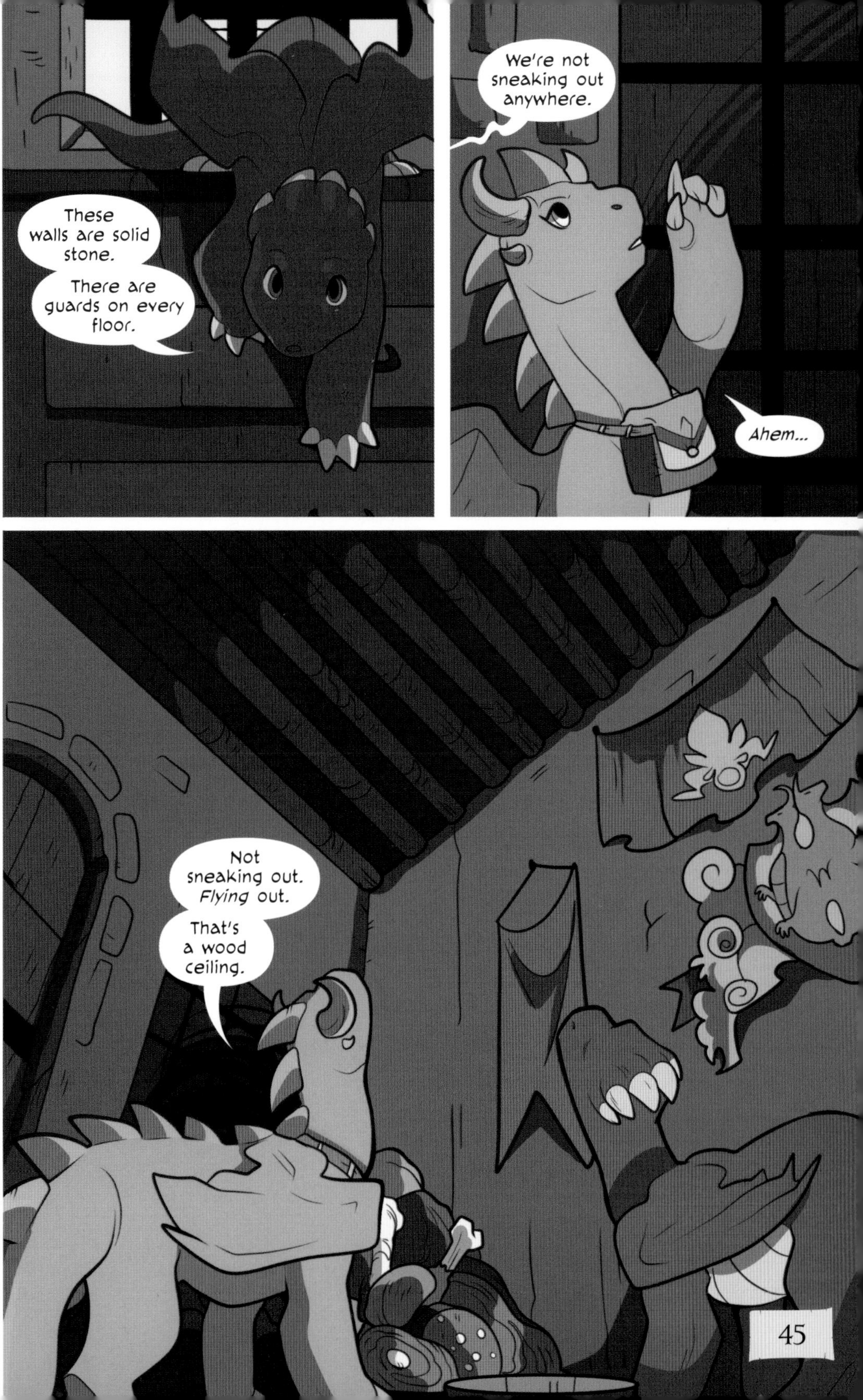
These walls are solid stone.
There are guards on every floor.
We're not sneaking out anywhere.
Ahem...
Not sneaking out. *Flying* out.
That's a wood ceiling.

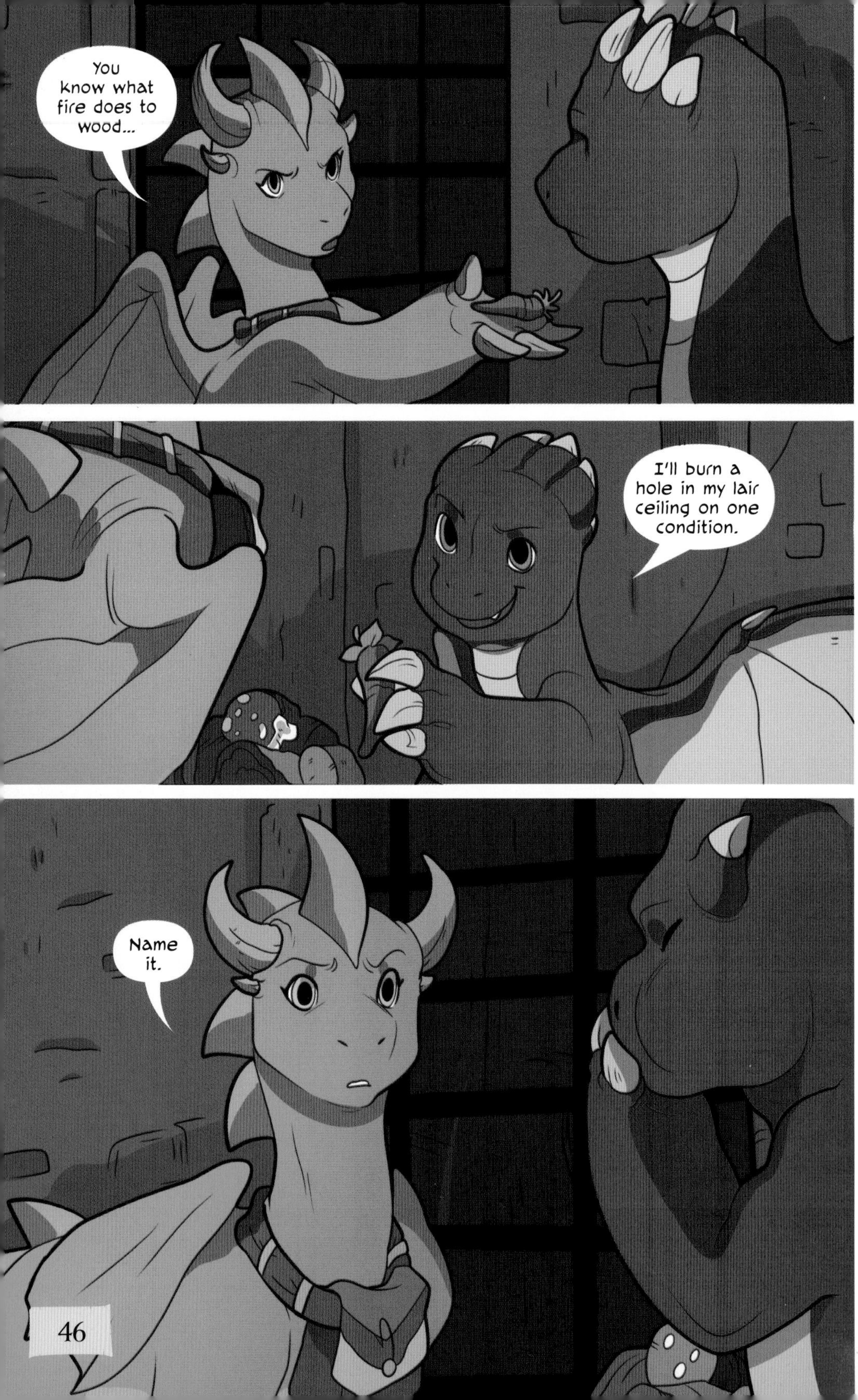
You know what fire does to wood...
I'll burn a hole in my lair ceiling on one condition.
Name it.

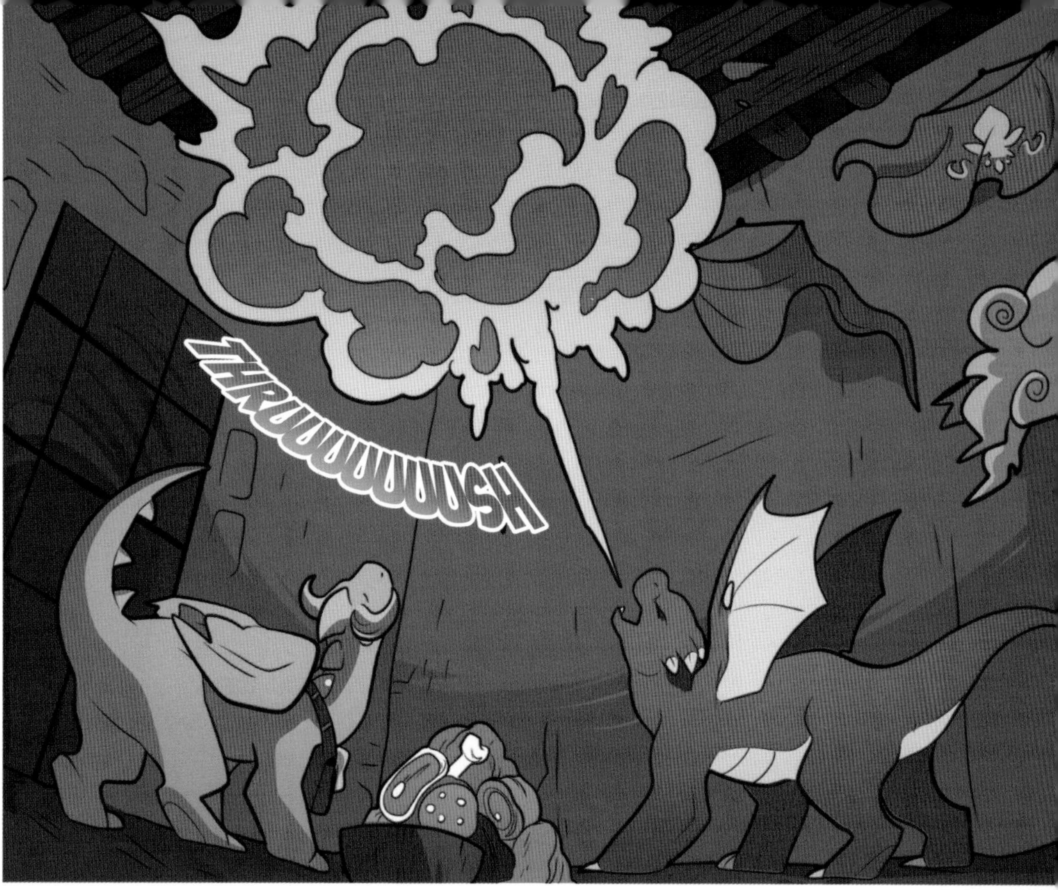
THROOOOOOOSH

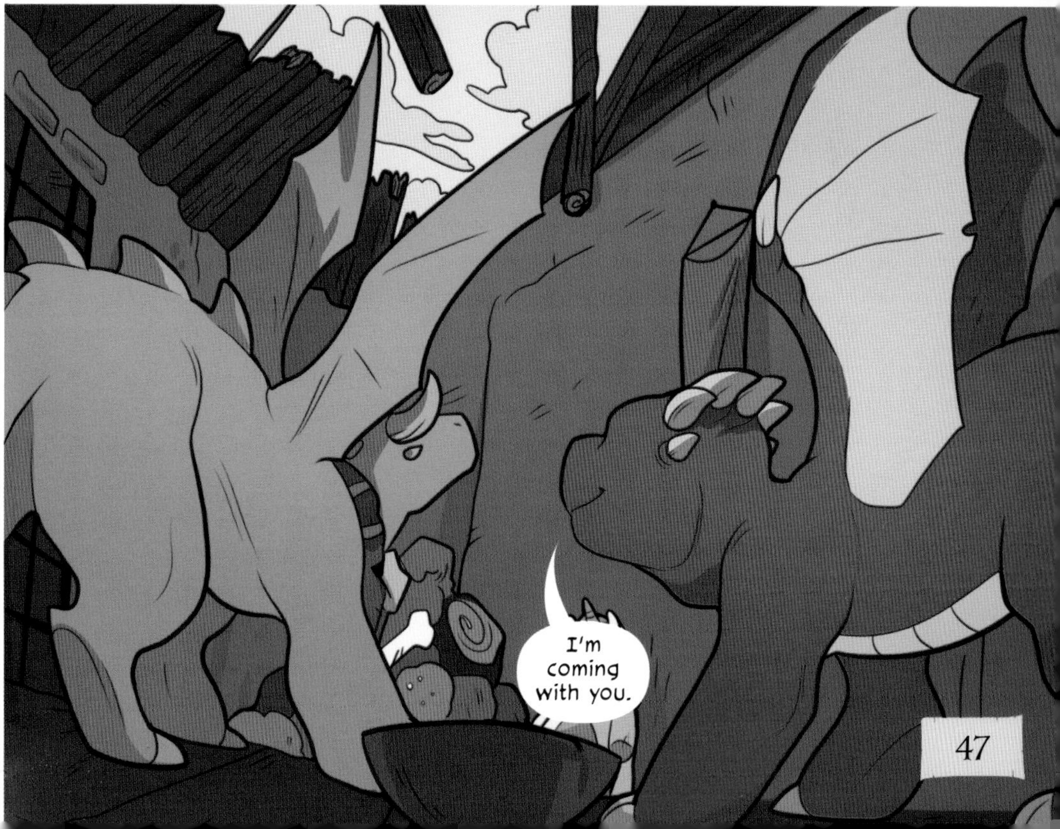
I'm coming with you.

Chapter 4

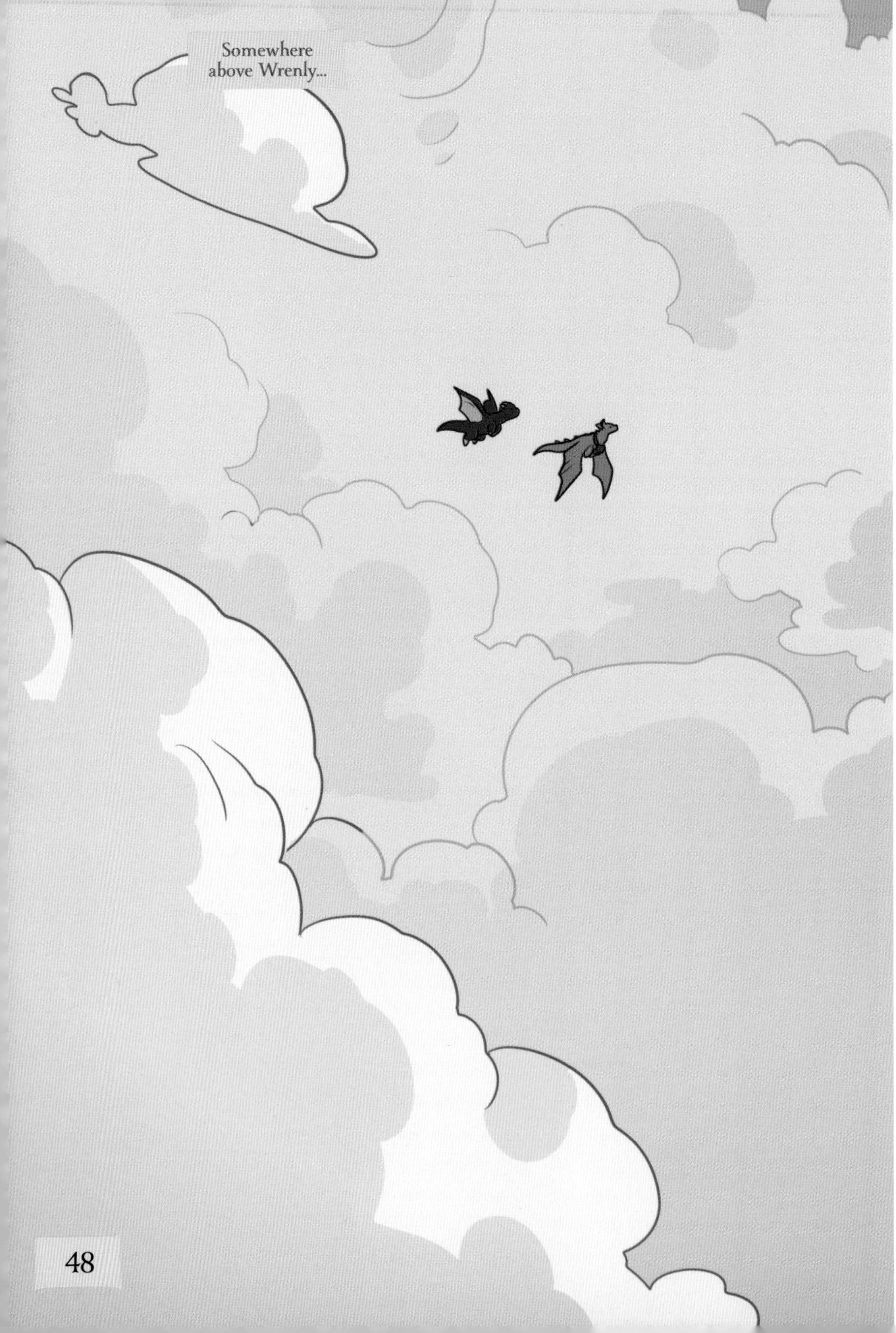
Somewhere above Wrenly...

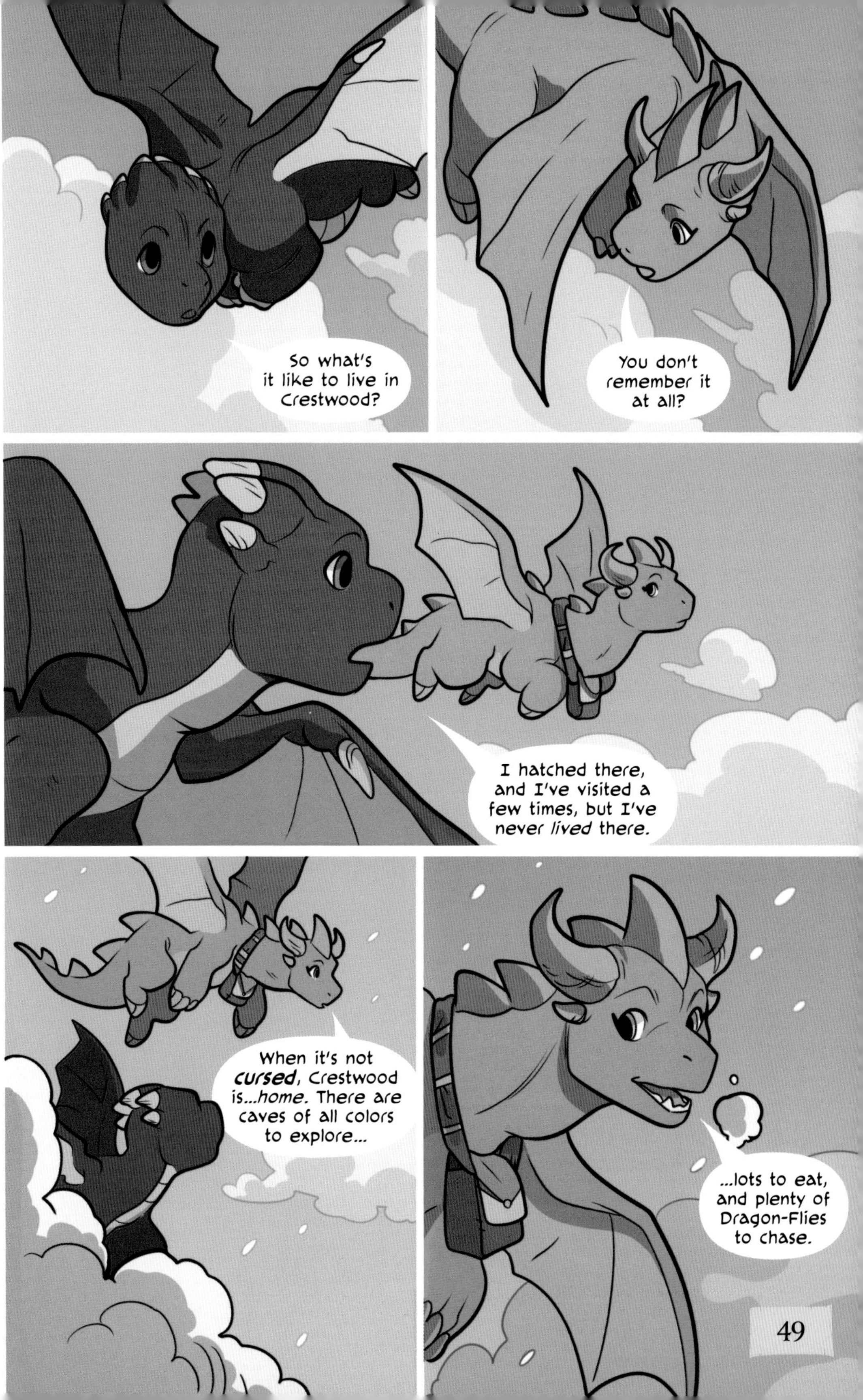
So what's it like to live in Crestwood?
You don't remember it at all?
I hatched there, and I've visited a few times, but I've never *lived* there.
When it's not ***cursed***, Crestwood is...*home*. There are caves of all colors to explore...
...lots to eat, and plenty of Dragon-Flies to chase.

51

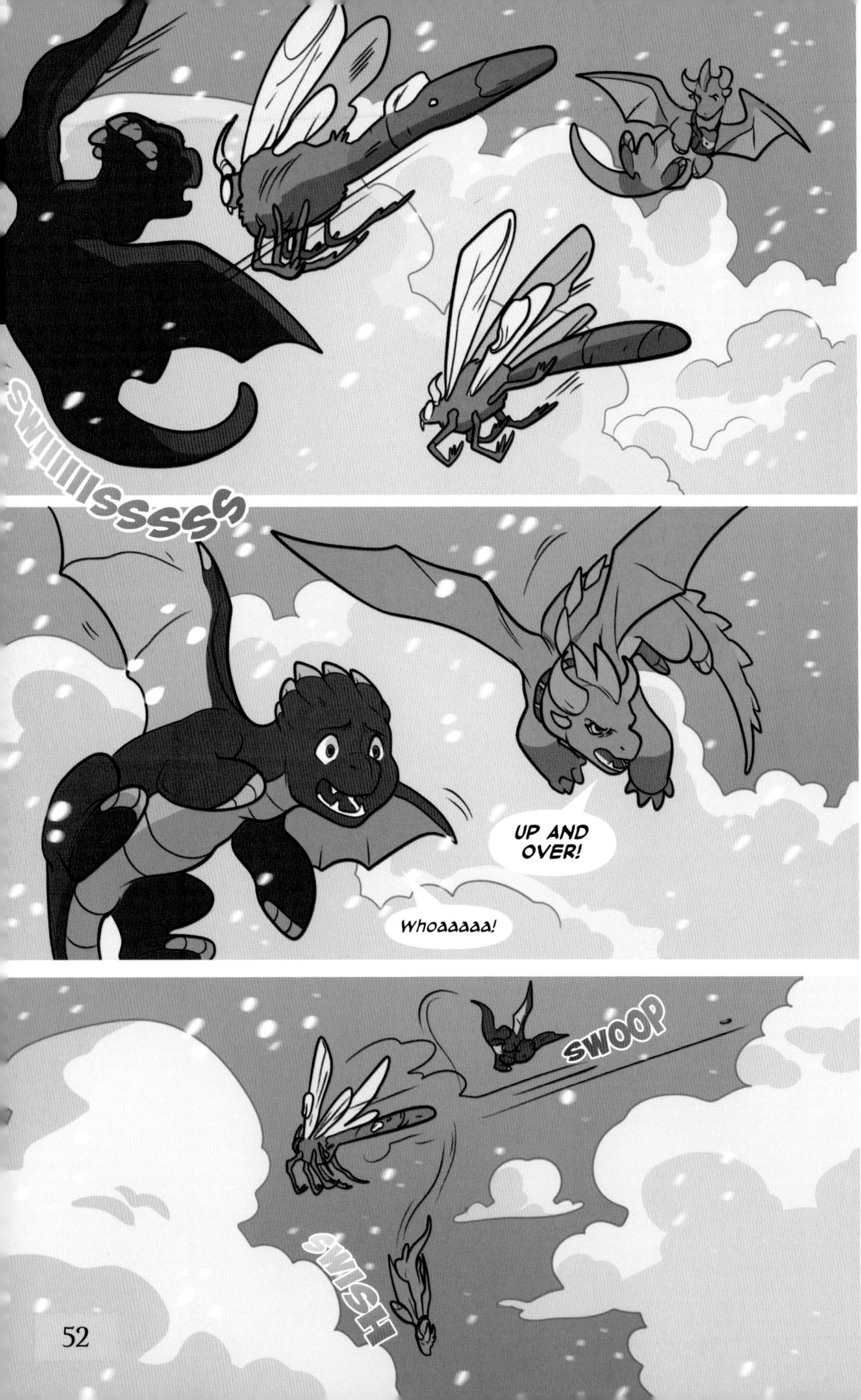
SWIIIIISSSSSS
UP AND OVER!
Whoaaaaa!
SWOOP
SWISH

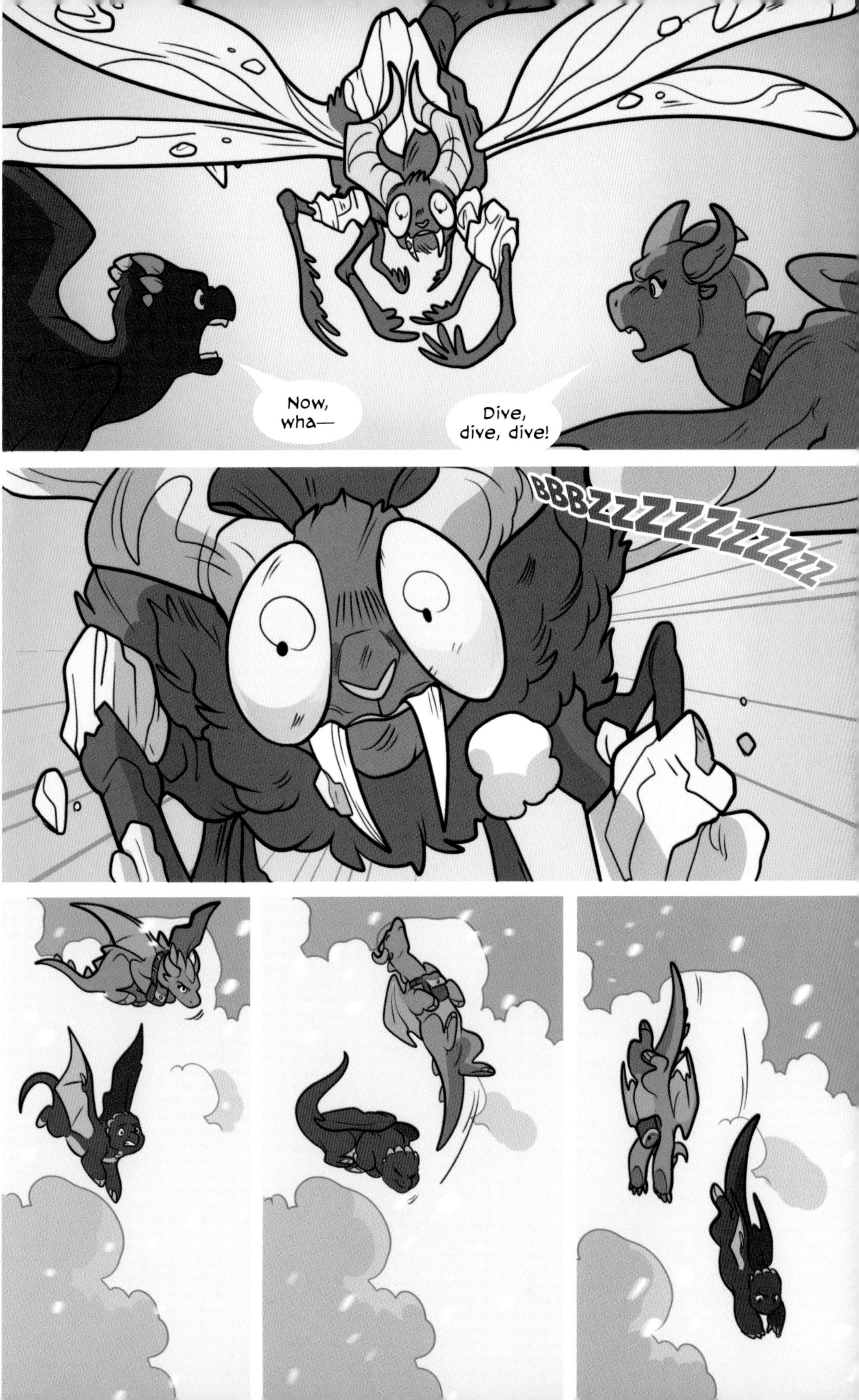
Now, wha—
Dive, dive, dive!
BBBZZZZZZZZZZZ

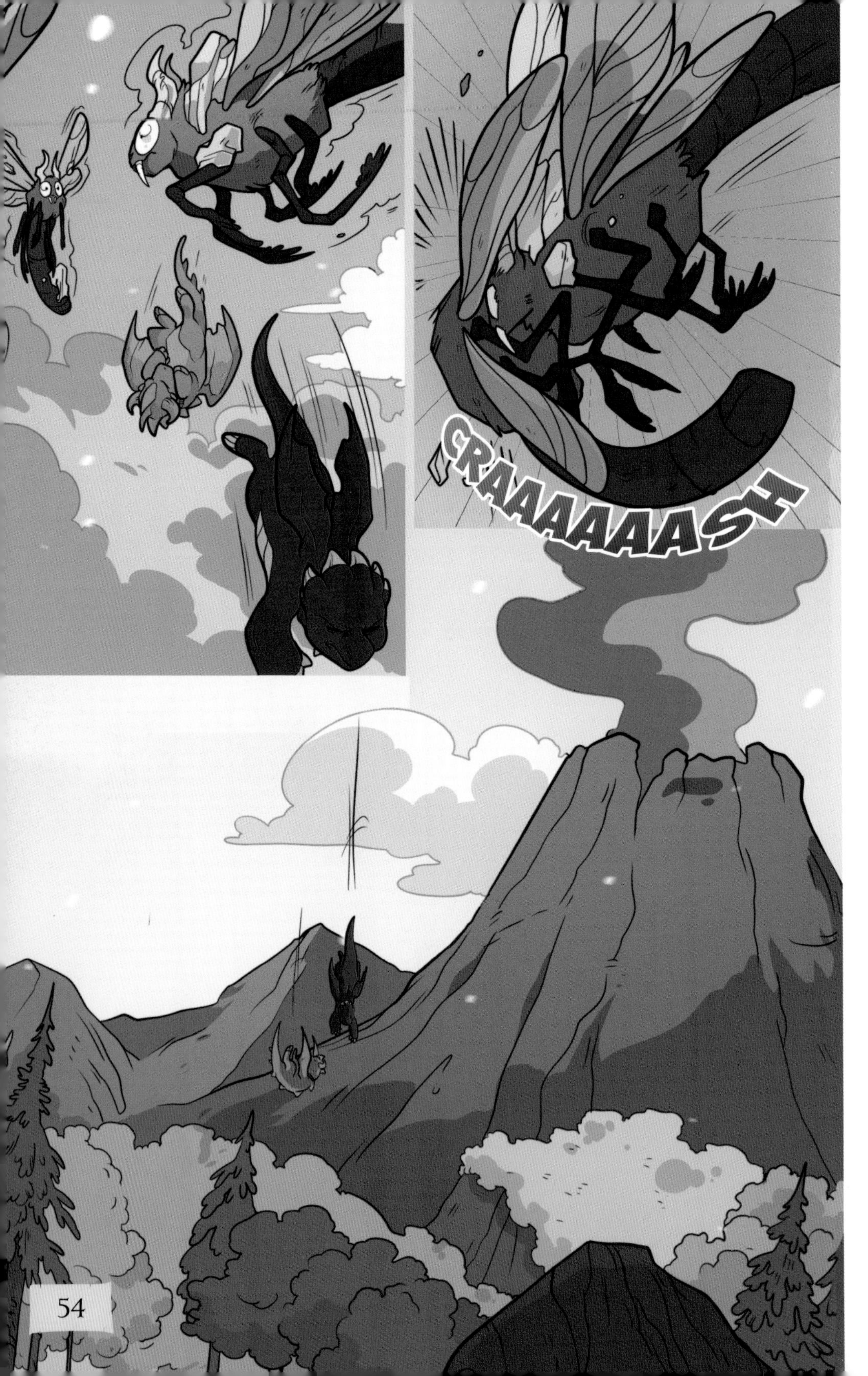
CRAAAAAASH

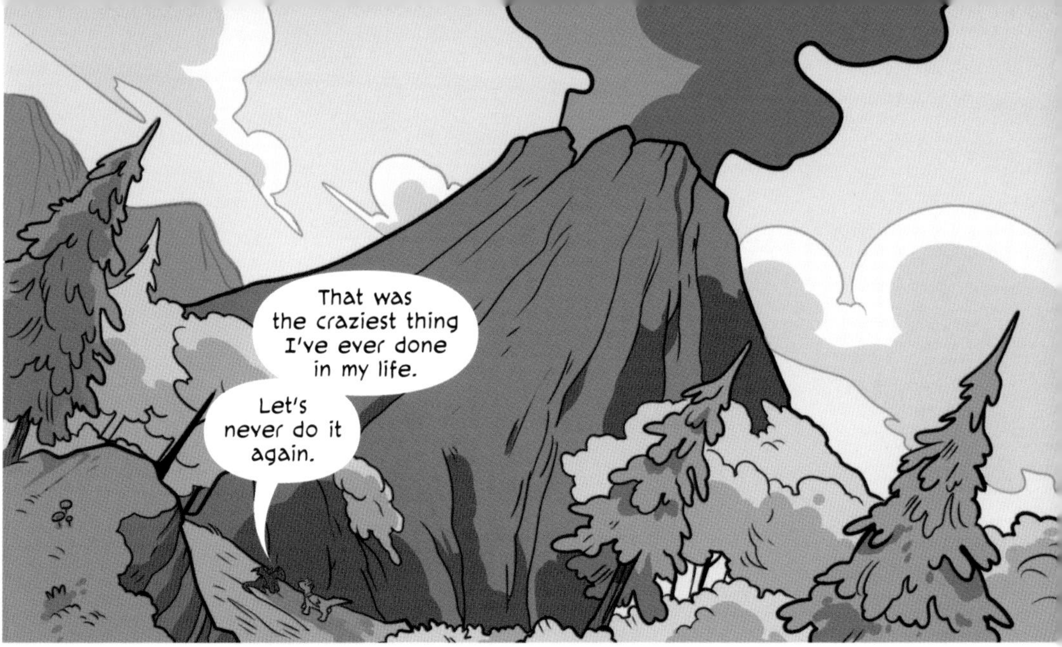
That was the craziest thing I've ever done in my life.
Let's never do it again.

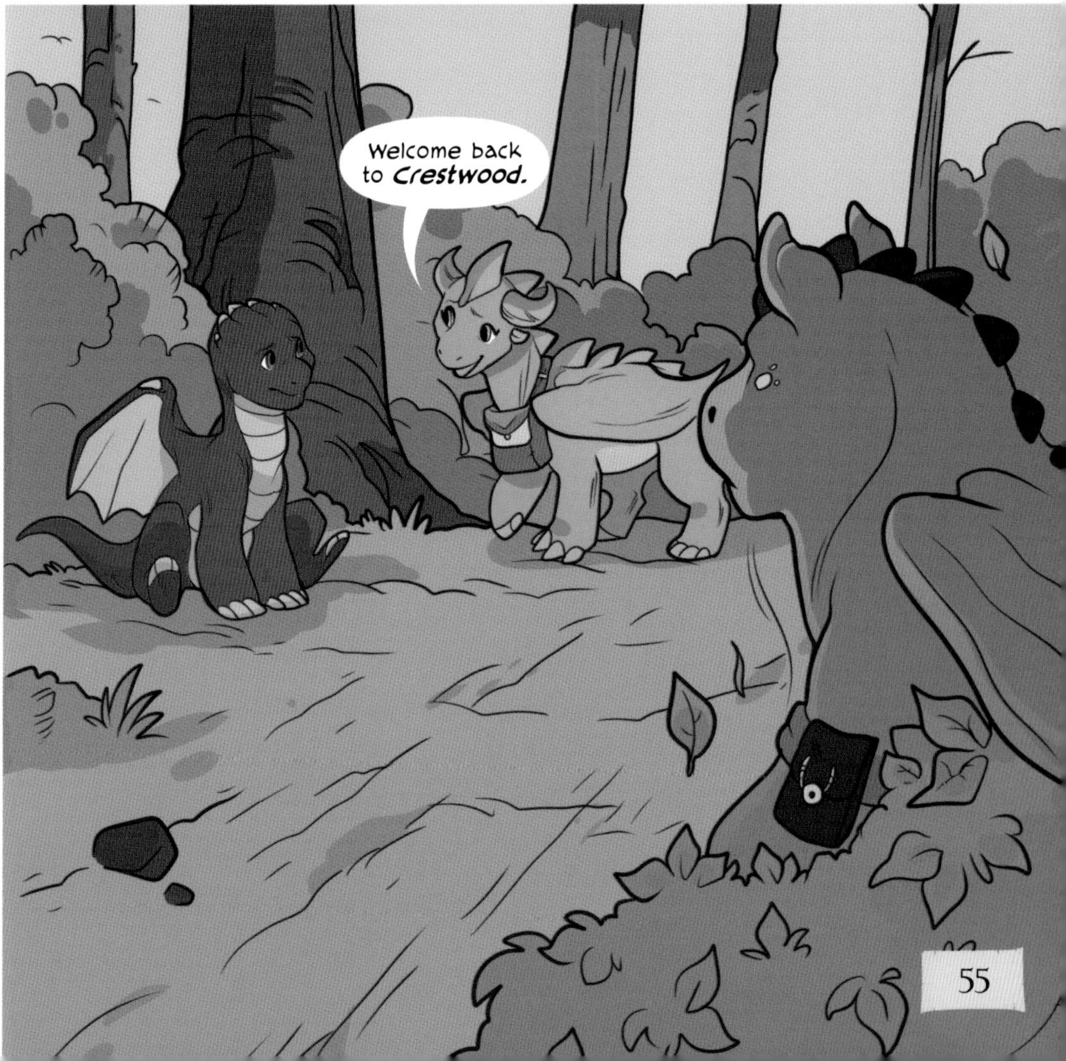
Welcome back to *Crestwood.*

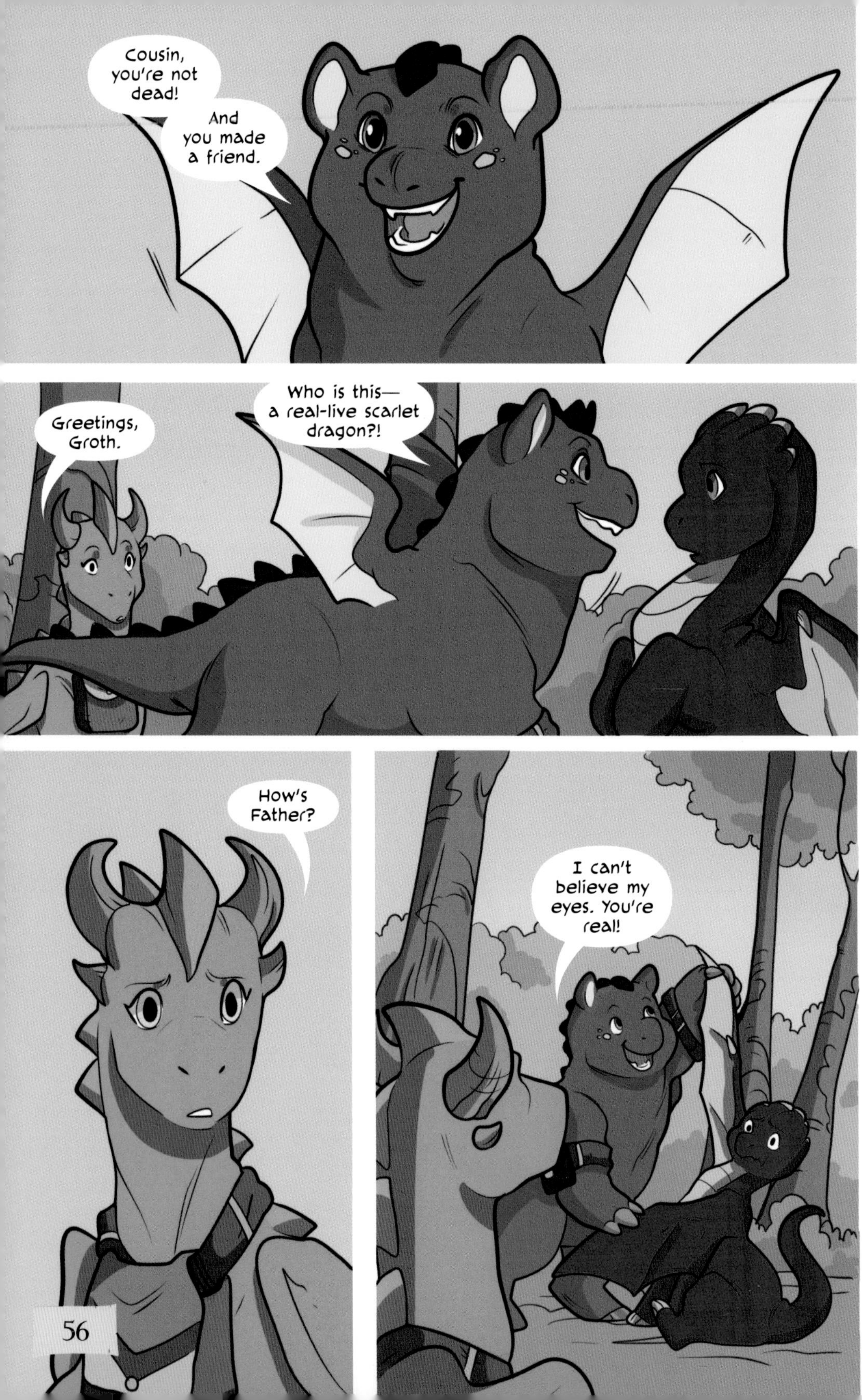
Cousin, you're not dead!
And you made a friend.
Greetings, Groth.
Who is this— a real-live scarlet dragon?!
How's Father?
I can't believe my eyes. You're real!

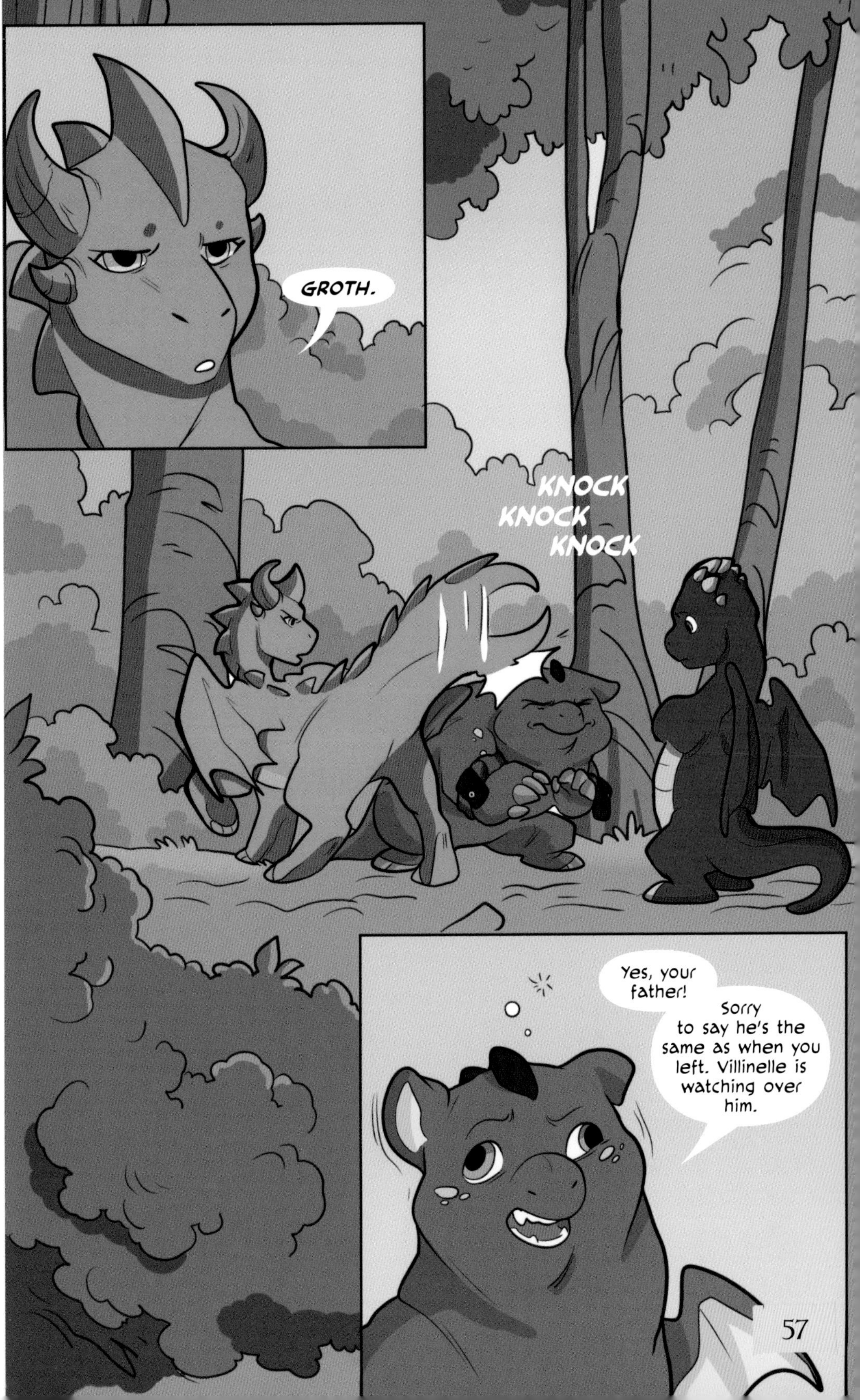
GROTH.
KNOCK
KNOCK
KNOCK
Yes, your father!
Sorry to say he's the same as when you left. Villinelle is watching over him.

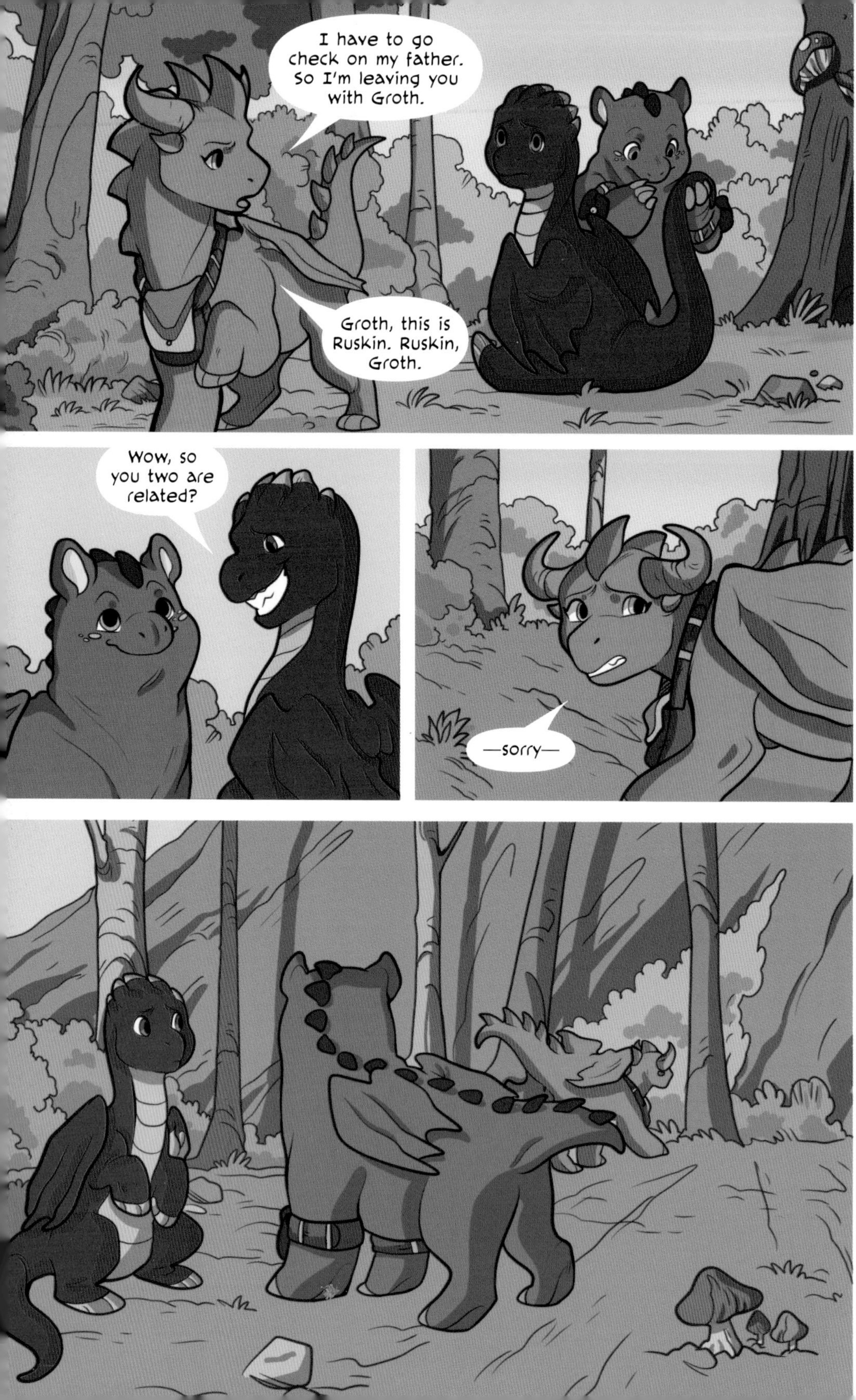
I have to go check on my father. So I'm leaving you with Groth.
Groth, this is Ruskin. Ruskin, Groth.
Wow, so you two are related?
—sorry—

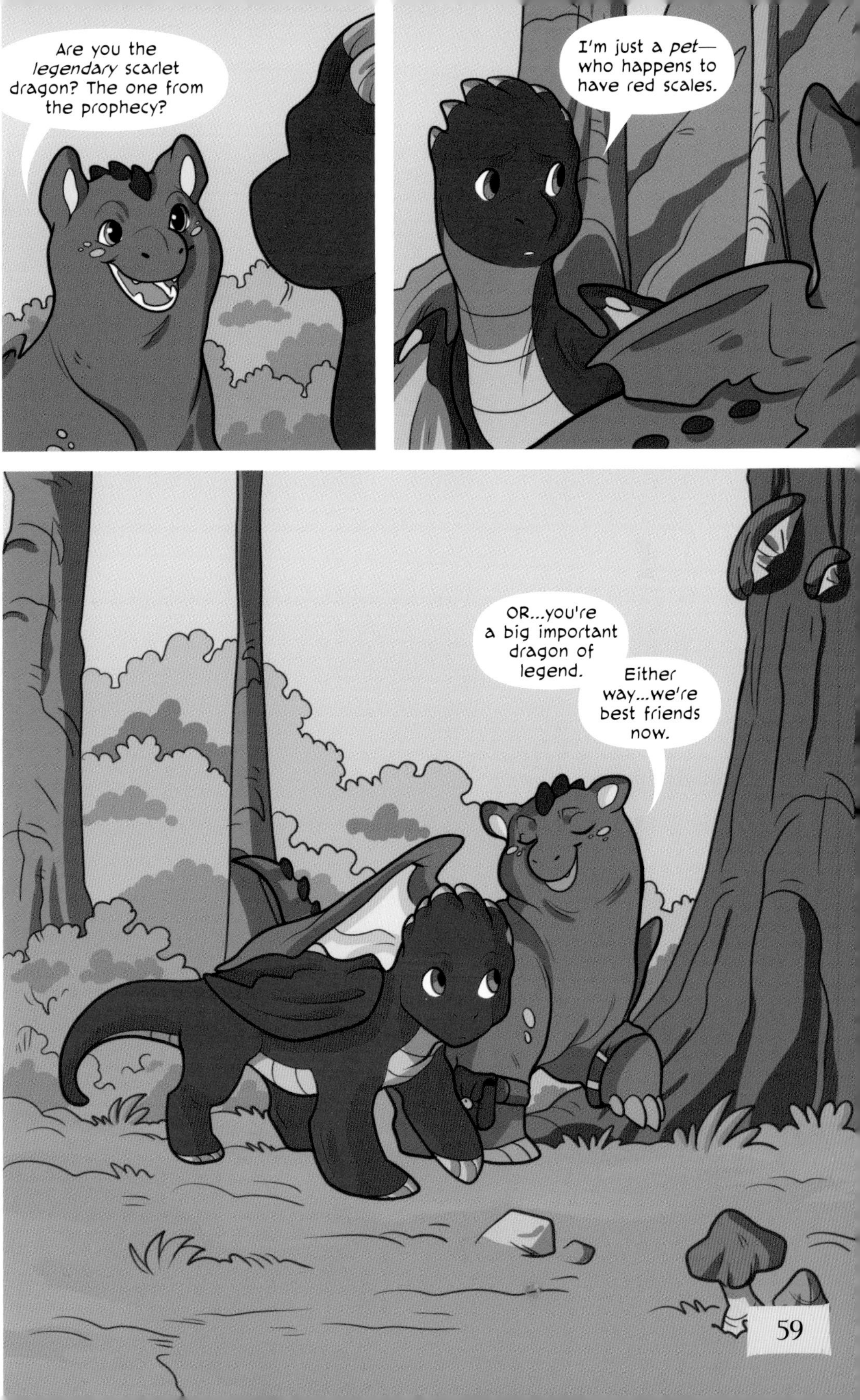
Are you the *legendary* scarlet dragon? The one from the prophecy?
I'm just a *pet*—who happens to have red scales.
OR...you're a big important dragon of legend.
Either way...we're best friends now.

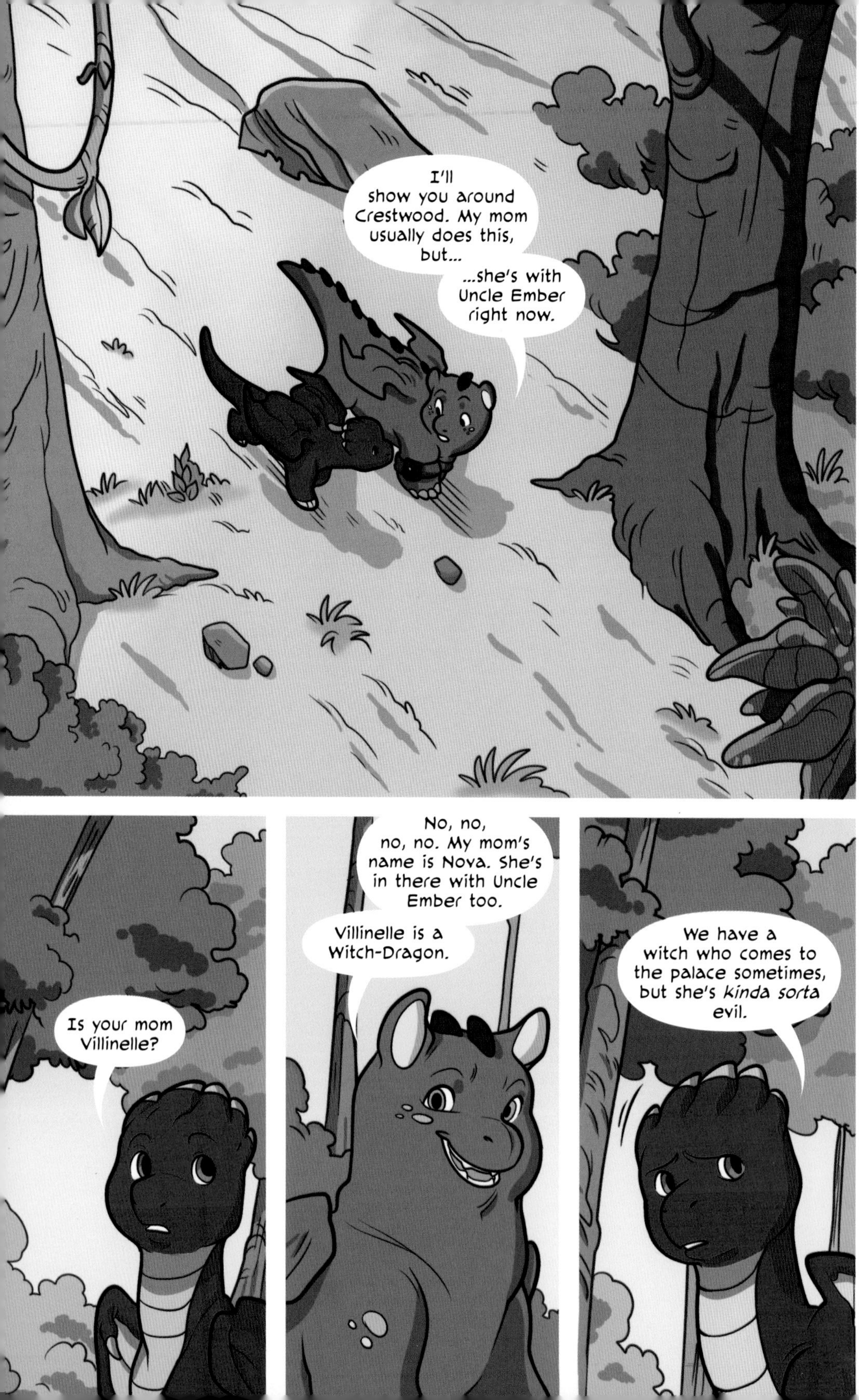
I'll show you around Crestwood. My mom usually does this, but...
...she's with Uncle Ember right now.
Is your mom Villinelle?
No, no, no, no. My mom's name is Nova. She's in there with Uncle Ember too.
Villinelle is a Witch-Dragon.
We have a witch who comes to the palace sometimes, but she's *kinda sorta* evil.

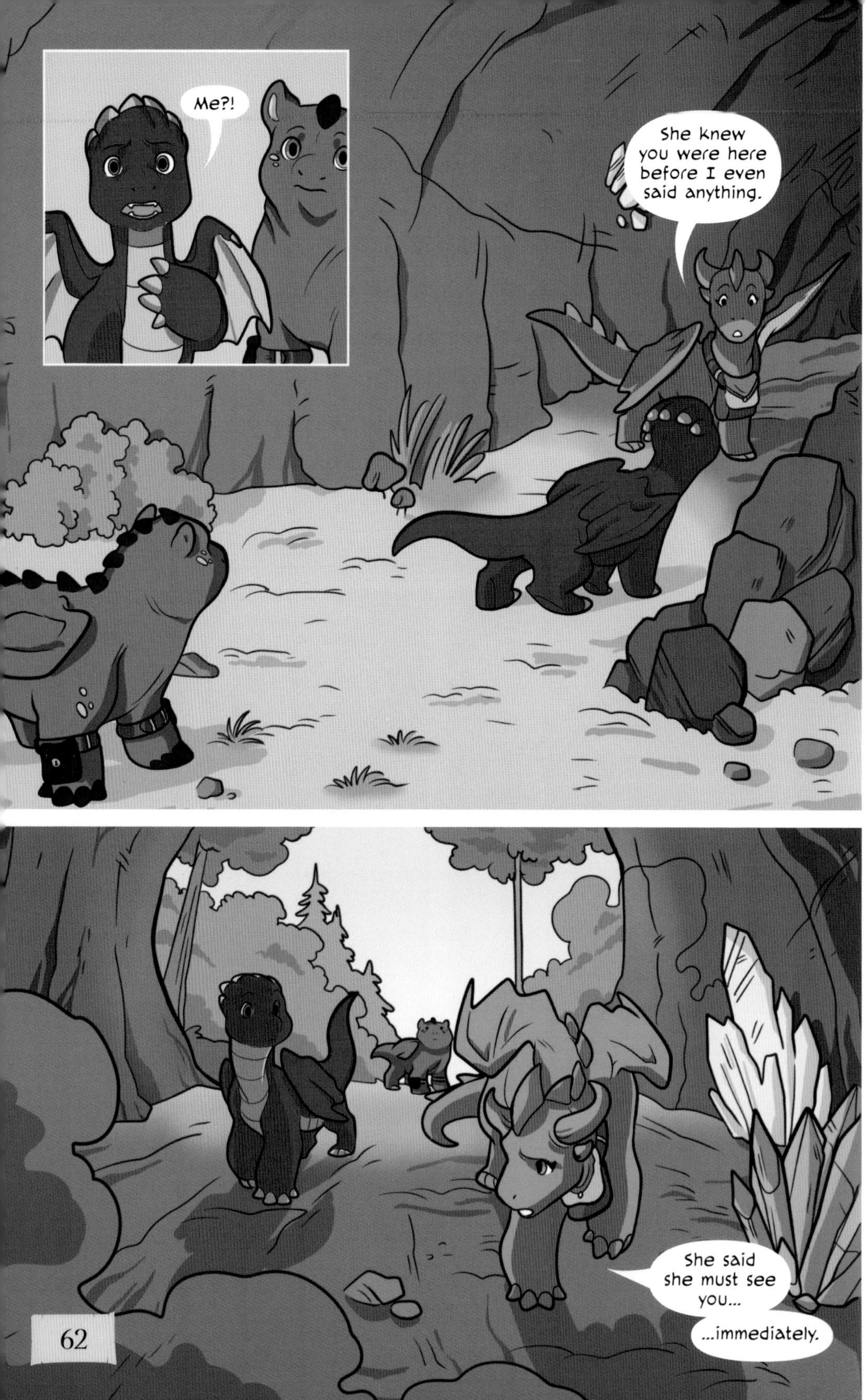
Me?!
She knew you were here before I even said anything.
She said she must see you...
...immediately.

Chapter 5

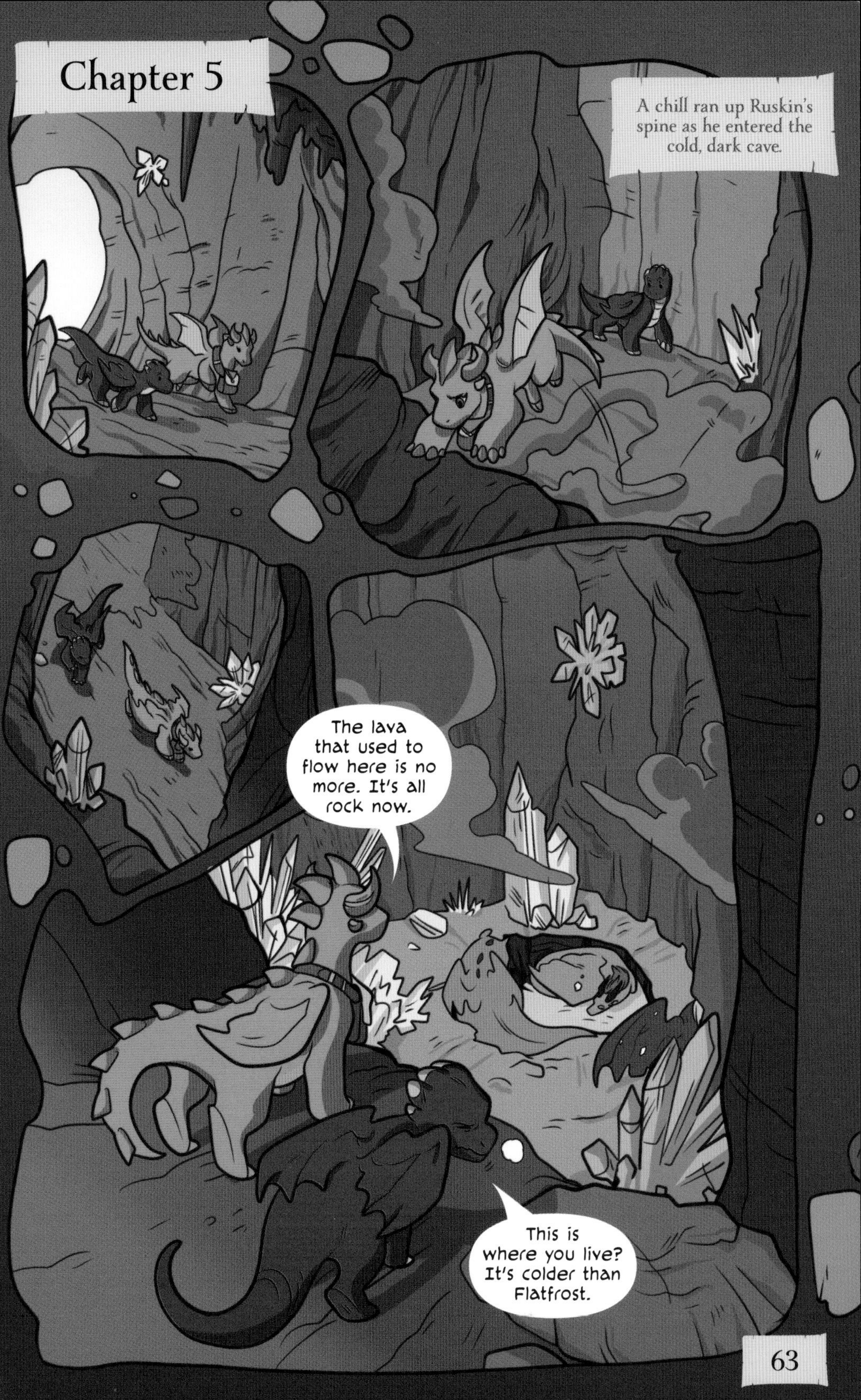
A chill ran up Ruskin's spine as he entered the cold, dark cave.
The lava that used to flow here is no more. It's all rock now.
This is where you live? It's colder than Flatfrost.

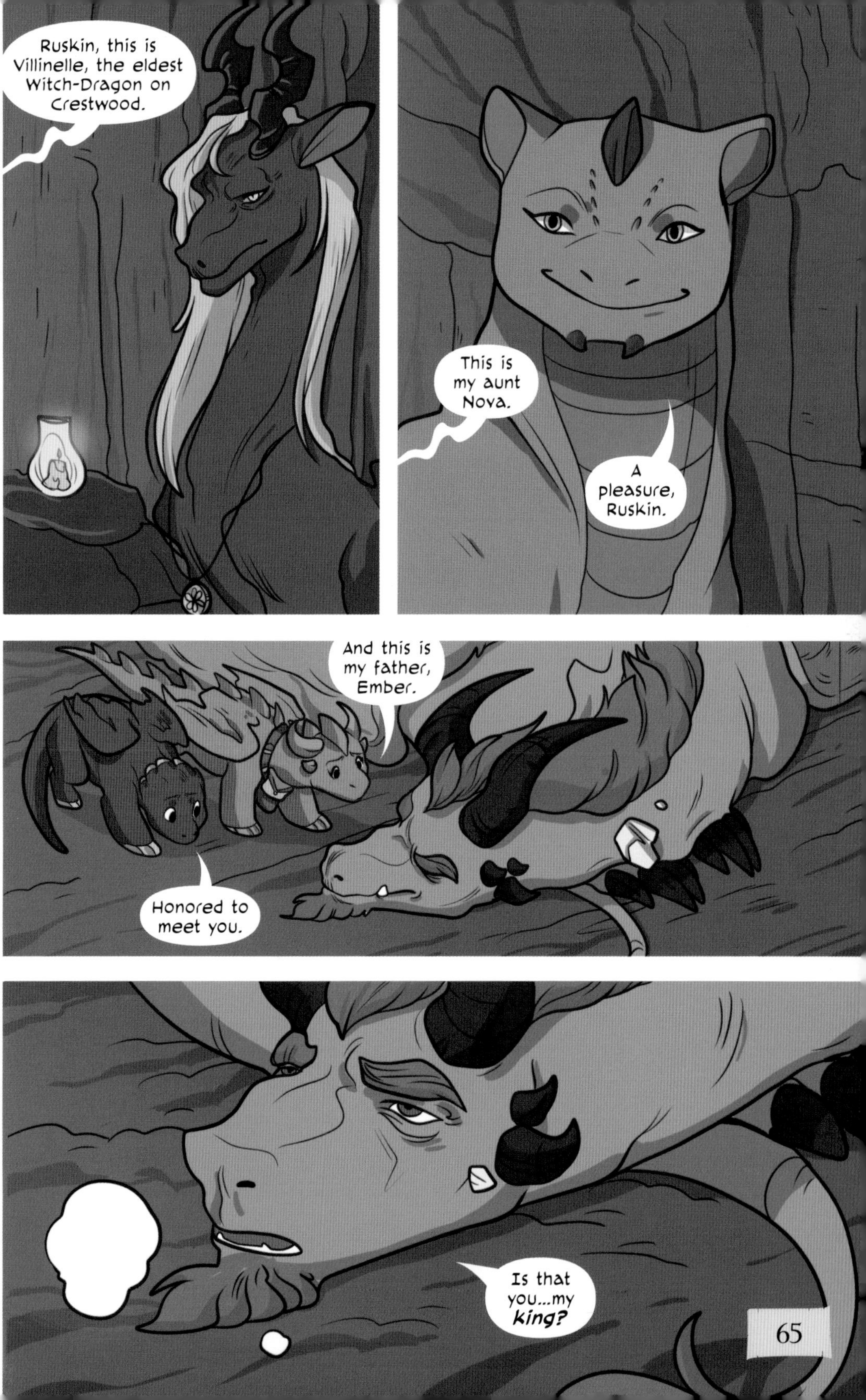
Ruskin, this is Villinelle, the eldest Witch-Dragon on Crestwood.
This is my aunt Nova.
A pleasure, Ruskin.
And this is my father, Ember.
Honored to meet you.
Is that you...my *king?*

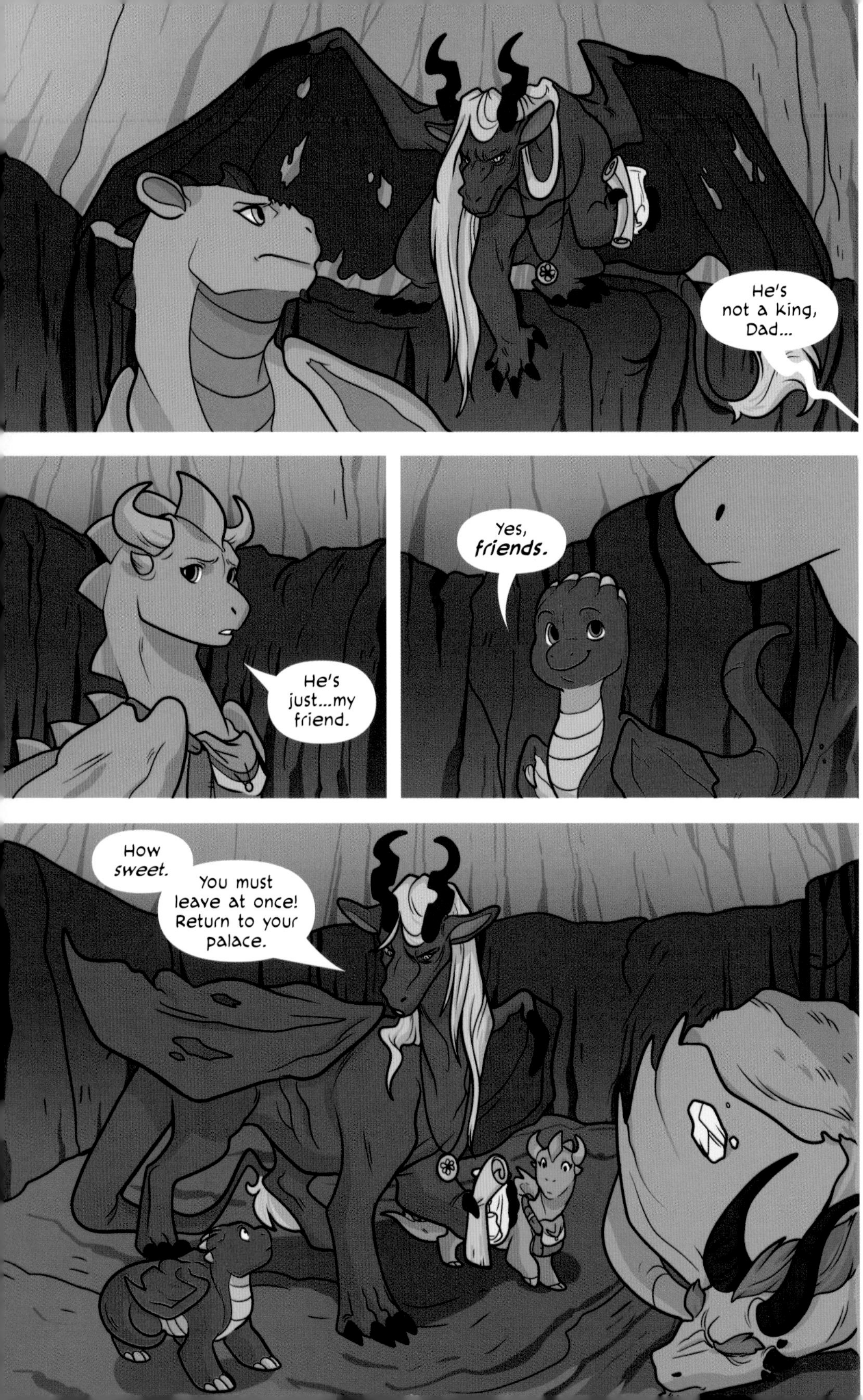
He's not a king, Dad...
He's just...my friend.
Yes, *friends.*
How *sweet.*
You must leave at once! Return to your palace.

67

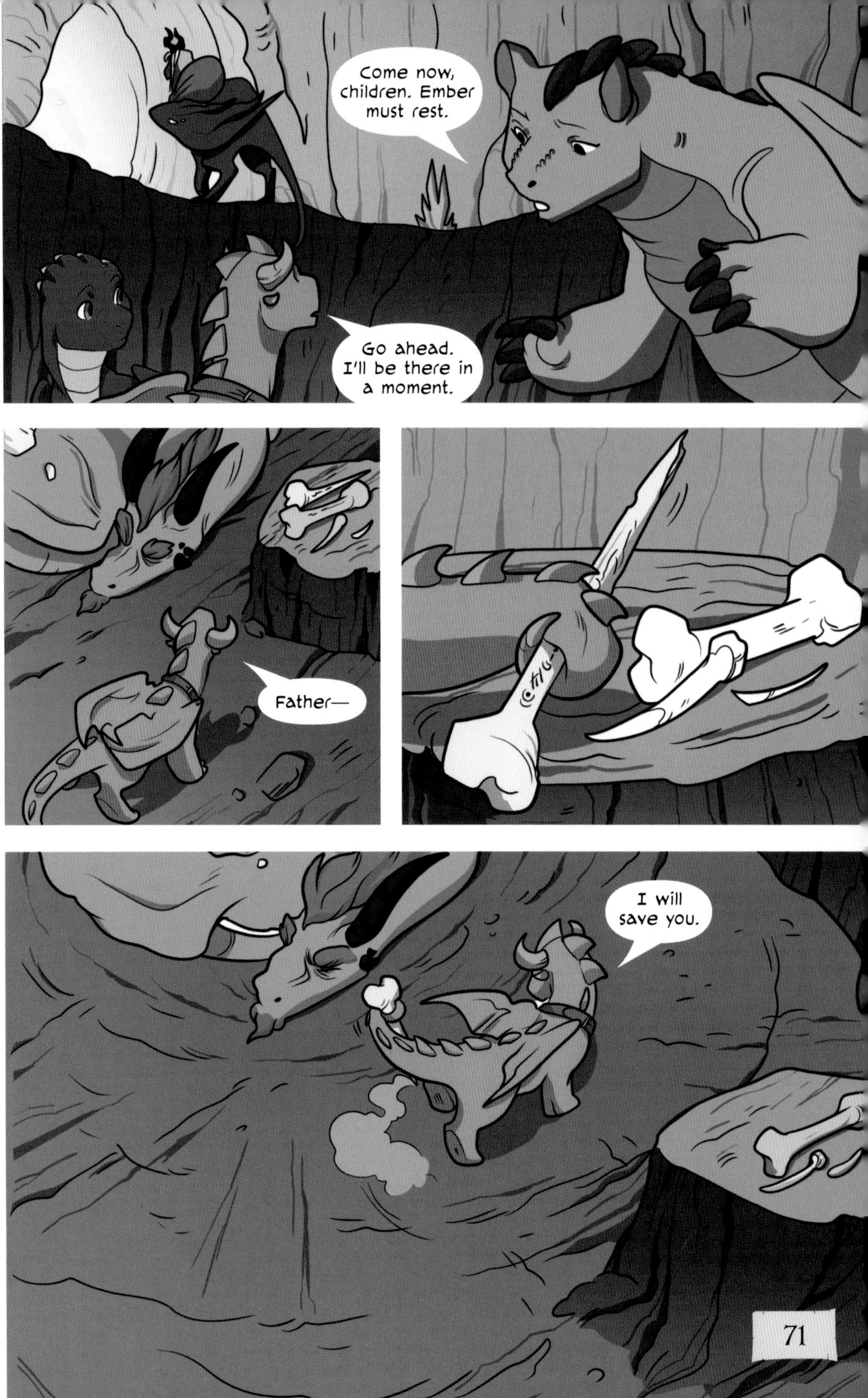
Come now, children. Ember must rest.
Go ahead. I'll be there in a moment.
Father—
I will save you.

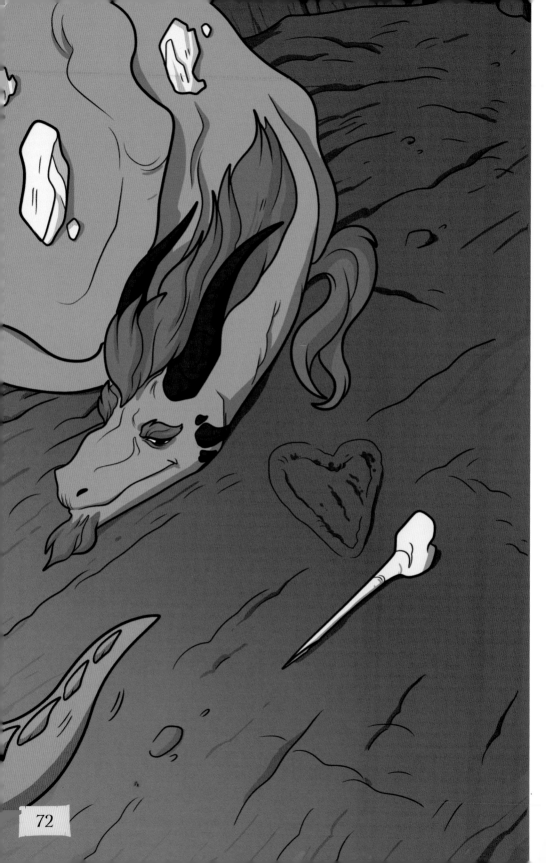

73

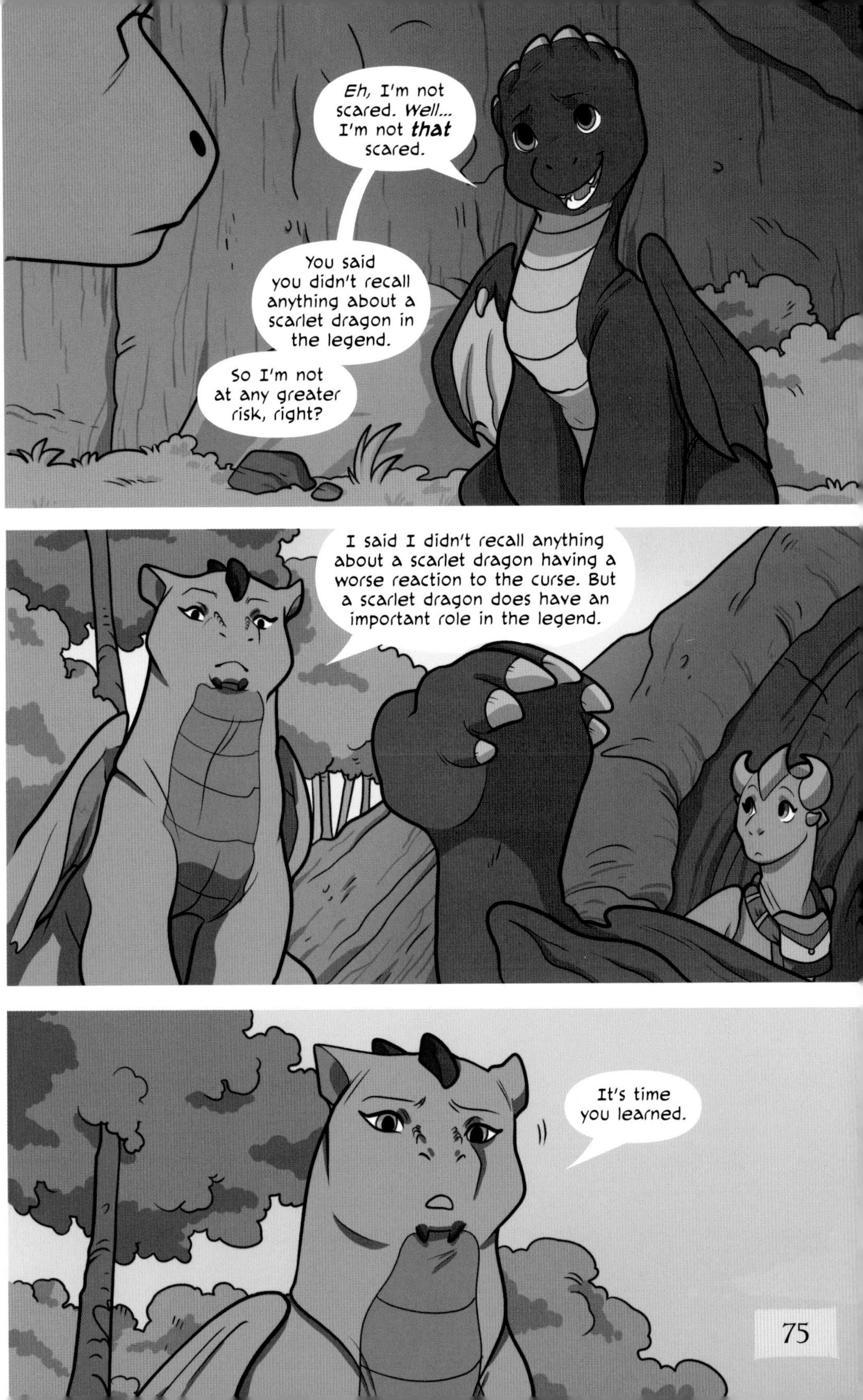
Eh, I'm not scared. *Well...* I'm not ***that*** scared.
You said you didn't recall anything about a scarlet dragon in the legend.
So I'm not at any greater risk, right?
I said I didn't recall anything about a scarlet dragon having a worse reaction to the curse. But a scarlet dragon does have an important role in the legend.
It's time you learned.

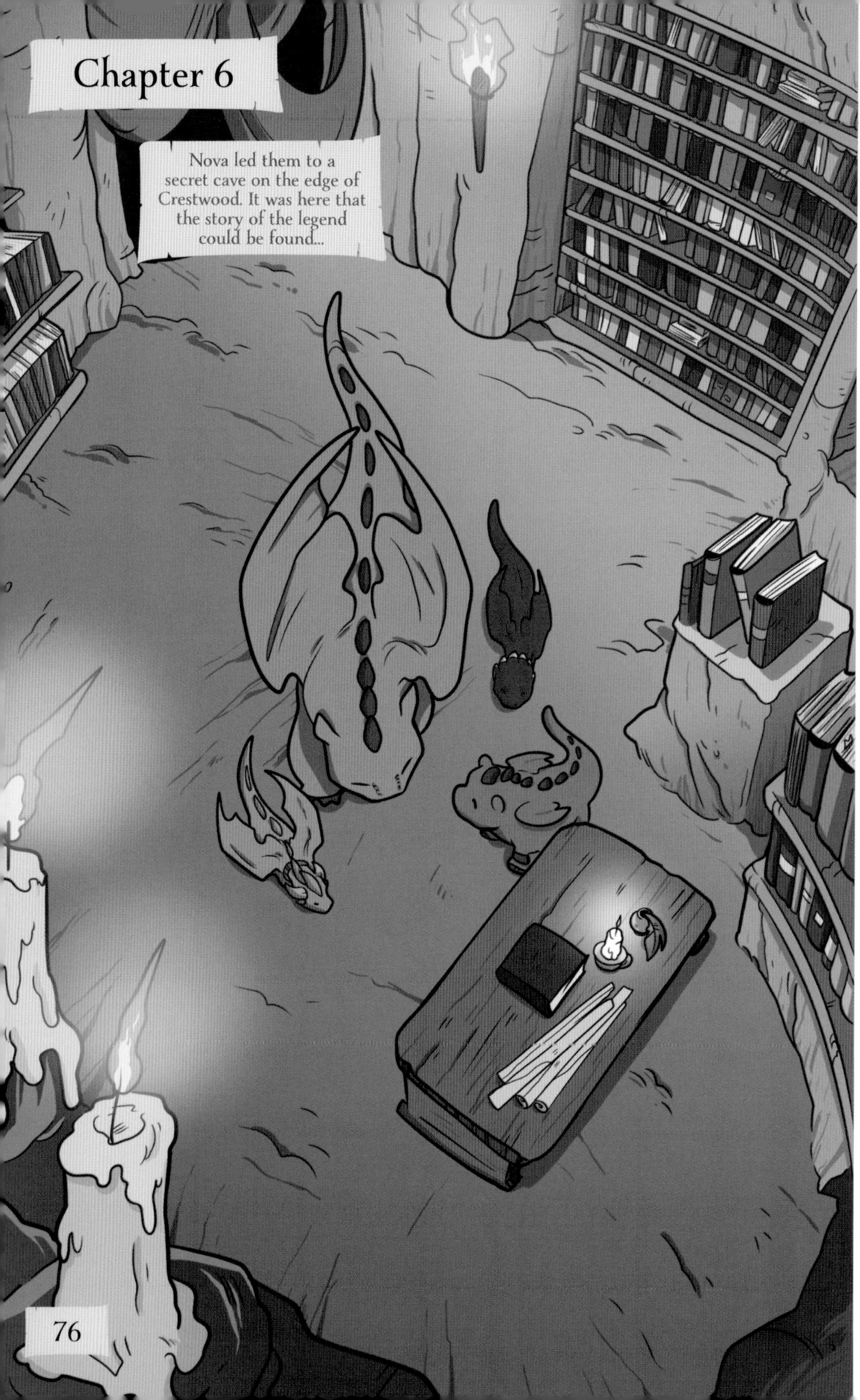
Chapter 6
Nova led them to a secret cave on the edge of Crestwood. It was here that the story of the legend could be found...

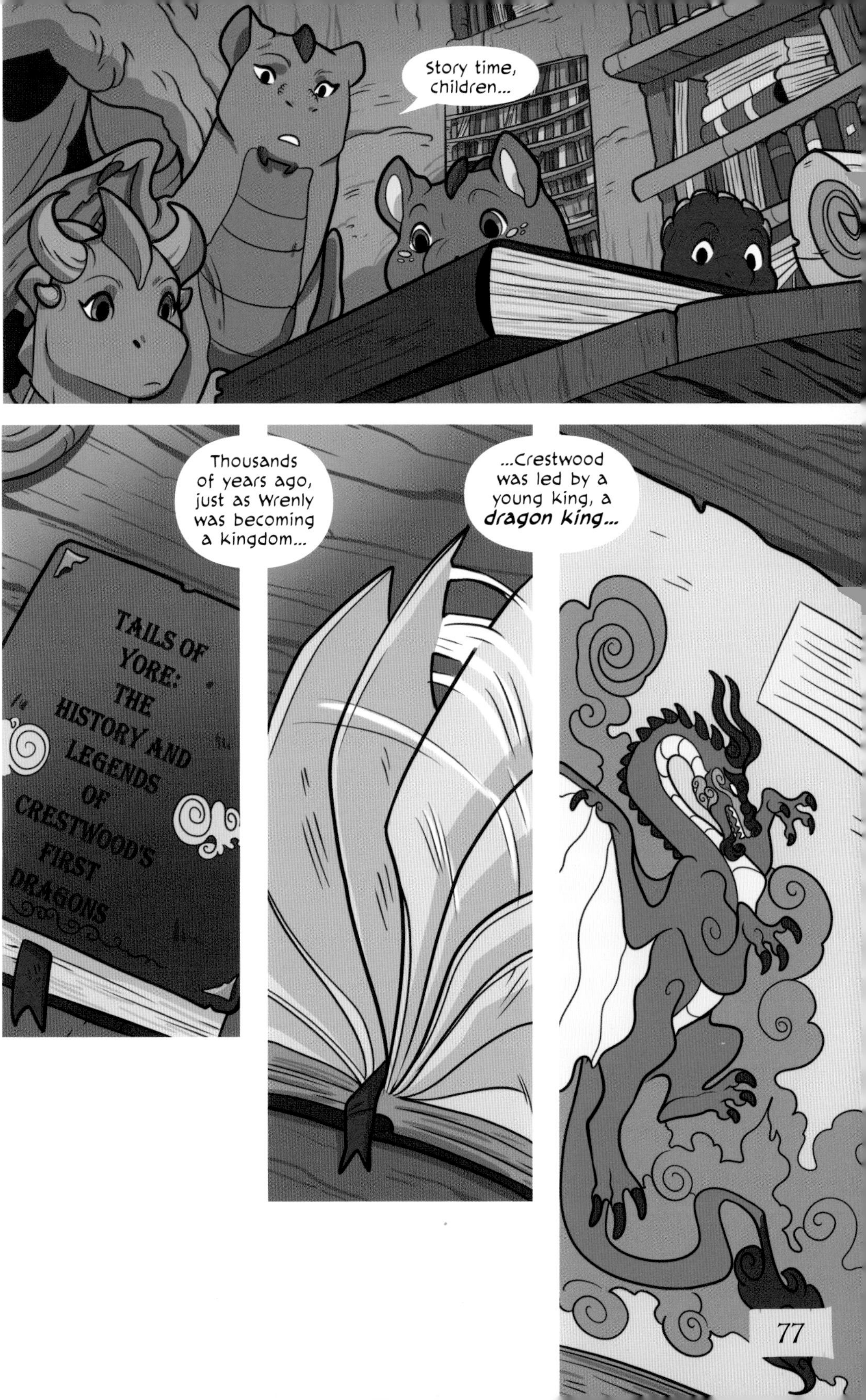
Story time, children...
Thousands of years ago, just as Wrenly was becoming a kingdom...
TAILS OF YORE: THE HISTORY AND LEGENDS OF CRESTWOOD'S FIRST DRAGONS
...Crestwood was led by a young king, a *dragon king...*

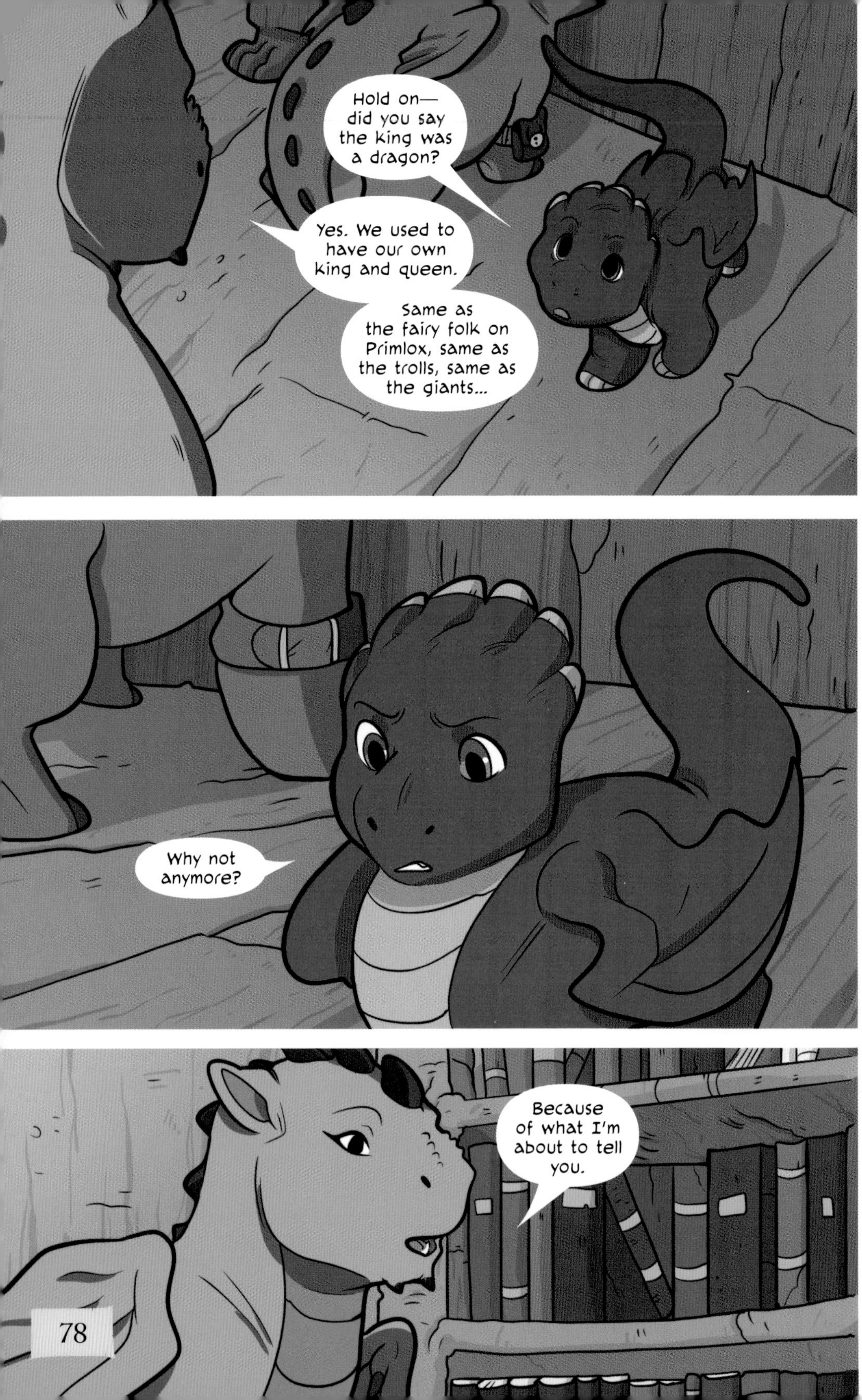
Hold on—
did you say
the king was
a dragon?
Yes. We used to
have our own
king and queen.
Same as
the fairy folk on
Primlox, same as
the trolls, same as
the giants...
Why not
anymore?
Because
of what I'm
about to tell
you.

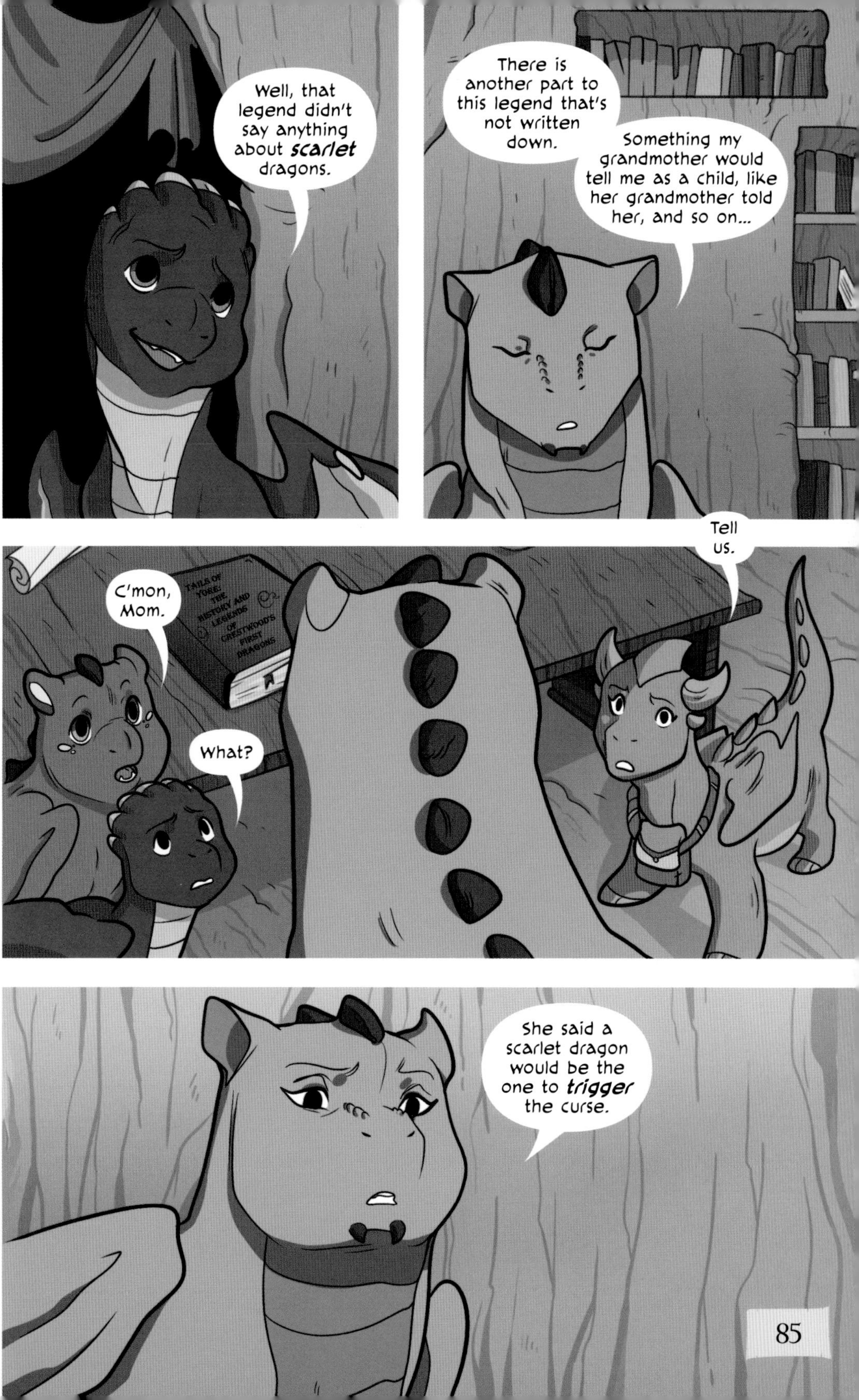
Well, that legend didn't say anything about *scarlet* dragons.
There is another part to this legend that's not written down.
Something my grandmother would tell me as a child, like her grandmother told her, and so on...
C'mon, Mom.
TAILS OF YORE: THE HISTORY AND LEGENDS OF CRESTWOOD'S FIRST DRAGONS
What?
Tell us.
She said a scarlet dragon would be the one to *trigger* the curse.

Chapter 7

89

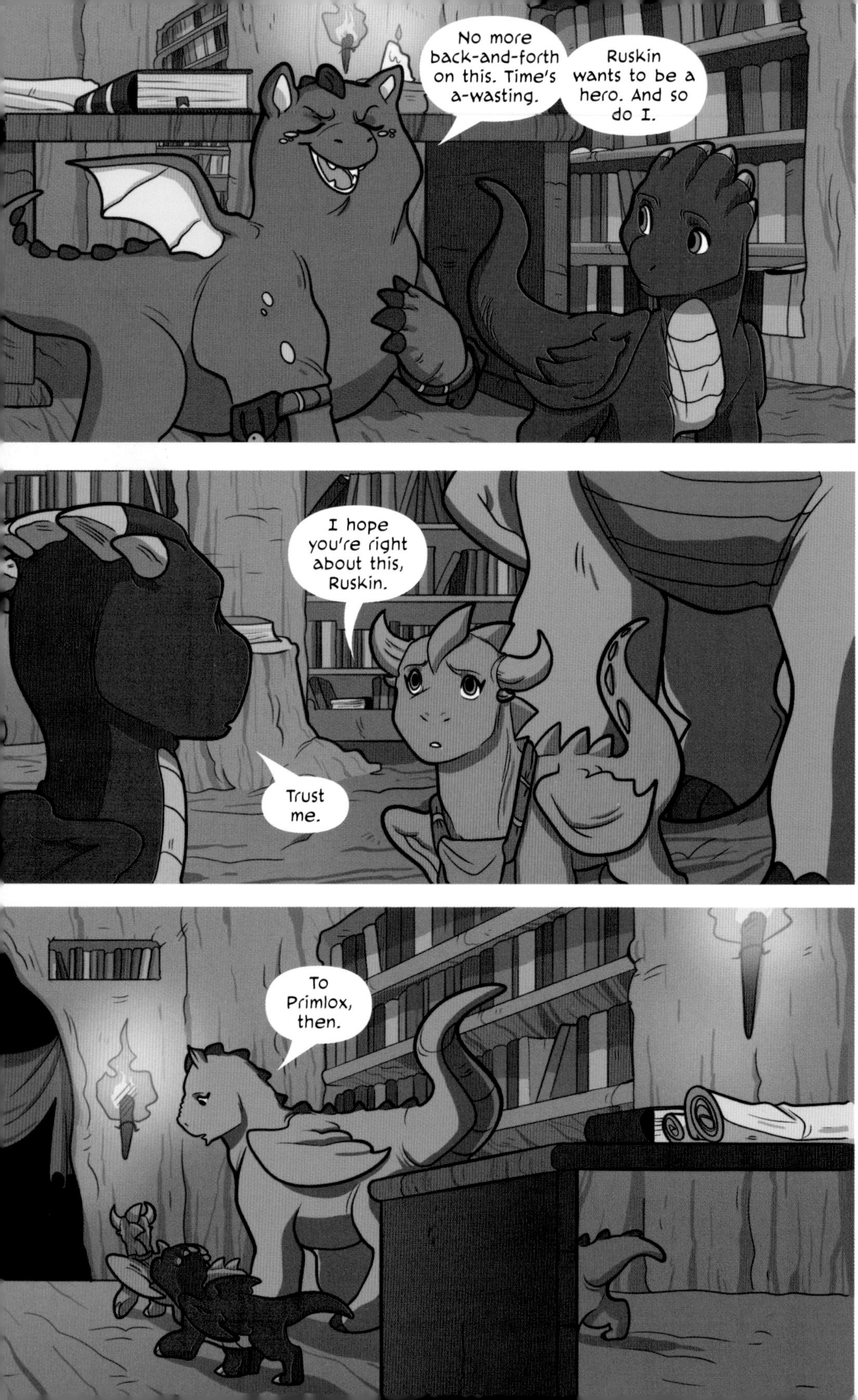
No more back-and-forth on this. Time's a-wasting.
Ruskin wants to be a hero. And so do I.
I hope you're right about this, Ruskin.
Trust me.
To Primlox, then.

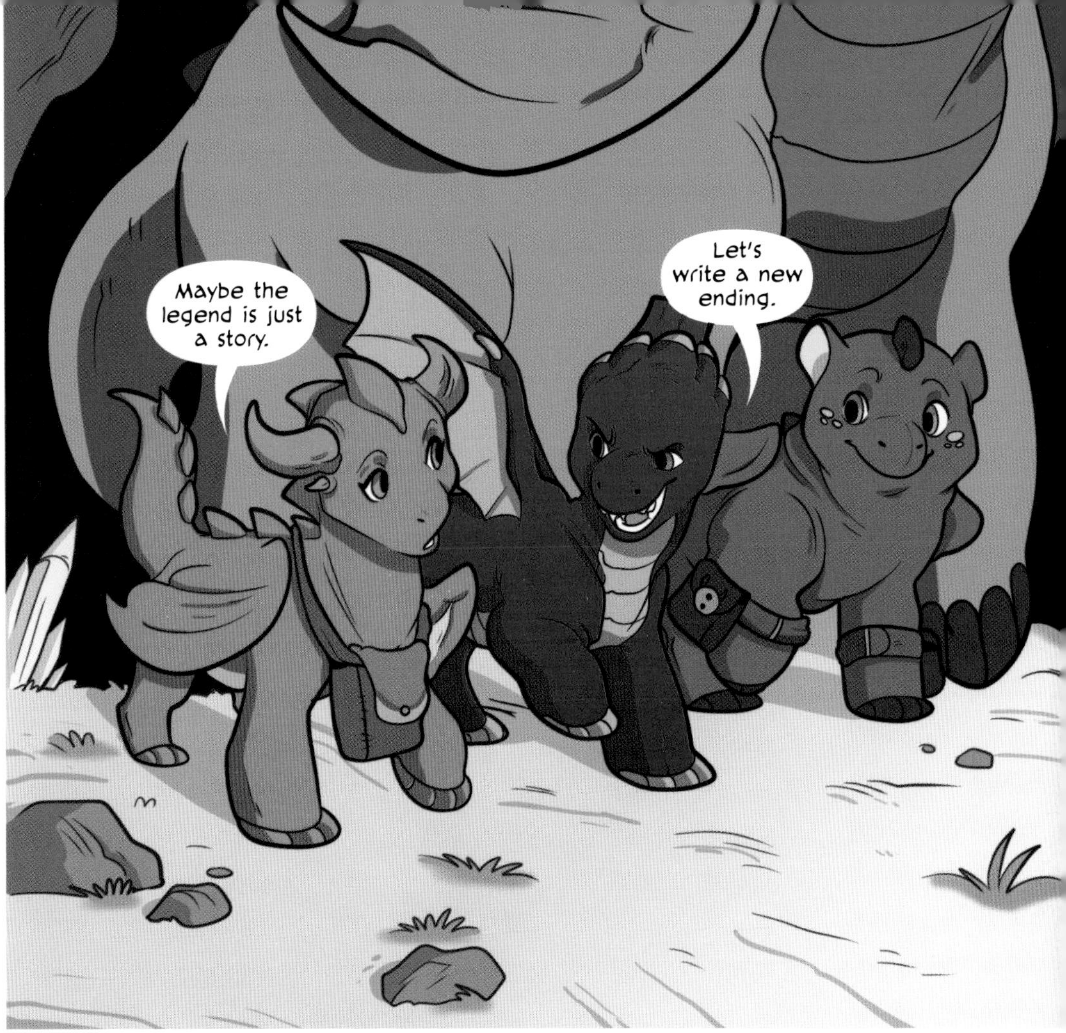
Maybe the legend is just a story.
Let's write a new ending.

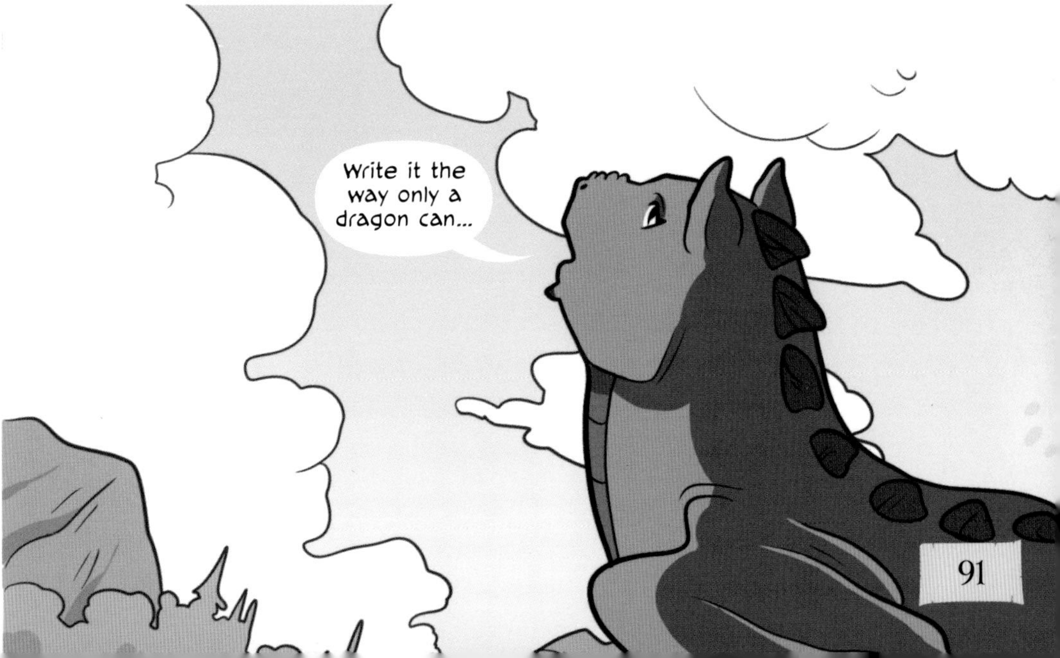
Write it the way only a dragon can...

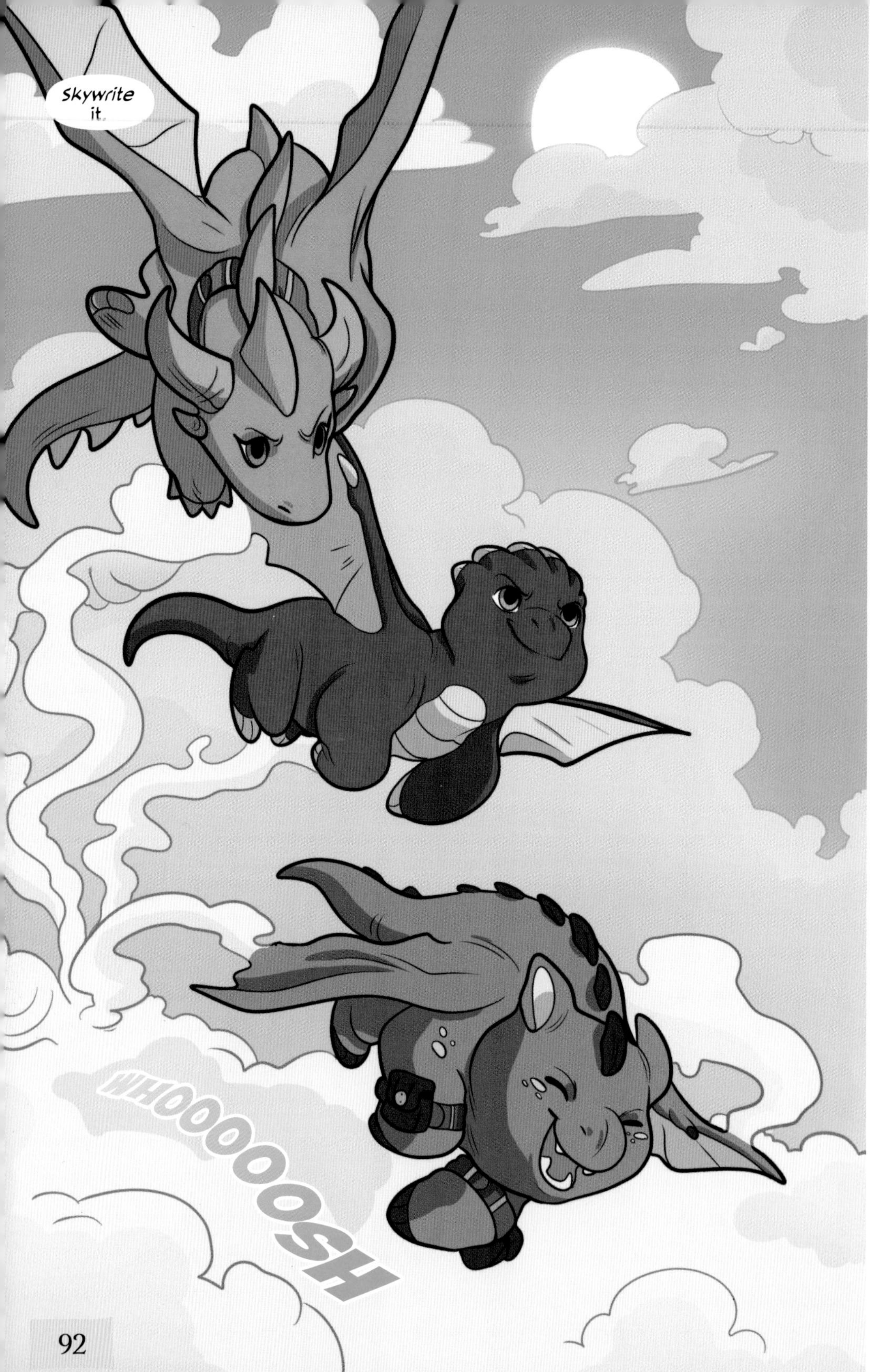
Skywrite it.
WHOOOOOOSH

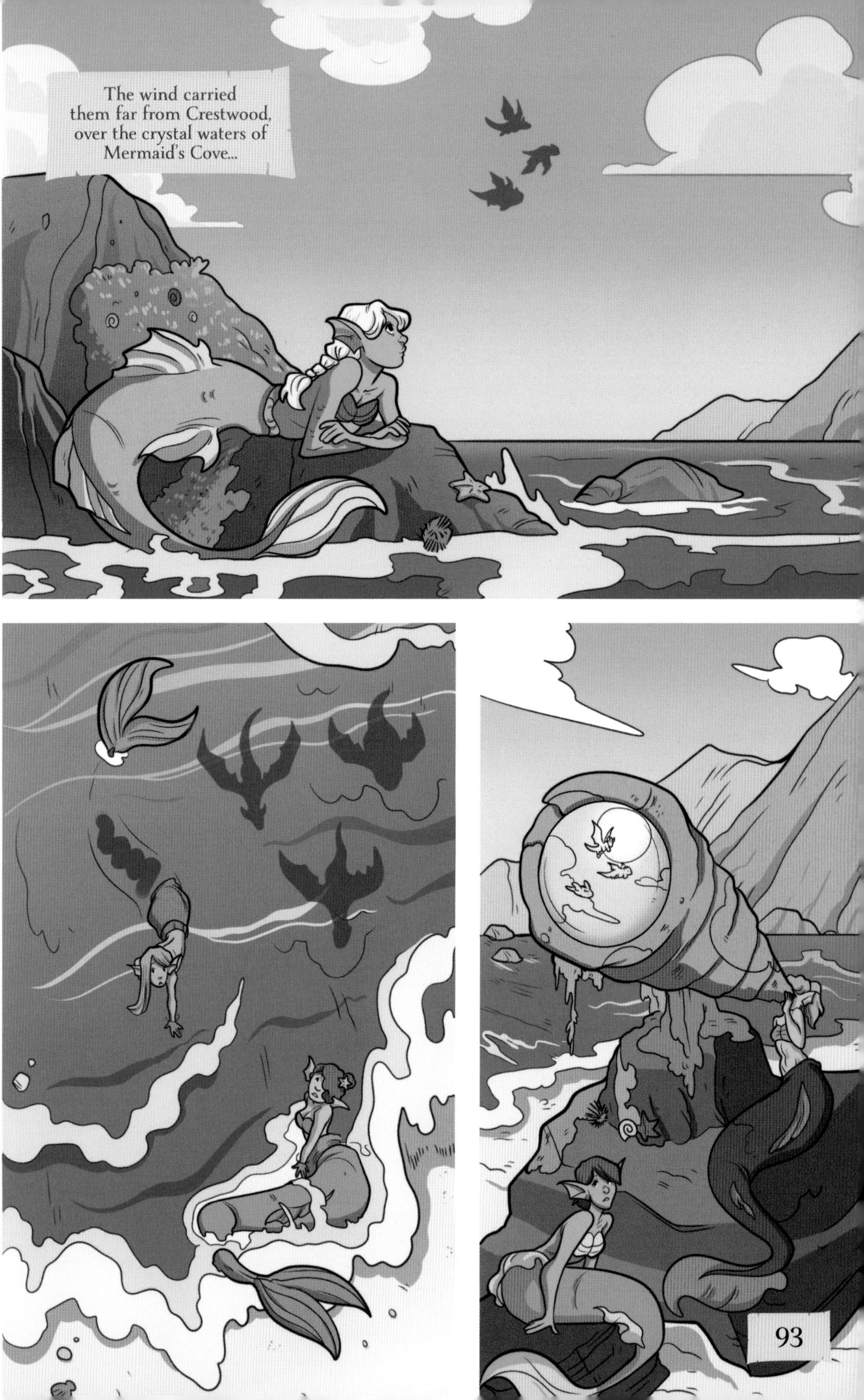
The wind carried them far from Crestwood, over the crystal waters of Mermaid's Cove...

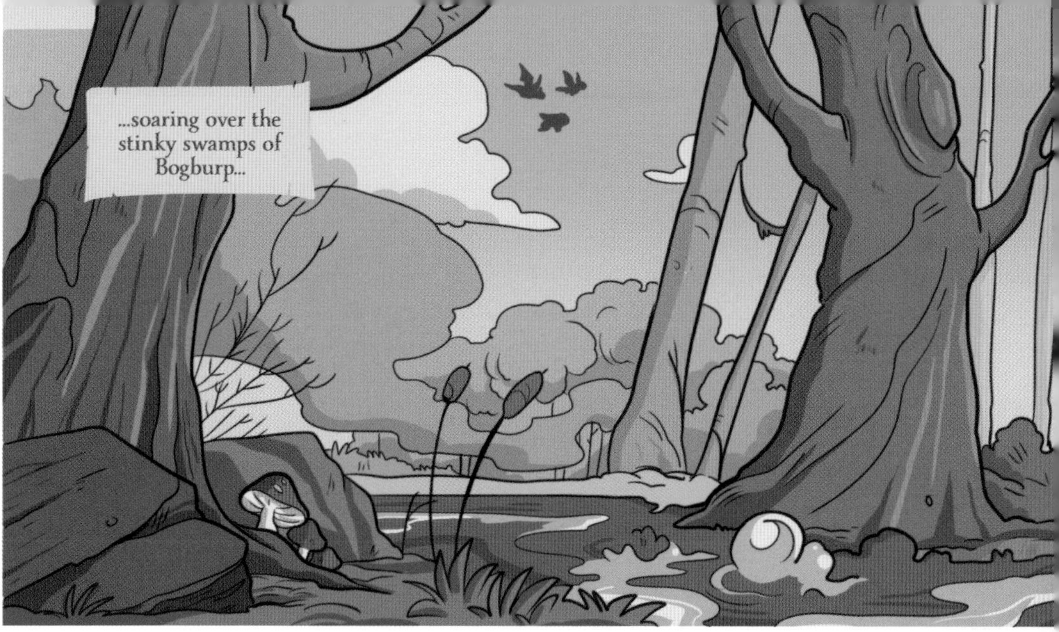
...soaring over the stinky swamps of Bogburp...

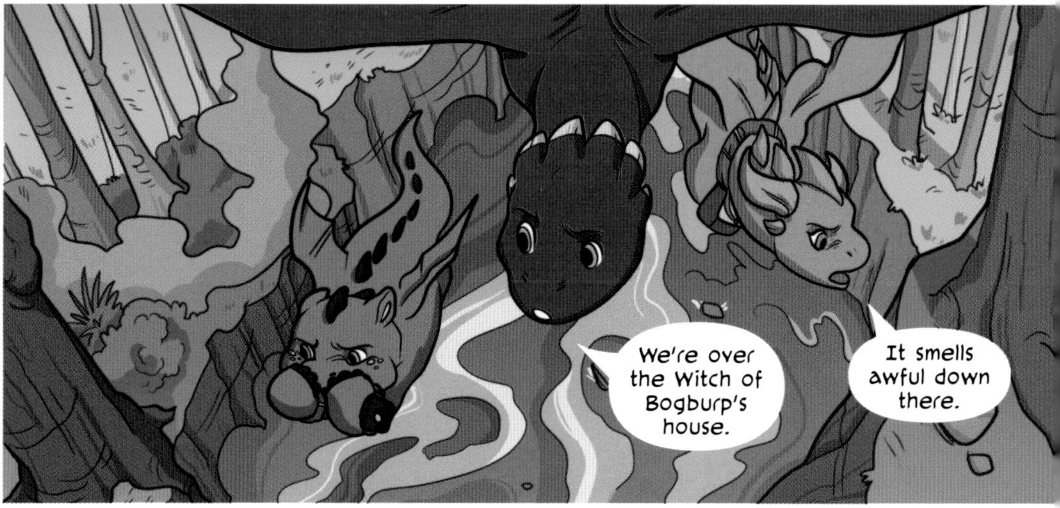
We're over the Witch of Bogburp's house.
It smells awful down there.

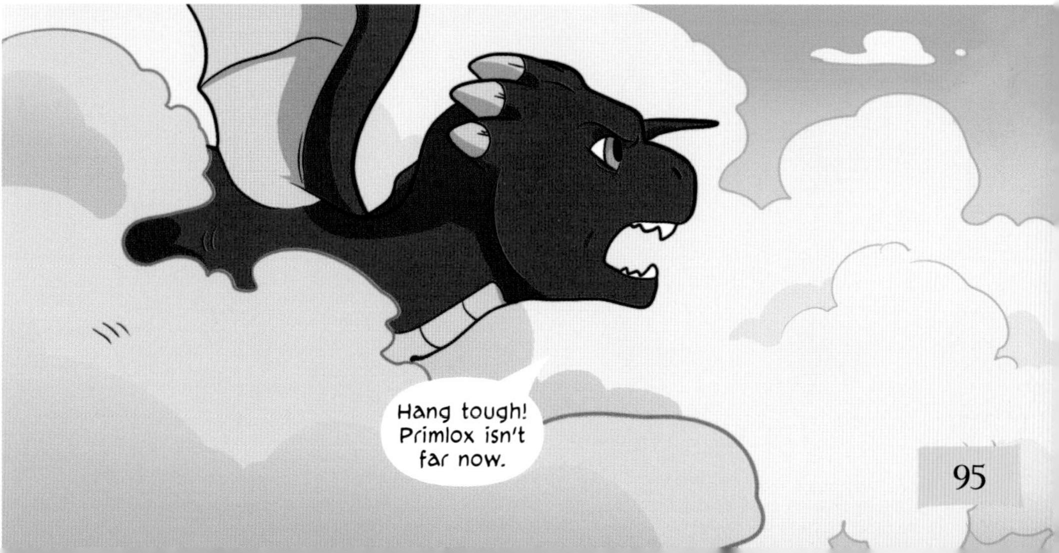
Hang tough! Primlox isn't far now.

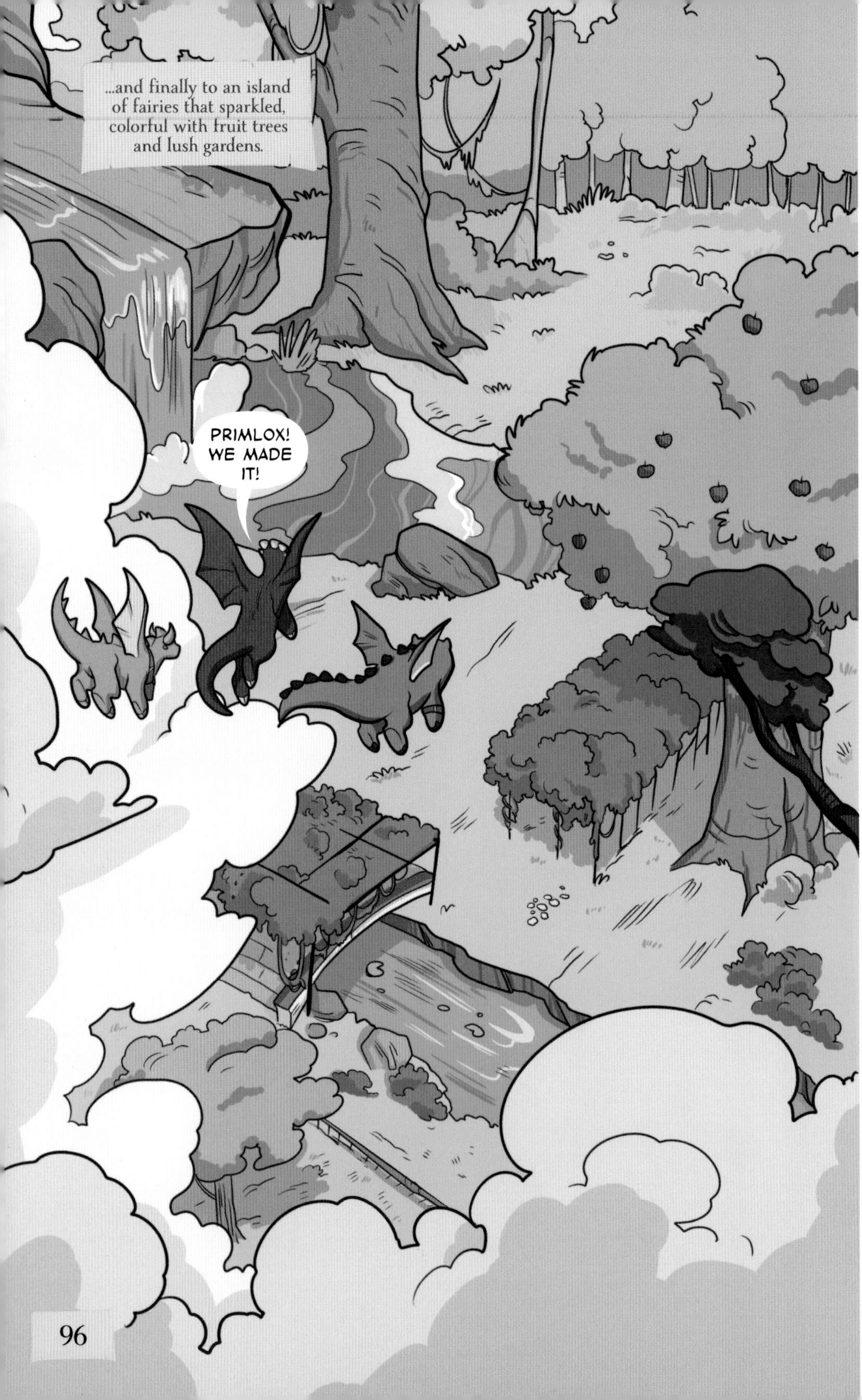
...and finally to an island of fairies that sparkled, colorful with fruit trees and lush gardens.
PRIMLOX! WE MADE IT!

Chapter 8

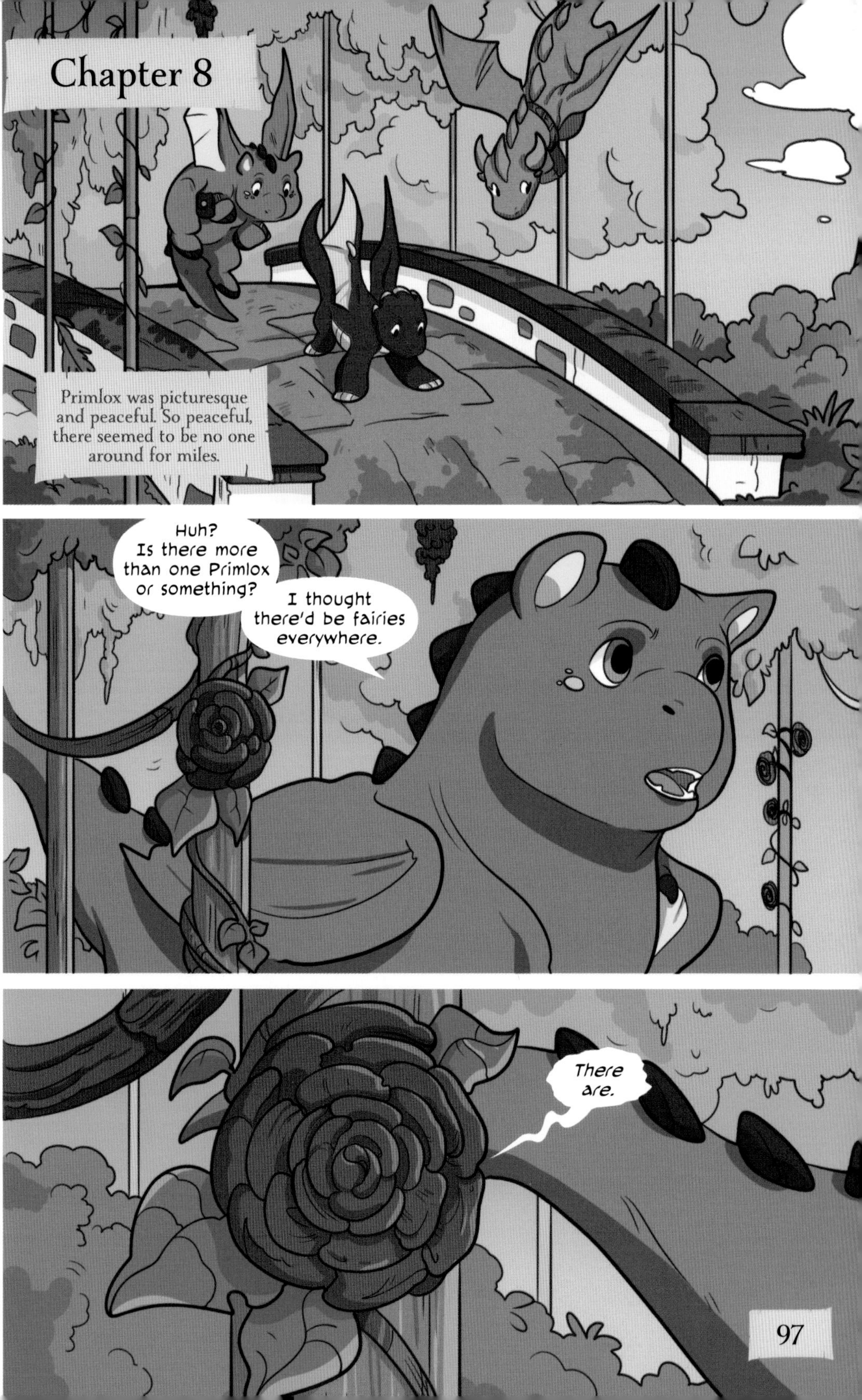
Primlox was picturesque and peaceful. So peaceful, there seemed to be no one around for miles.
Huh? Is there more than one Primlox or something?
I thought there'd be fairies everywhere.
There are.

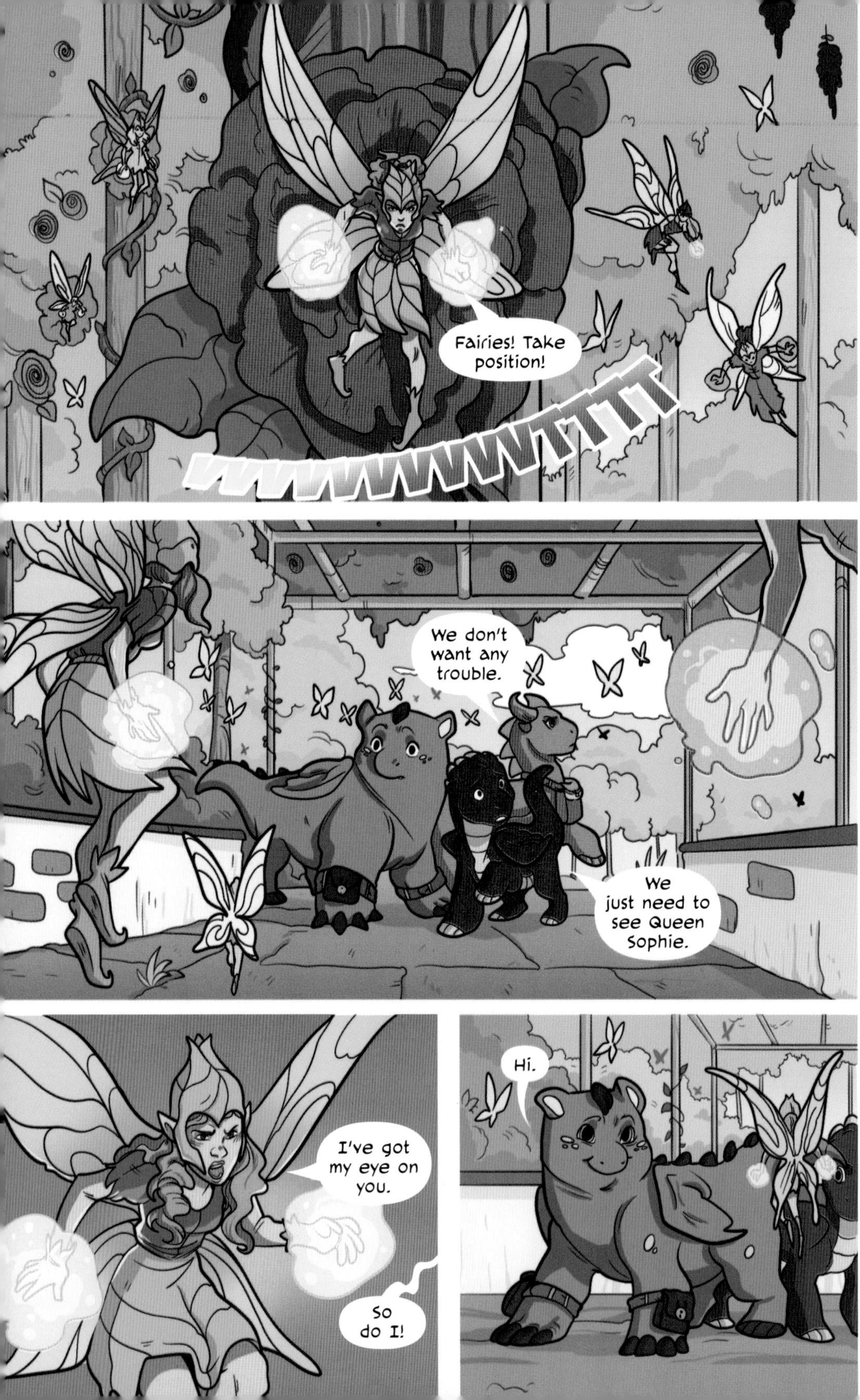
Fairies! Take position!
VVVVVVVVVVVTTTTT
We don't want any trouble.
We just need to see Queen Sophie.
I've got my eye on you.
So do I!
Hi.

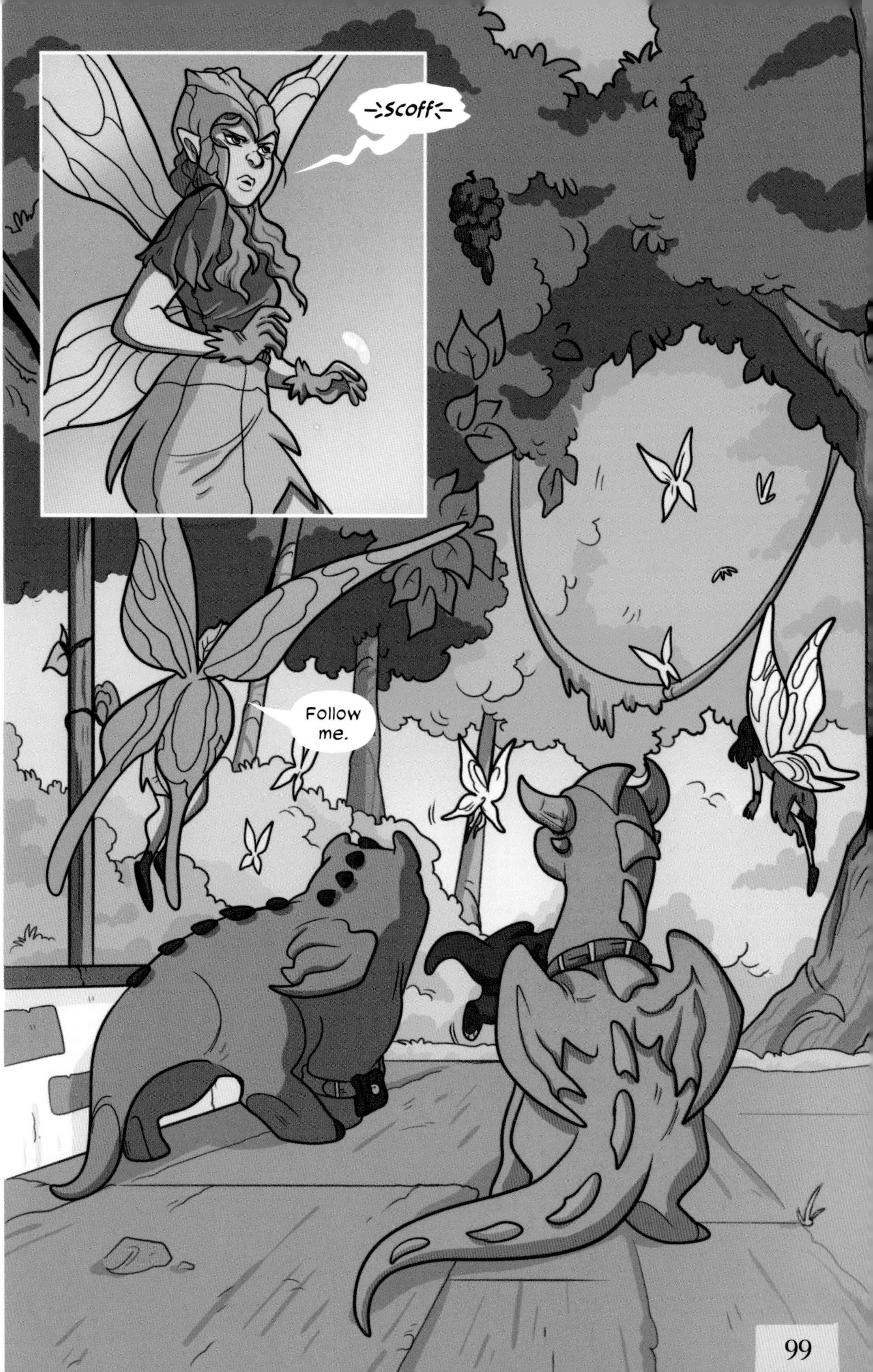
-Scoff-
Follow me.

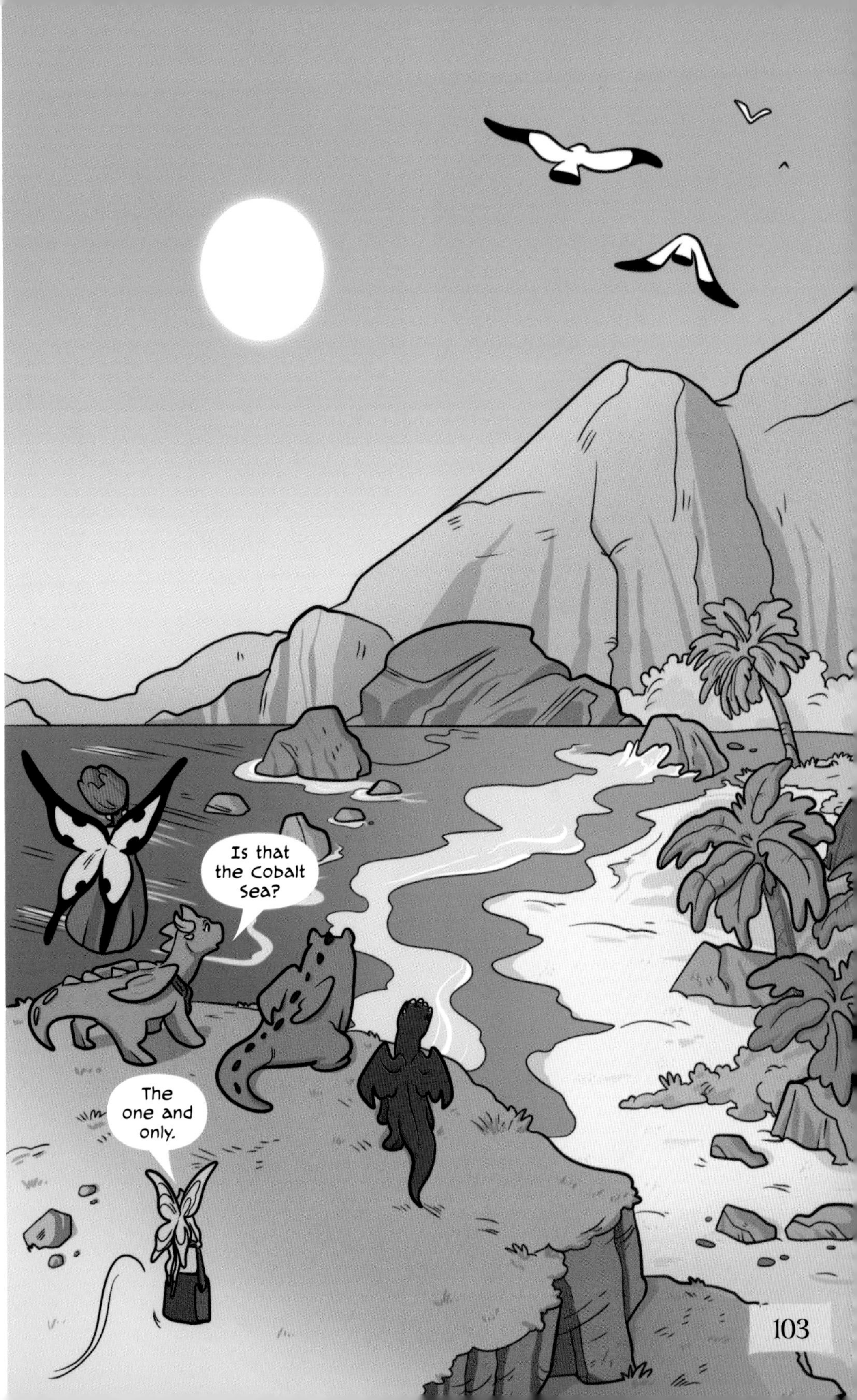
Is that the Cobalt Sea?
The one and only.

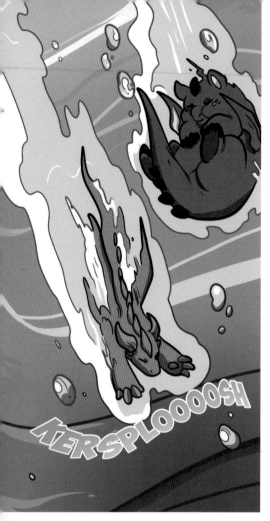

KERSPLOOOOSH

FSHHHHHHHH

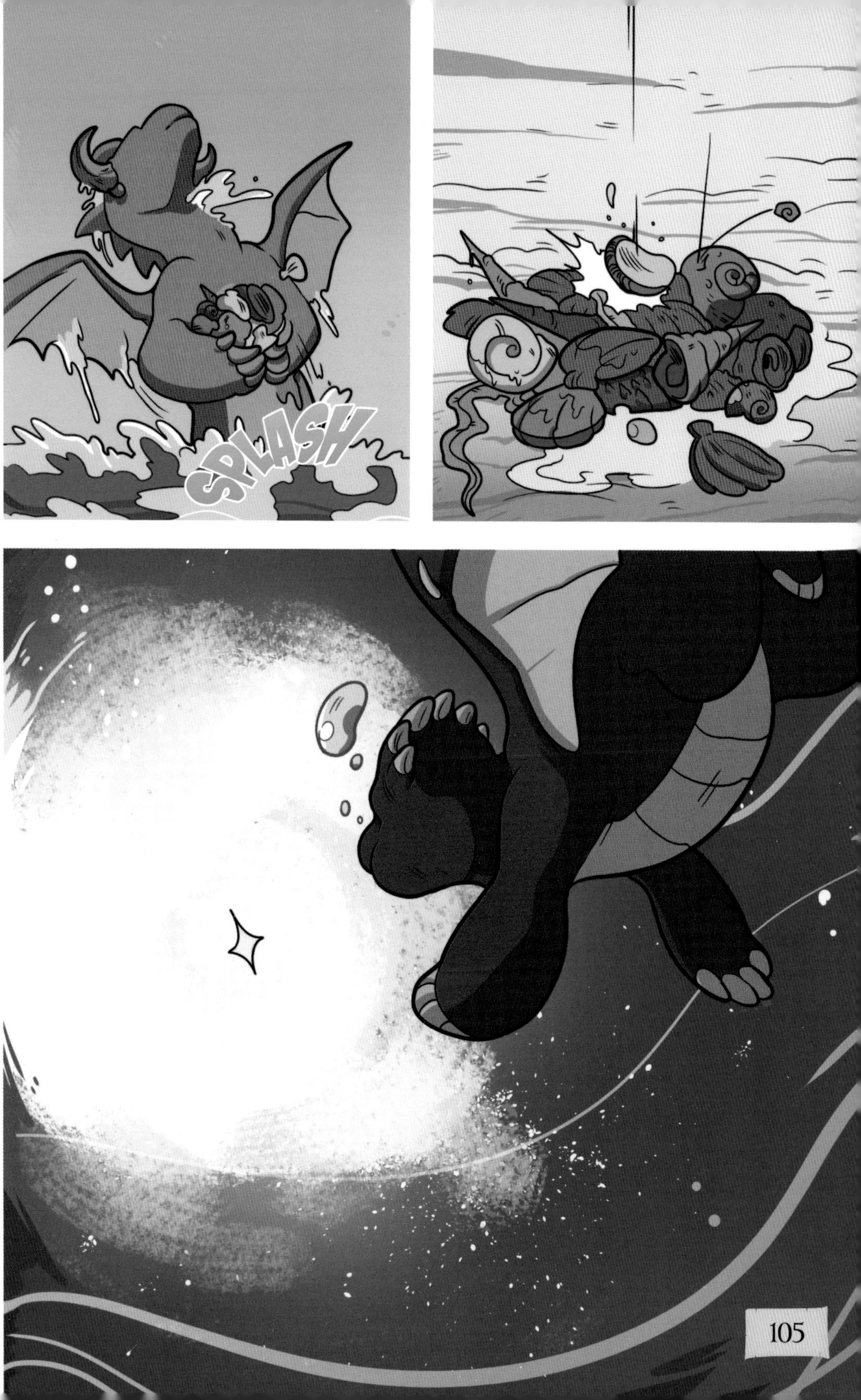
SPLASH

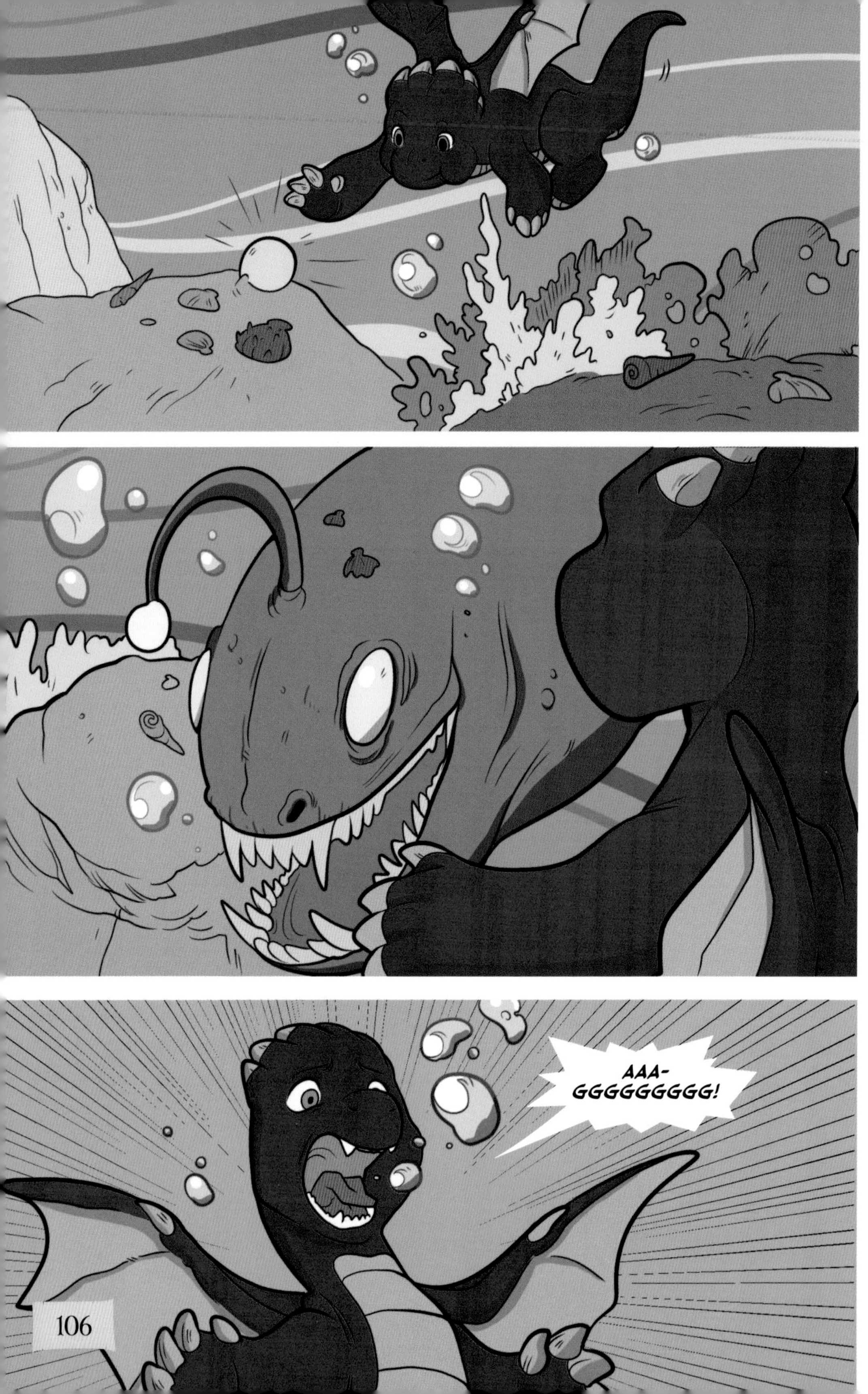
AAA-
GGGGGGGGG!

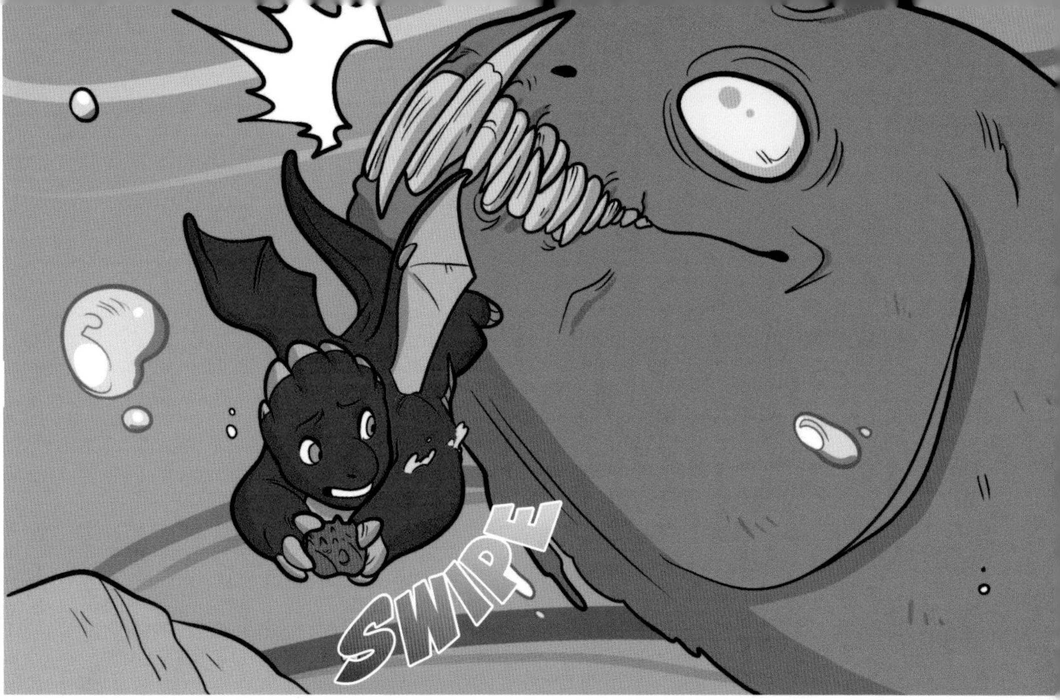
SWIPE

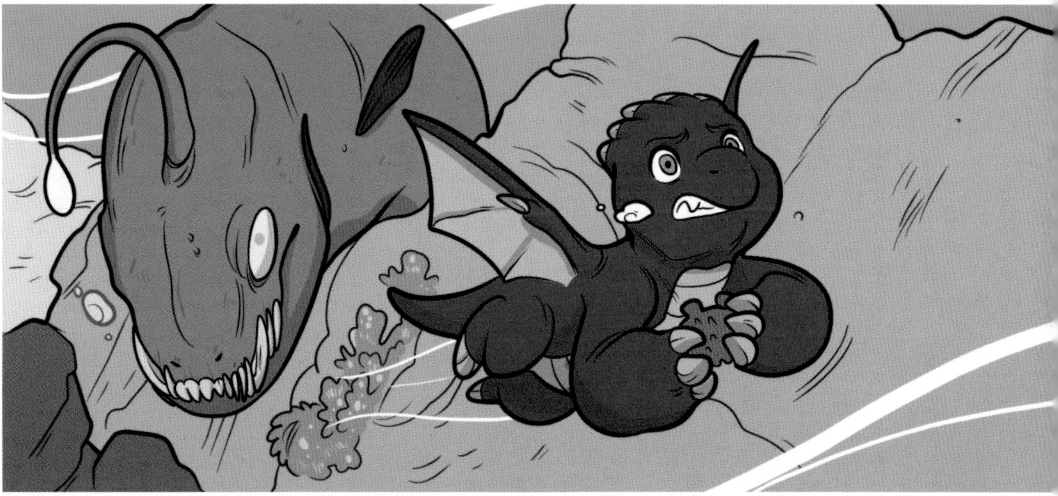

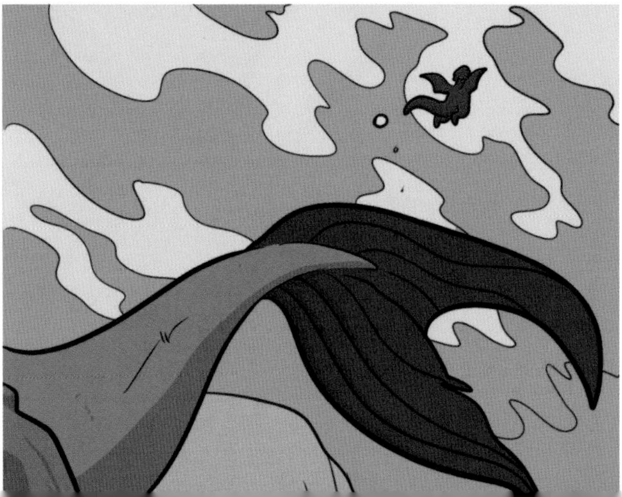

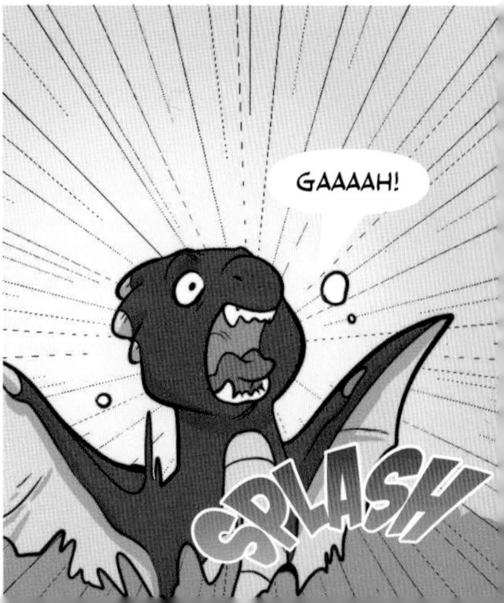
GAAAAH!
SPLASH

108

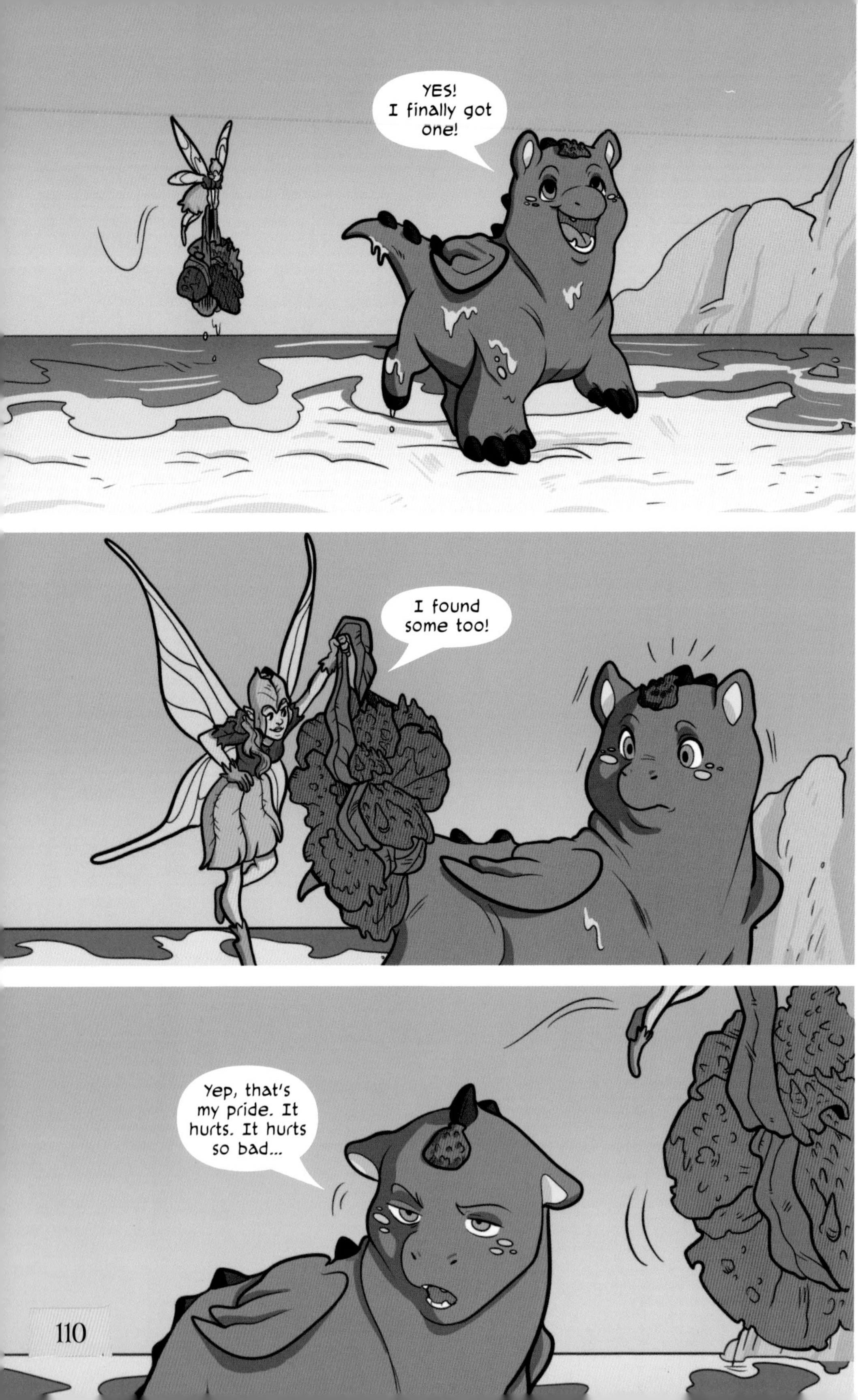
YES! I finally got one!
I found some too!
Yep, that's my pride. It hurts. It hurts so bad...

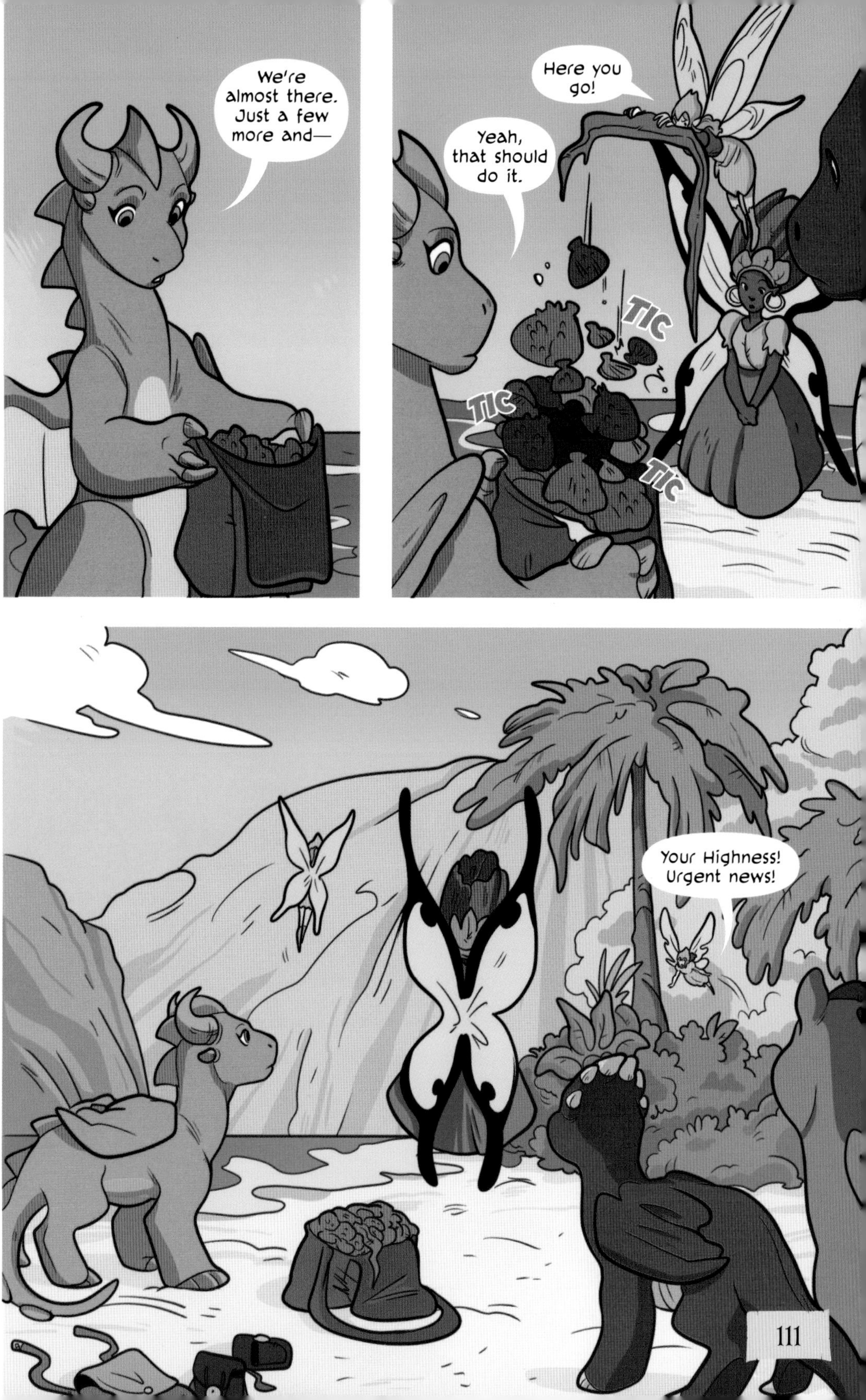
We're almost there. Just a few more and—
Here you go!
Yeah, that should do it.
TIC
TIC
TIC
Your Highness! Urgent news!

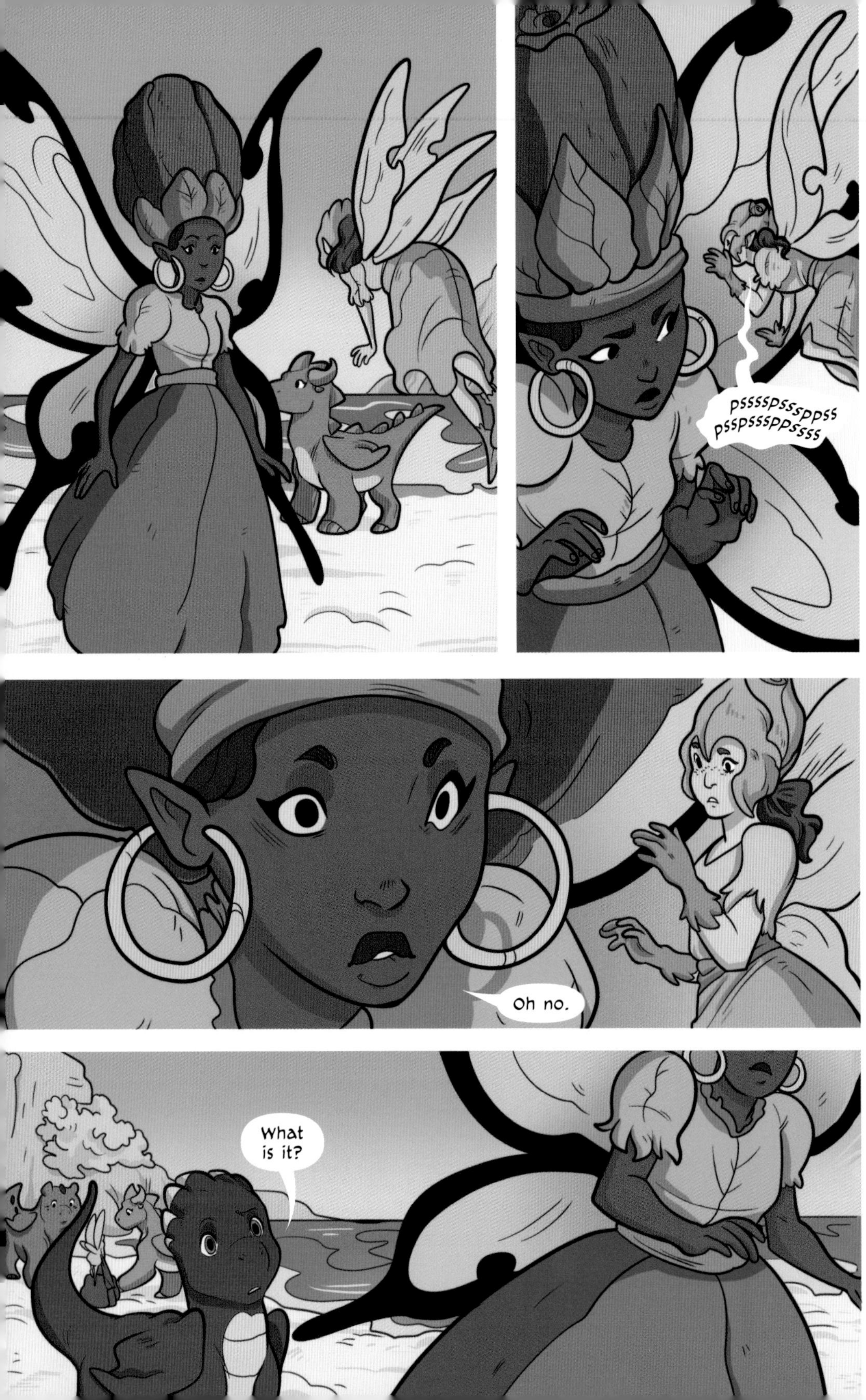
psssspsssppss
psspssspPssss
Oh no.
What is it?

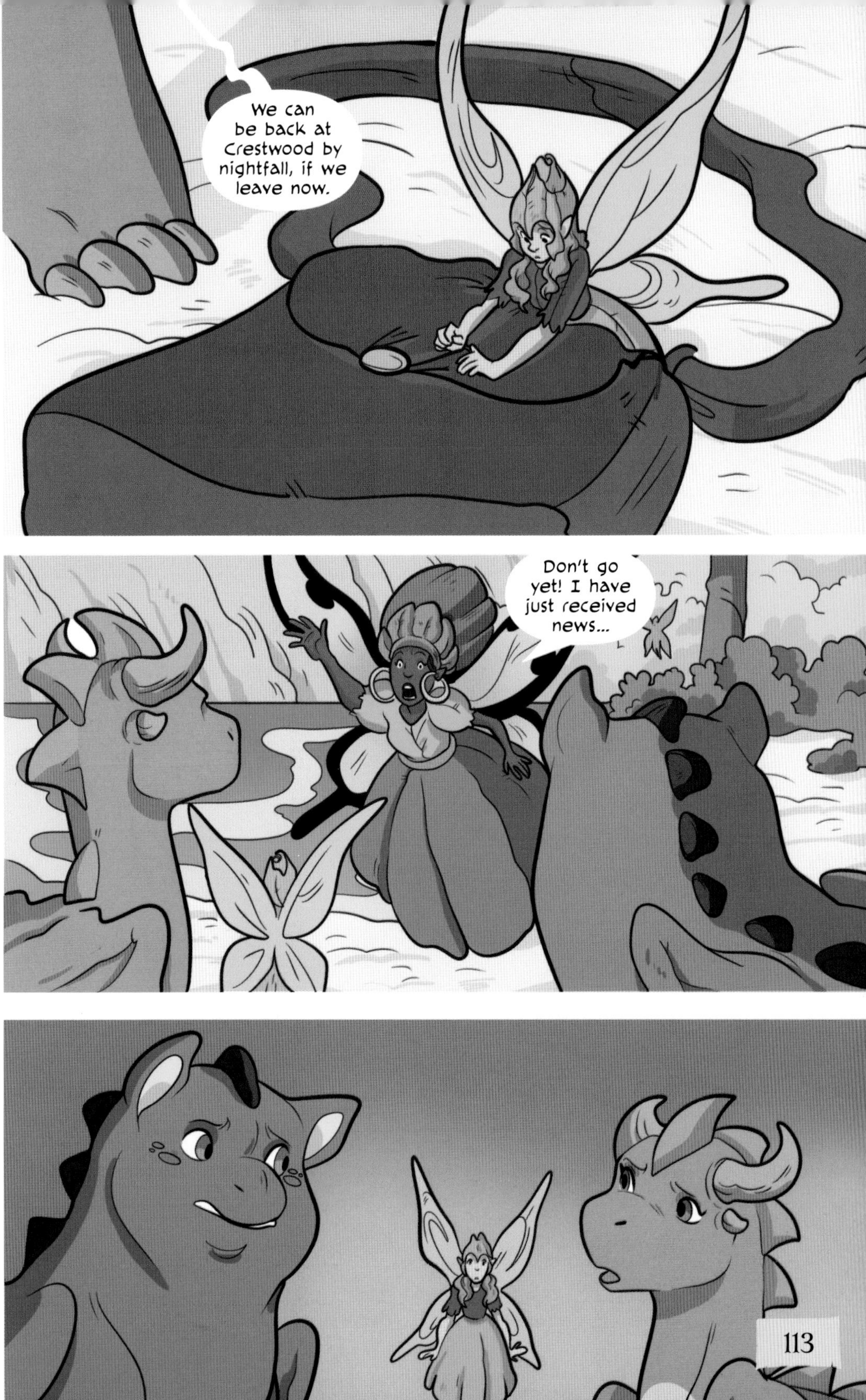
We can be back at Crestwood by nightfall, if we leave now.
Don't go yet! I have just received news...

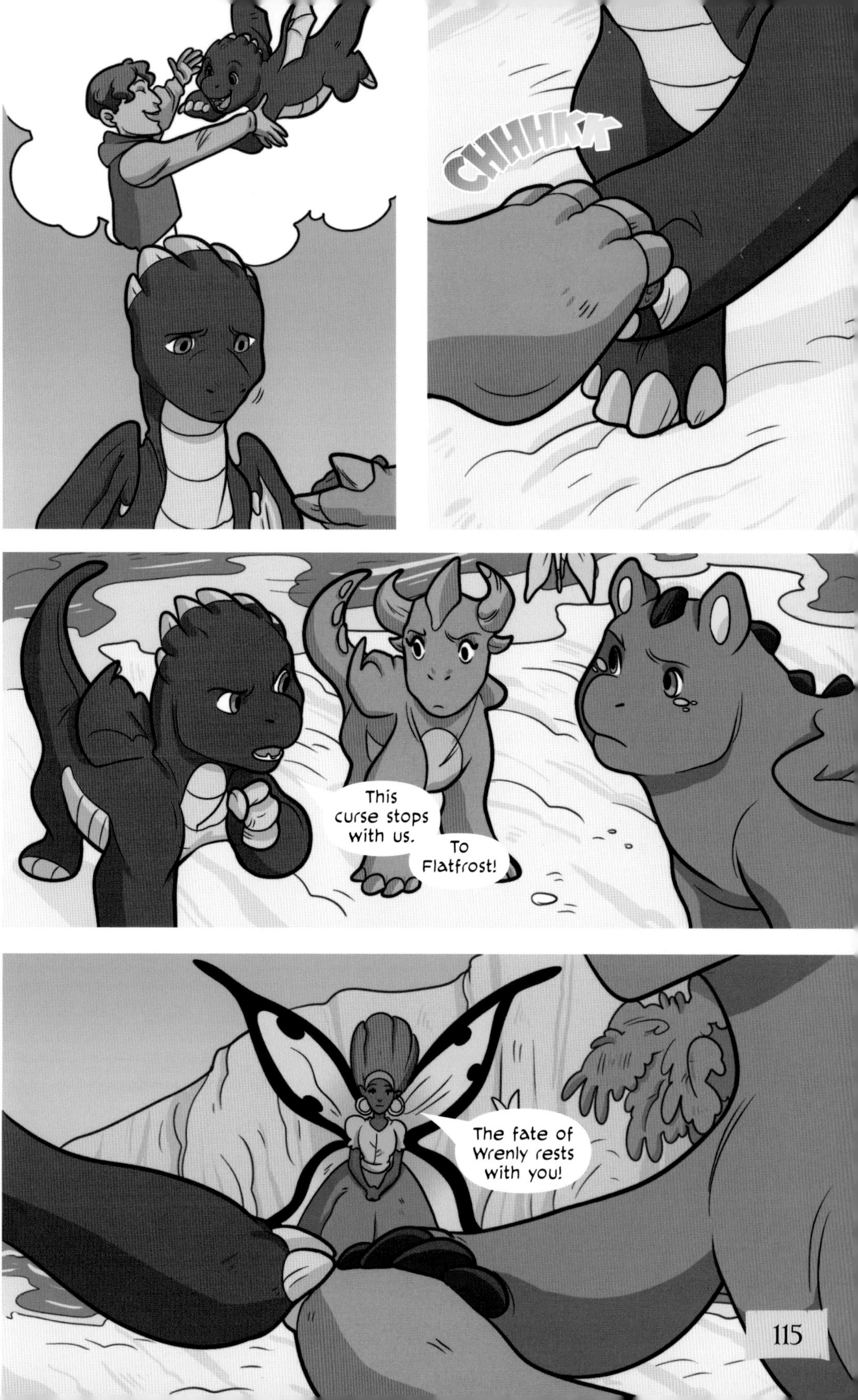
CHHHKK
This curse stops with us.
To Flatfrost!
The fate of Wrenly rests with you!

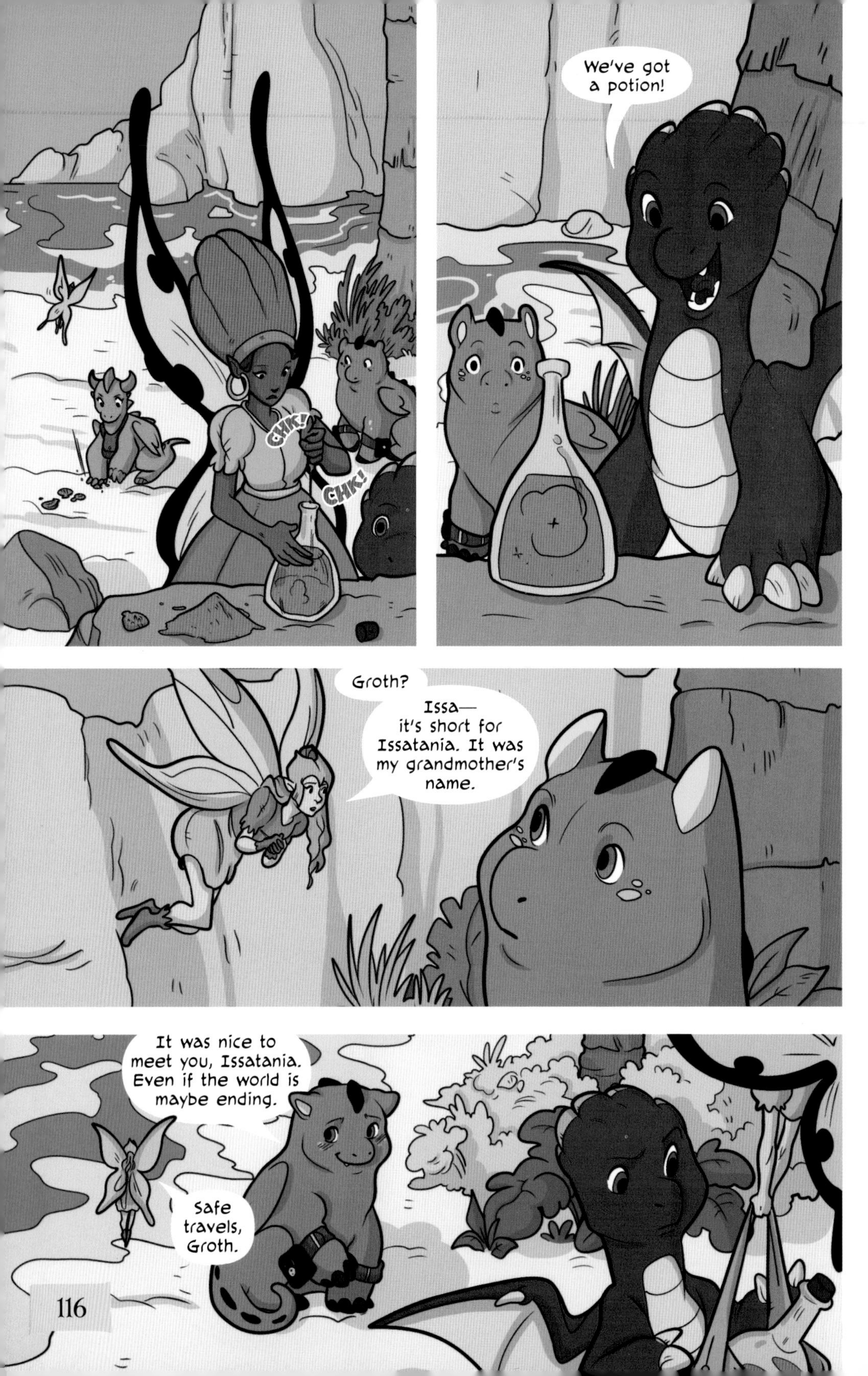
CHK!
CHK!
We've got a potion!
Groth?
Issa— it's short for Issatania. It was my grandmother's name.
It was nice to meet you, Issatania. Even if the world is maybe ending.
Safe travels, Groth.

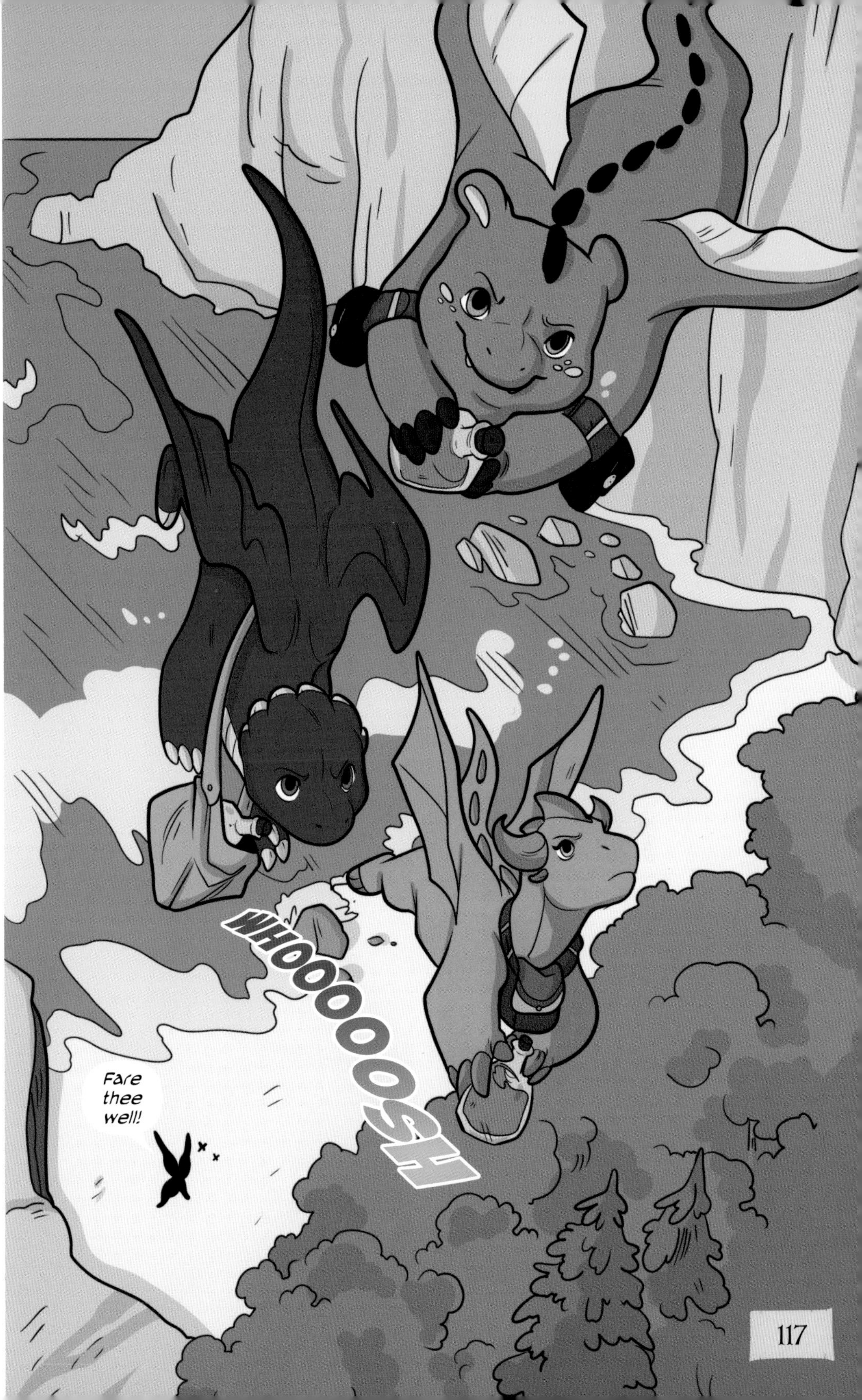
WHOOOOOOSH
Fare thee well!

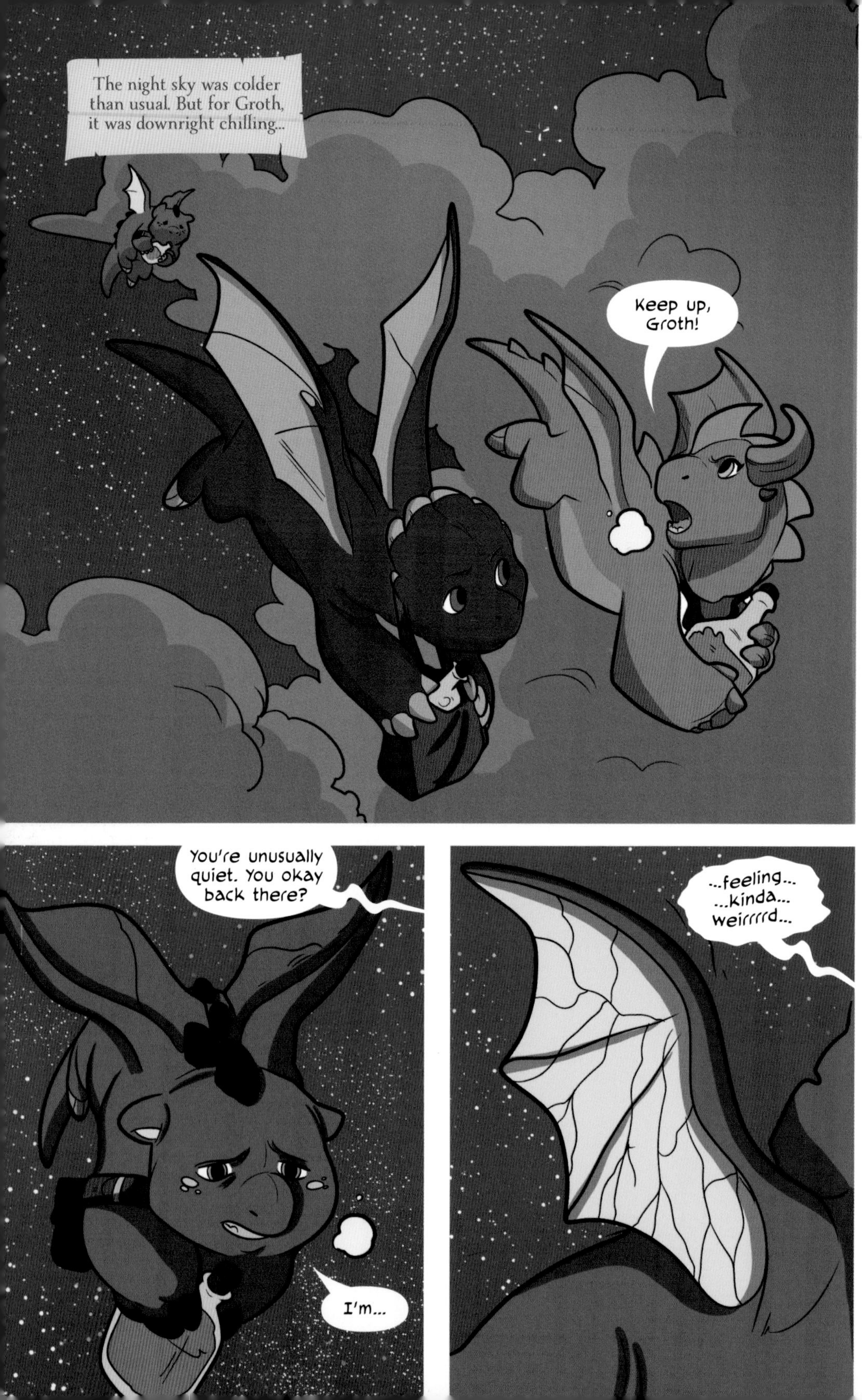
The night sky was colder than usual. But for Groth, it was downright chilling...
Keep up, Groth!
You're unusually quiet. You okay back there?
I'm...
...feeling... ...kinda... weirrrrrd...

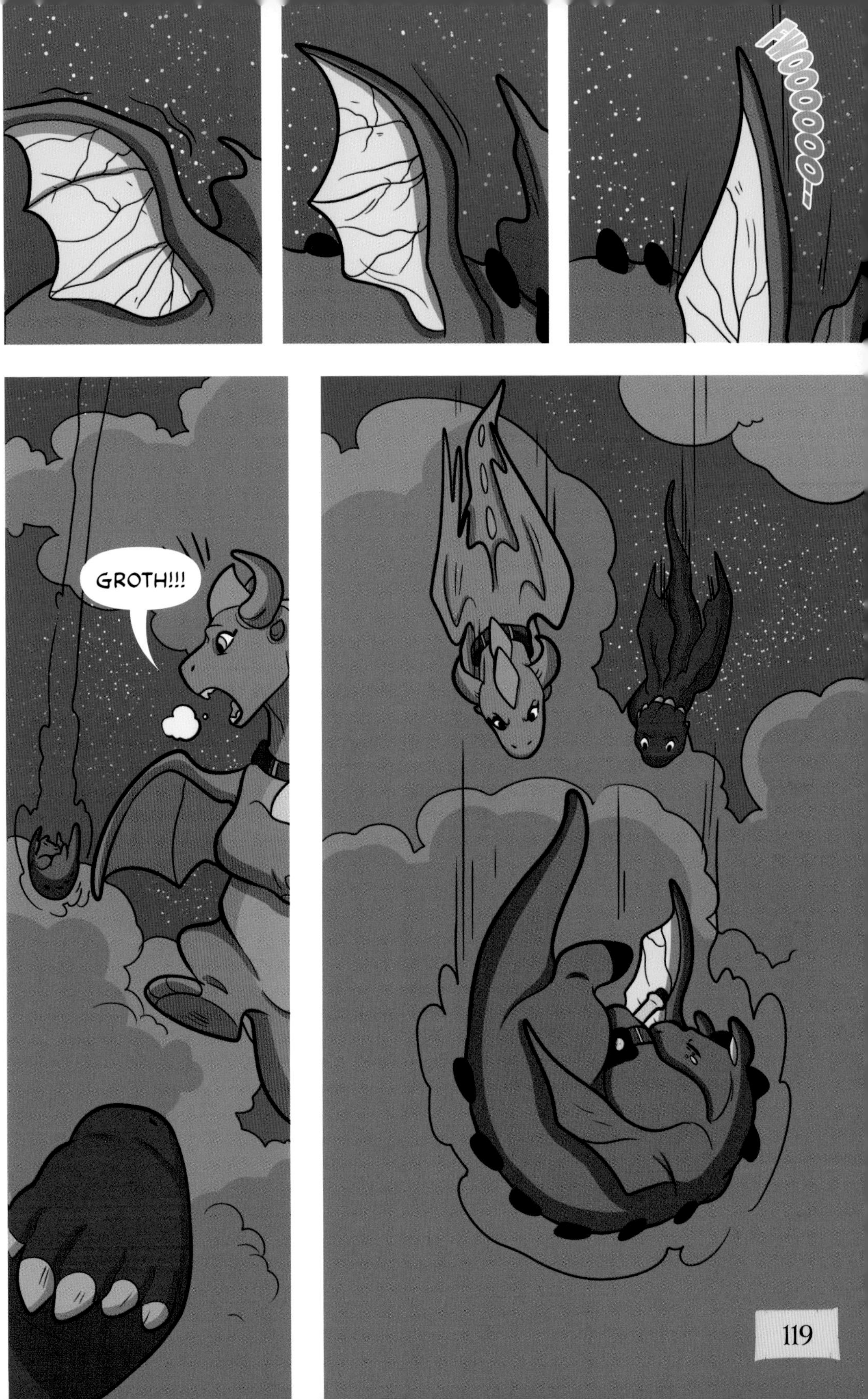
FWOOOOOO--
GROTH!!!

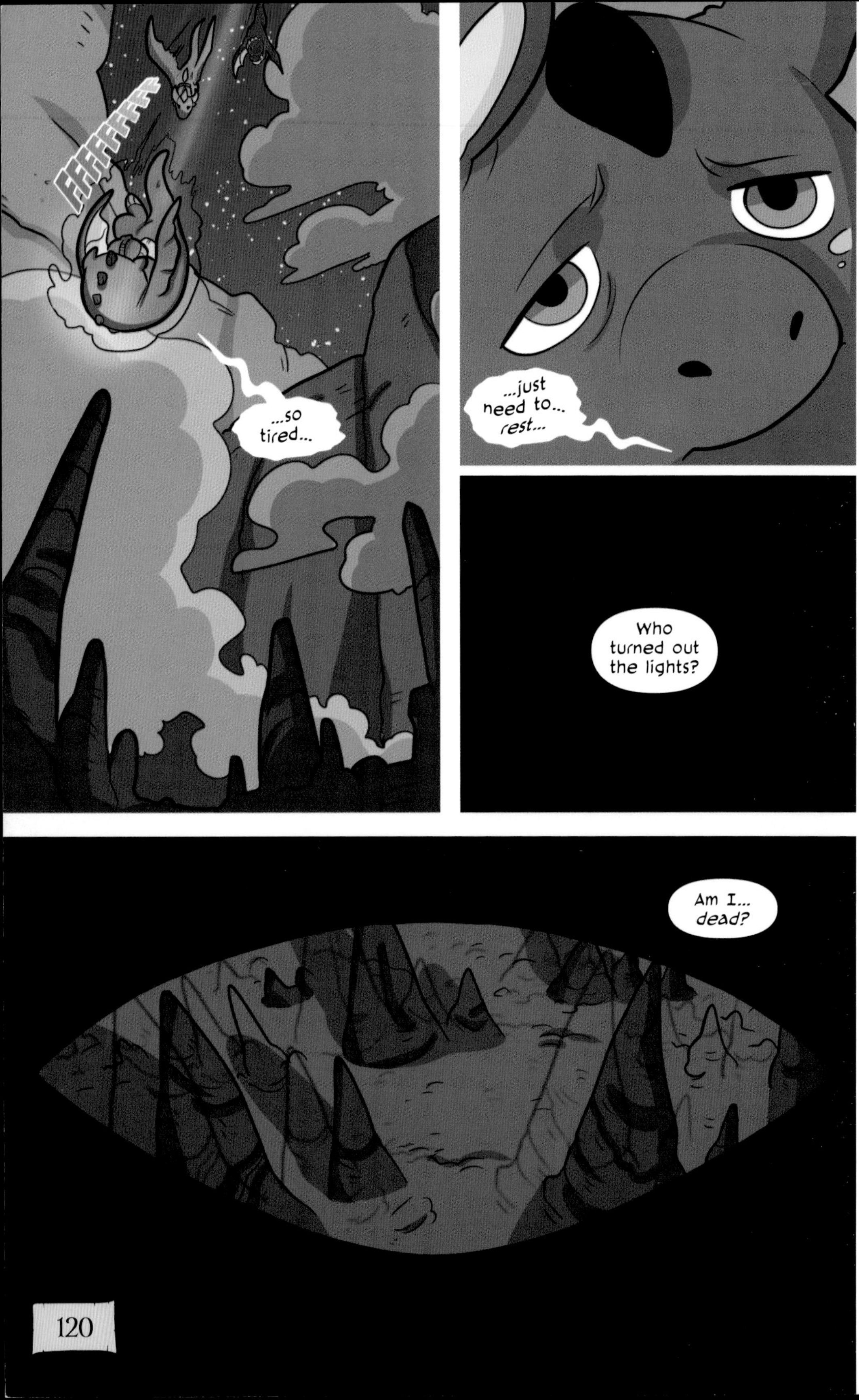
...so tired...
...just need to... rest...
Who turned out the lights?
Am I... dead?

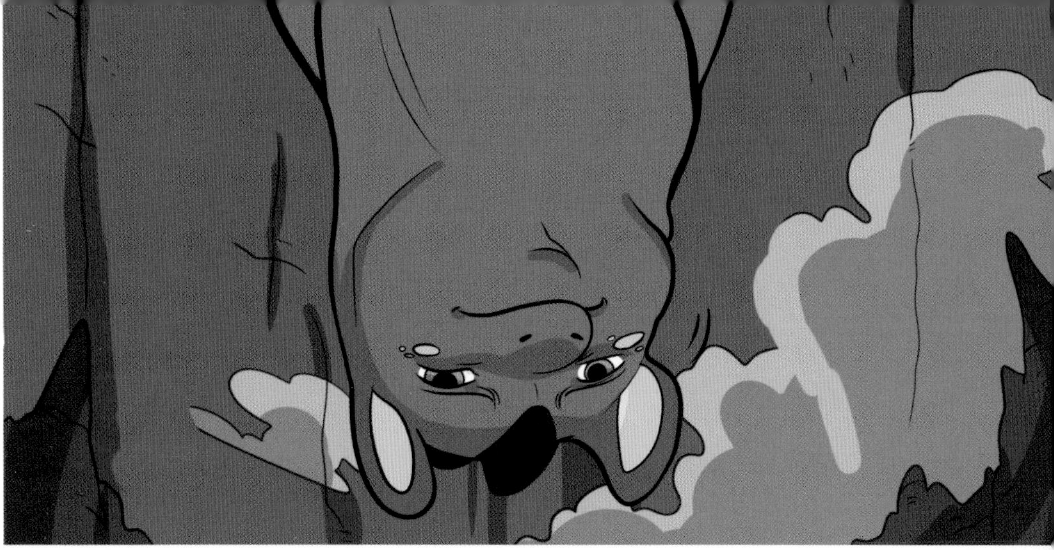

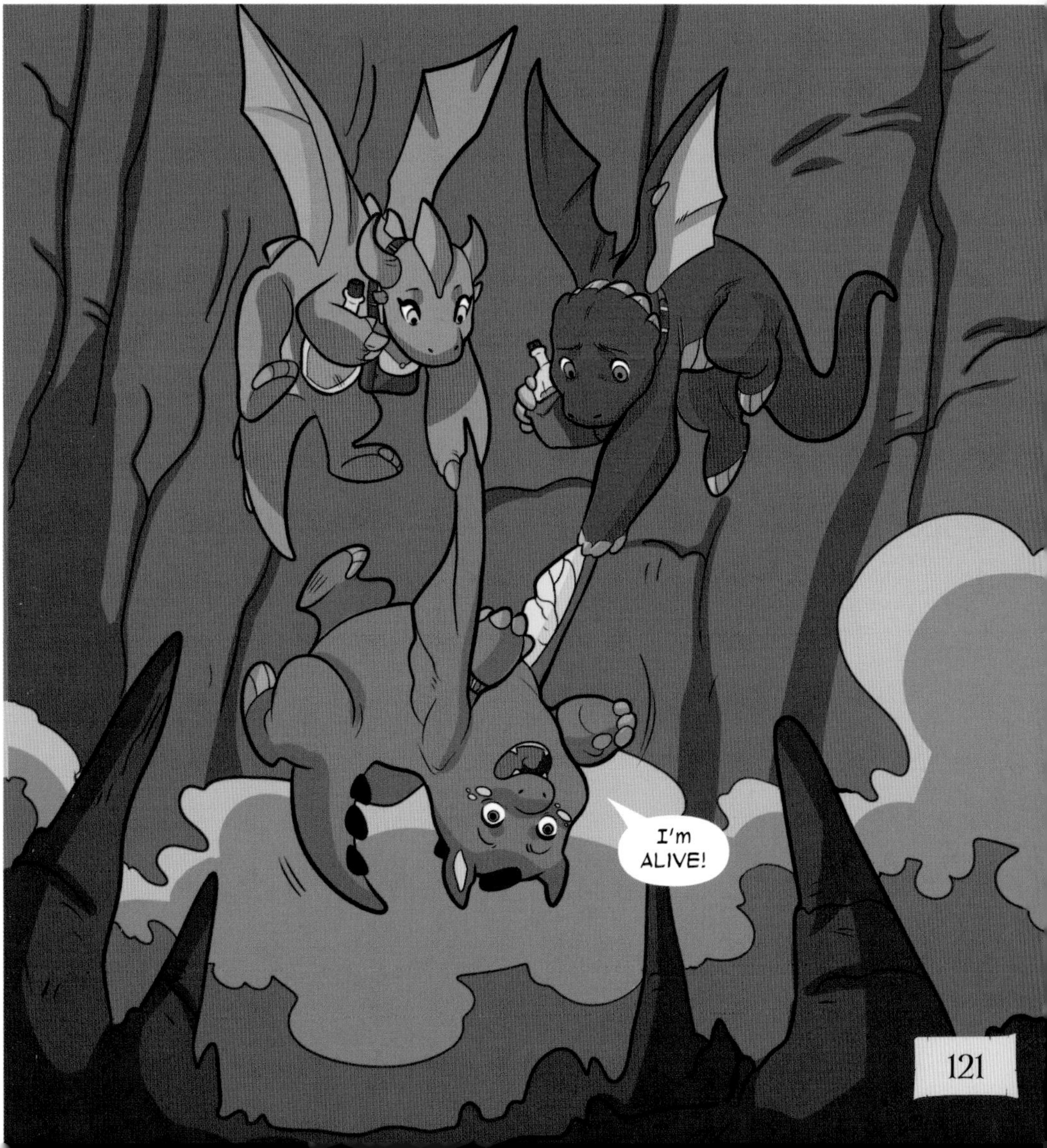
I'm ALIVE!

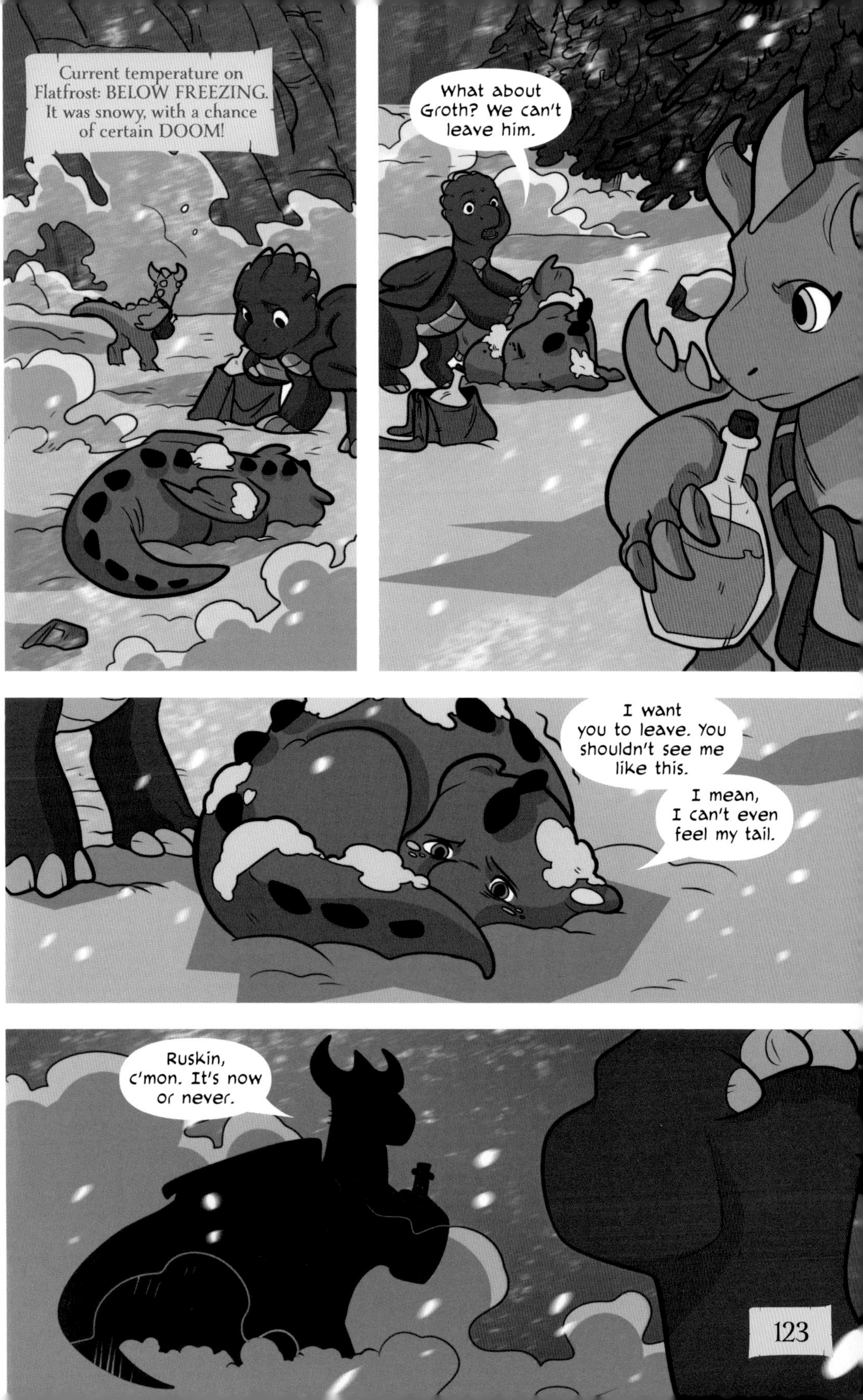

Current temperature on Flatfrost: BELOW FREEZING. It was snowy, with a chance of certain DOOM!
What about Groth? We can't leave him.
I want you to leave. You shouldn't see me like this.
I mean, I can't even feel my tail.
Ruskin, c'mon. It's now or never.

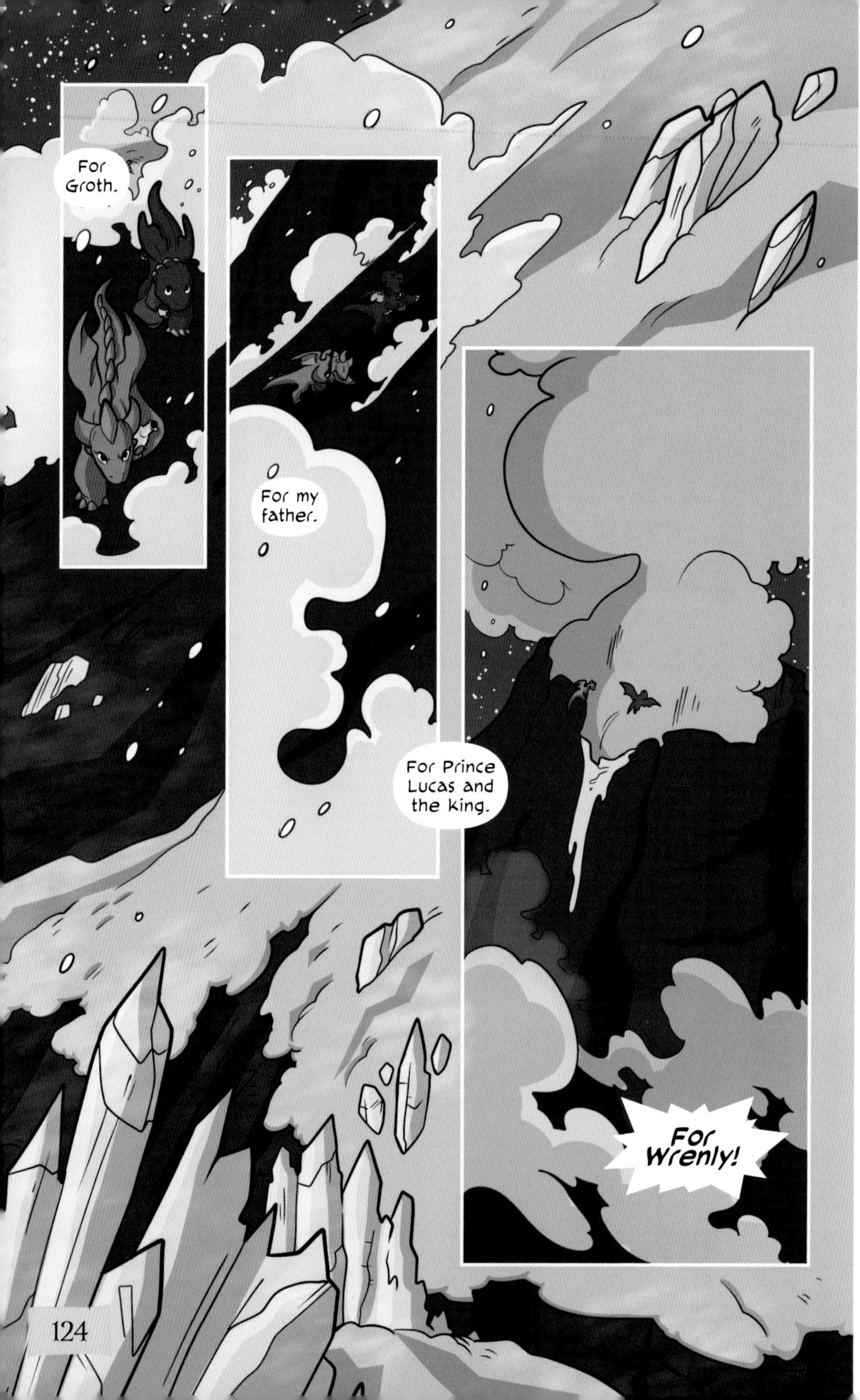
For Groth.
For my father.
For Prince Lucas and the king.
For Wrenly!

Chapter 10

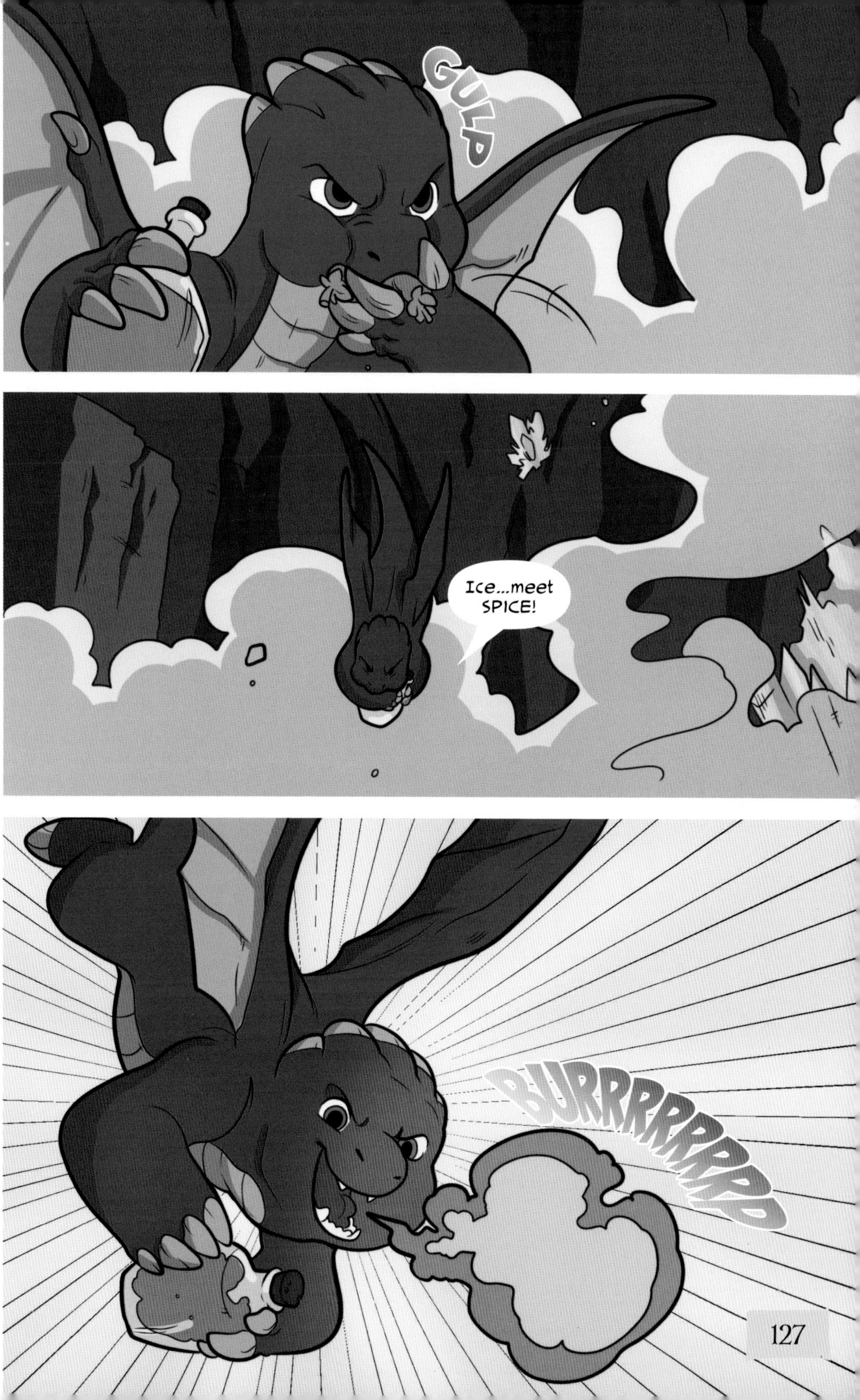
GULP
Ice...meet SPICE!
BURRRRRRRP

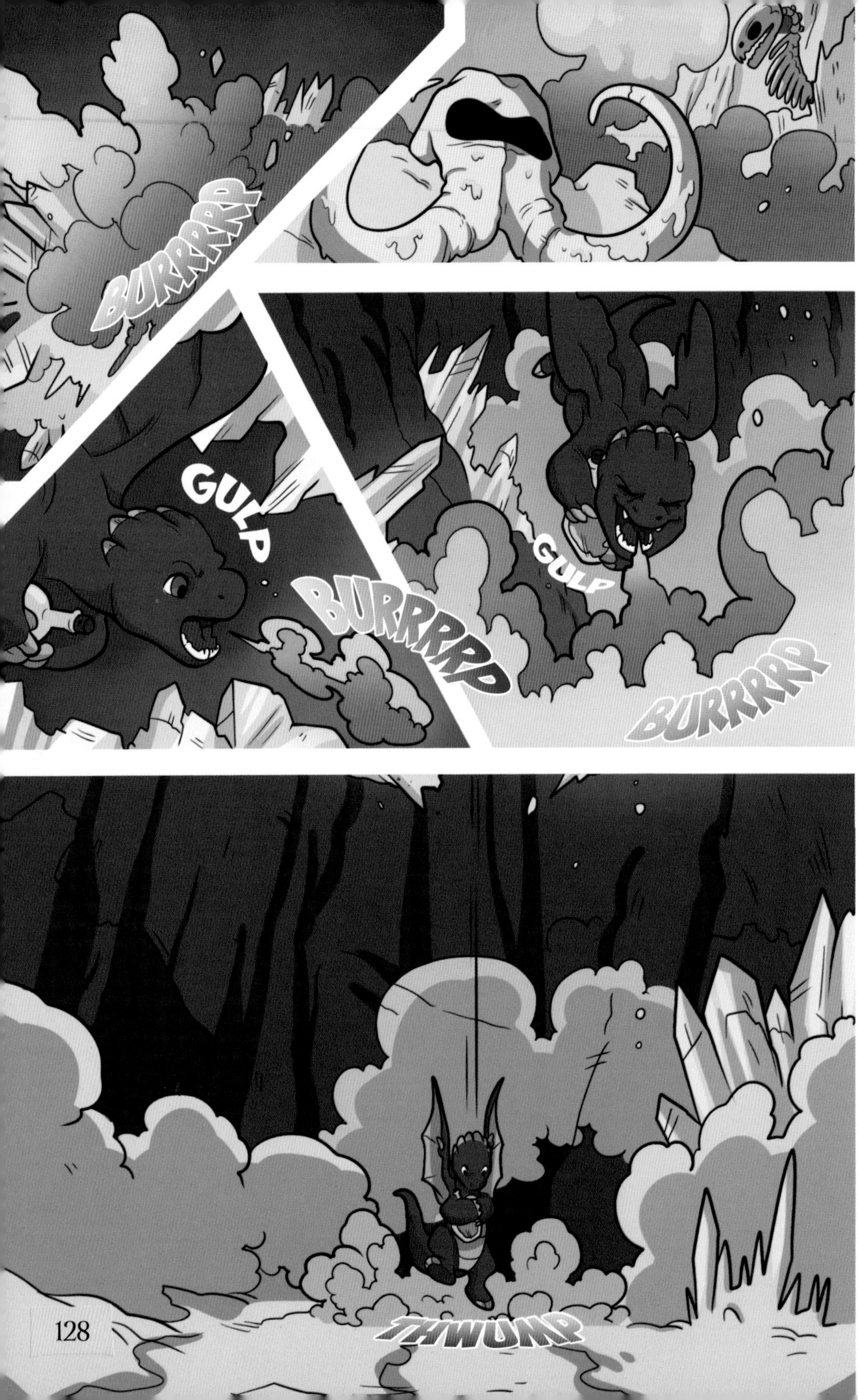
BURRRRRP
GULP
BURRRRRP
GULP
BURRRRP
THWUMP

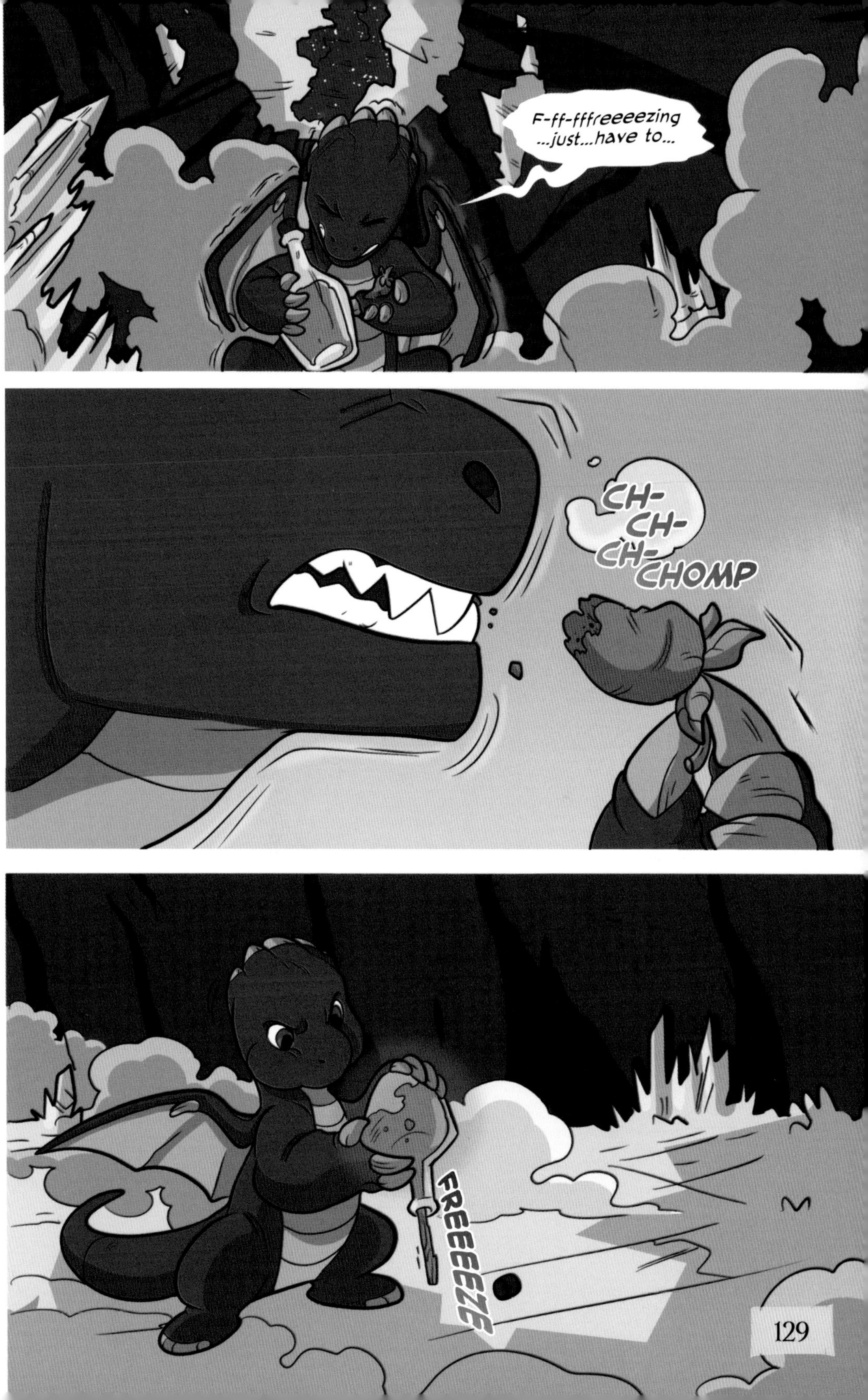
F-ff-fffreeeezing ...just...have to...
CH-CH-CH-CHOMP
FREEEEZE

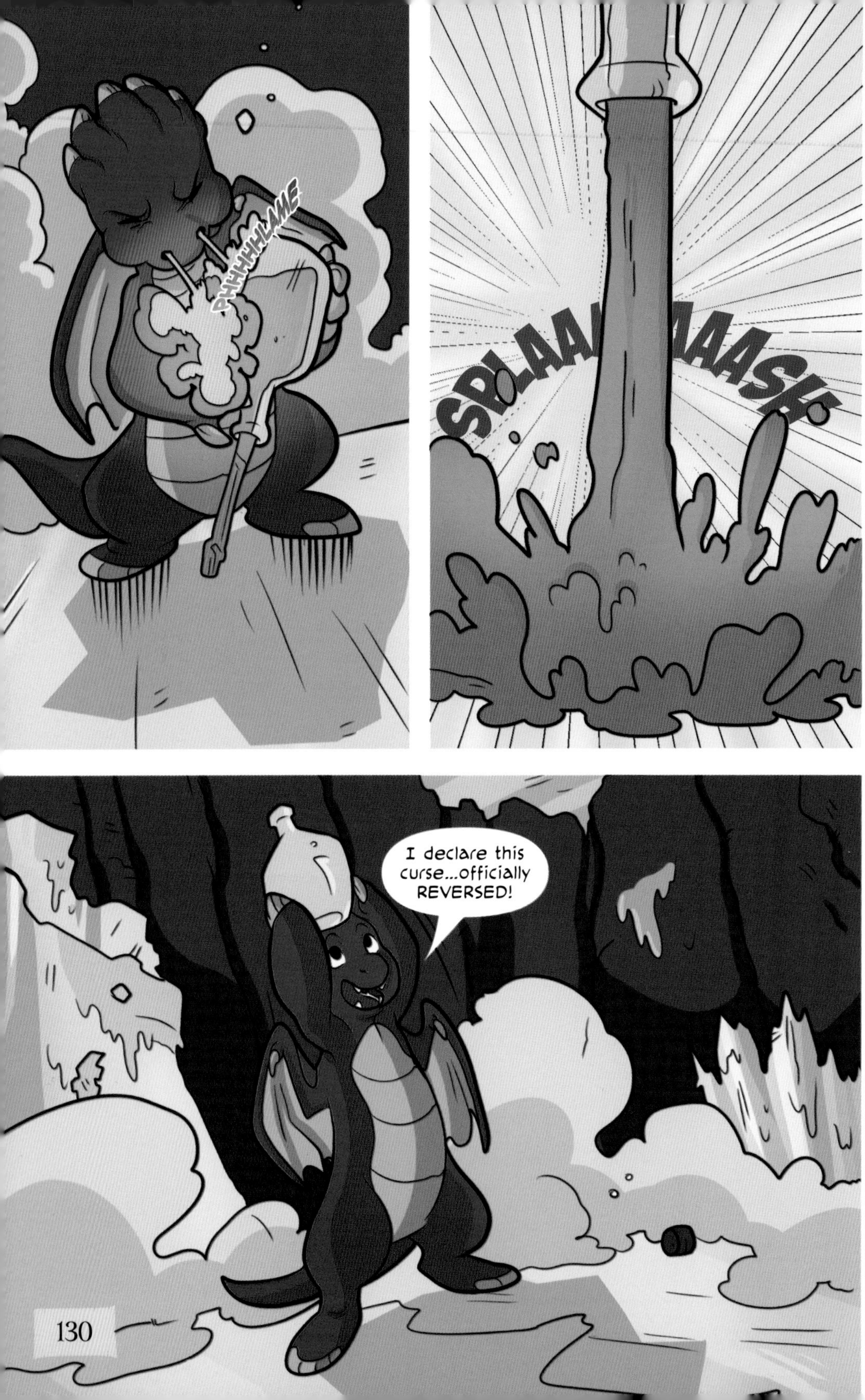
PHHHHHLAME
SPLAAAAAAASH
I declare this curse...officially REVERSED!

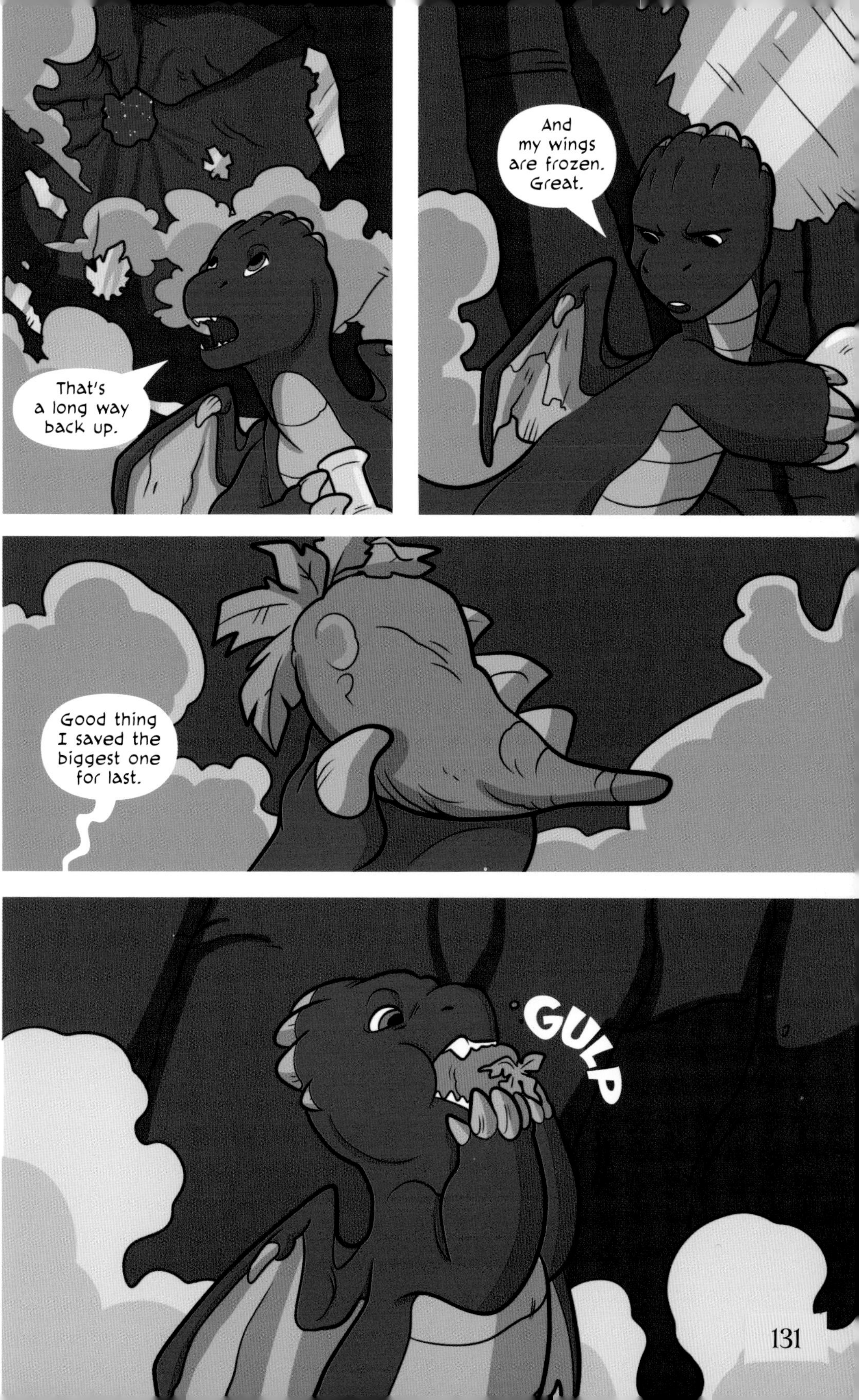
That's a long way back up.
And my wings are frozen. Great.
Good thing I saved the biggest one for last.
GULP

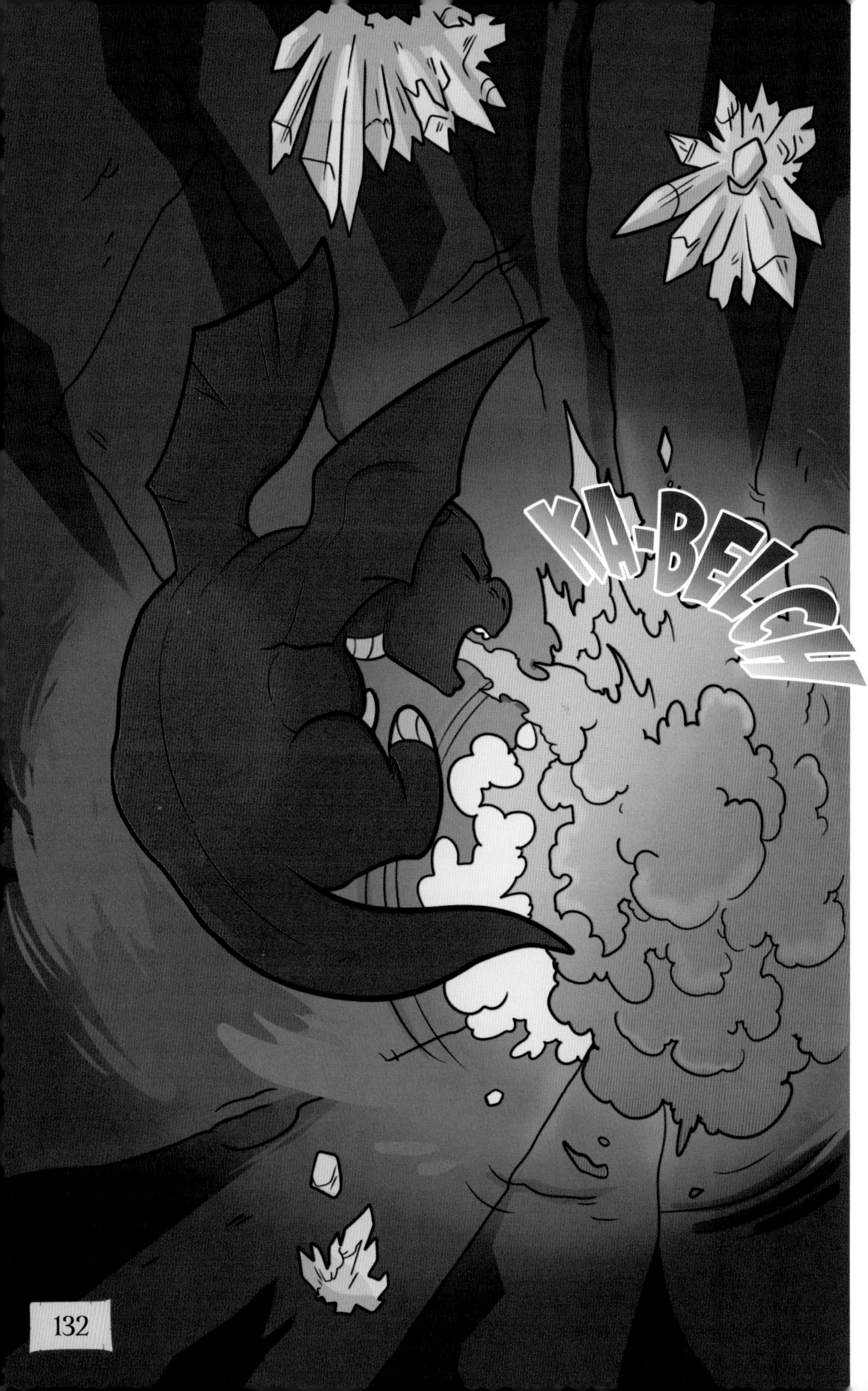
KA-BELCH

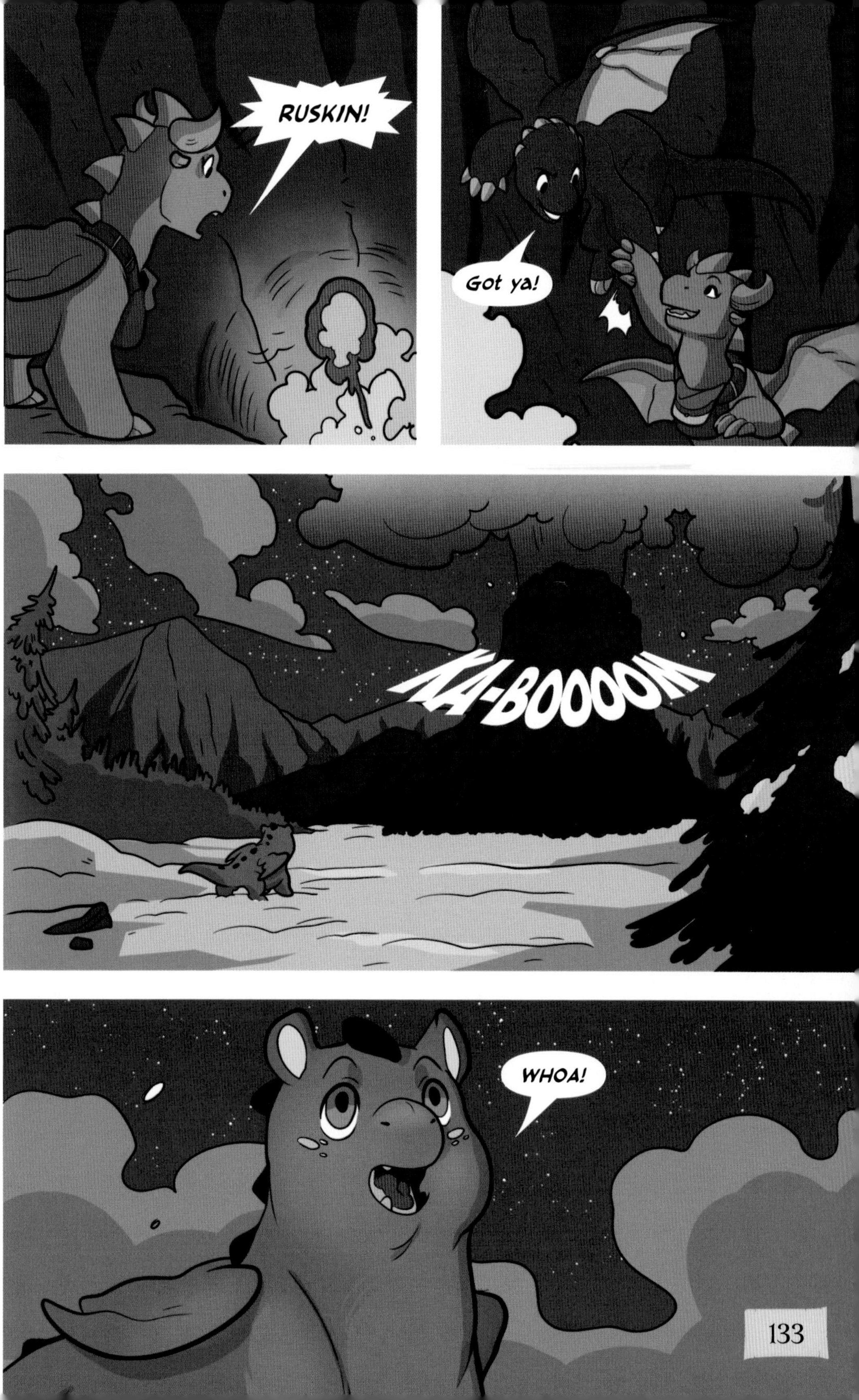
RUSKIN!
Got ya!
KA-BOOOOM
WHOA!

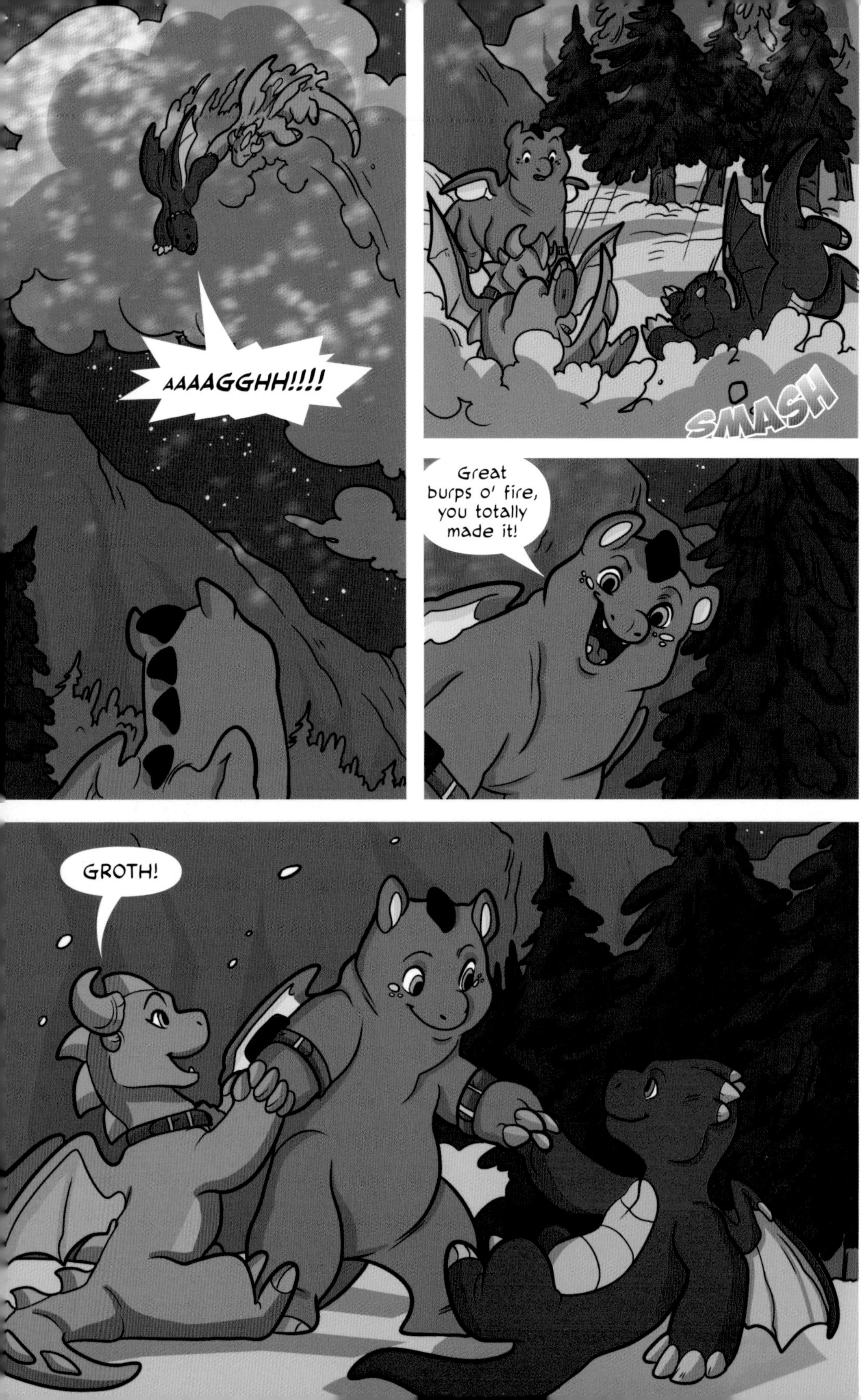
AAAAGGHH!!!!
SMASH
Great burps o' fire, you totally made it!
GROTH!

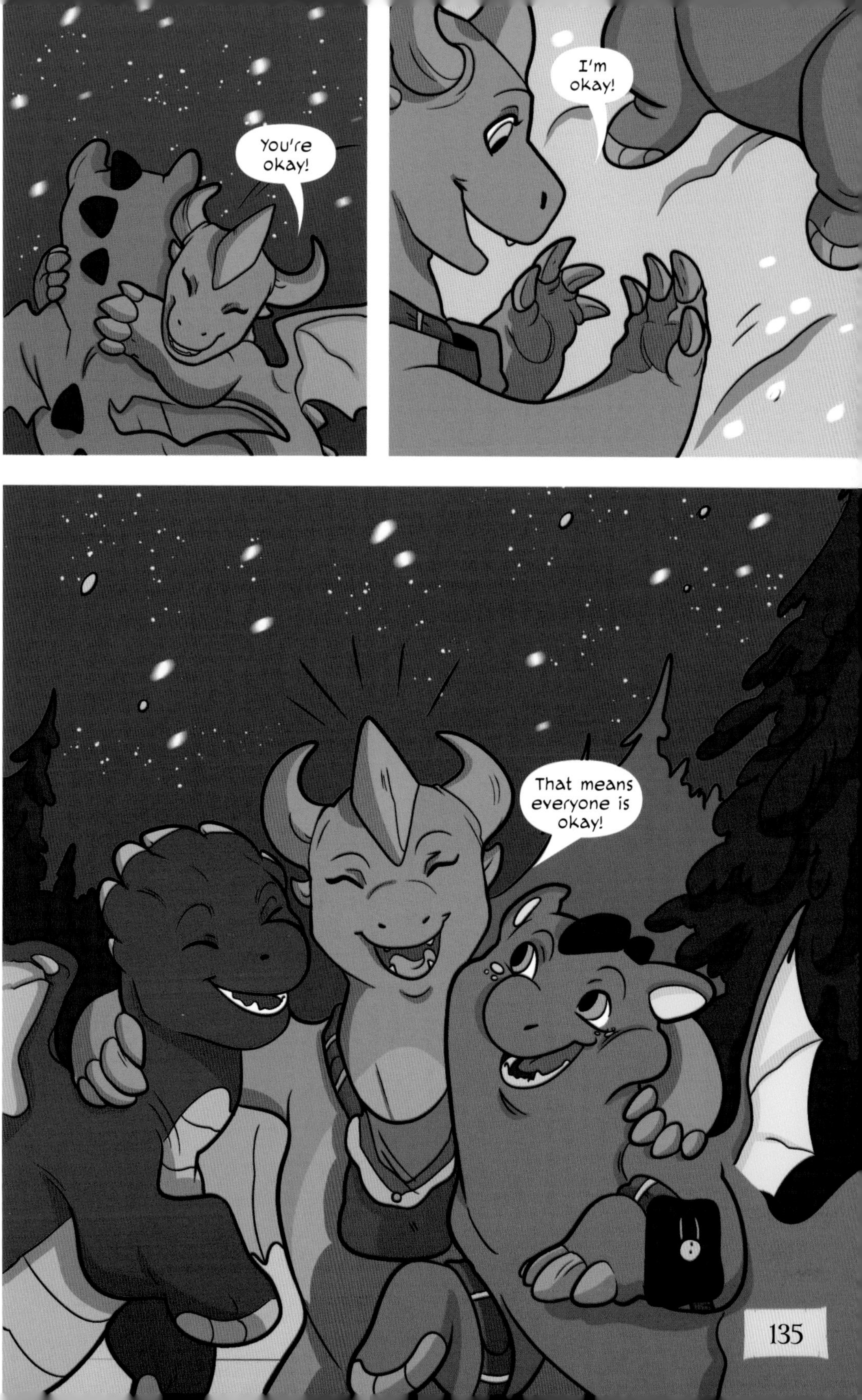
You're okay!
I'm okay!
That means everyone is okay!

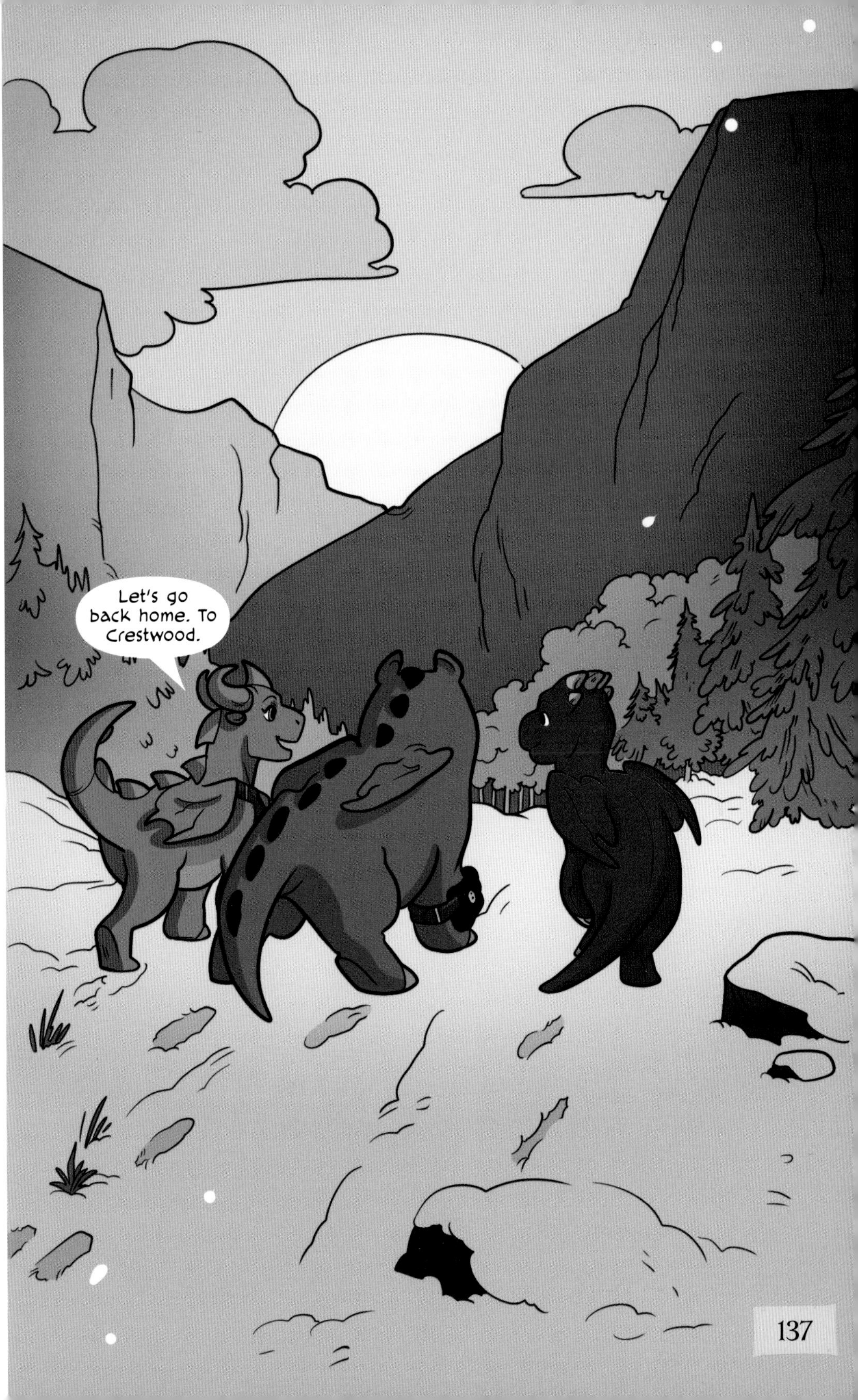
Let's go back home. To Crestwood.

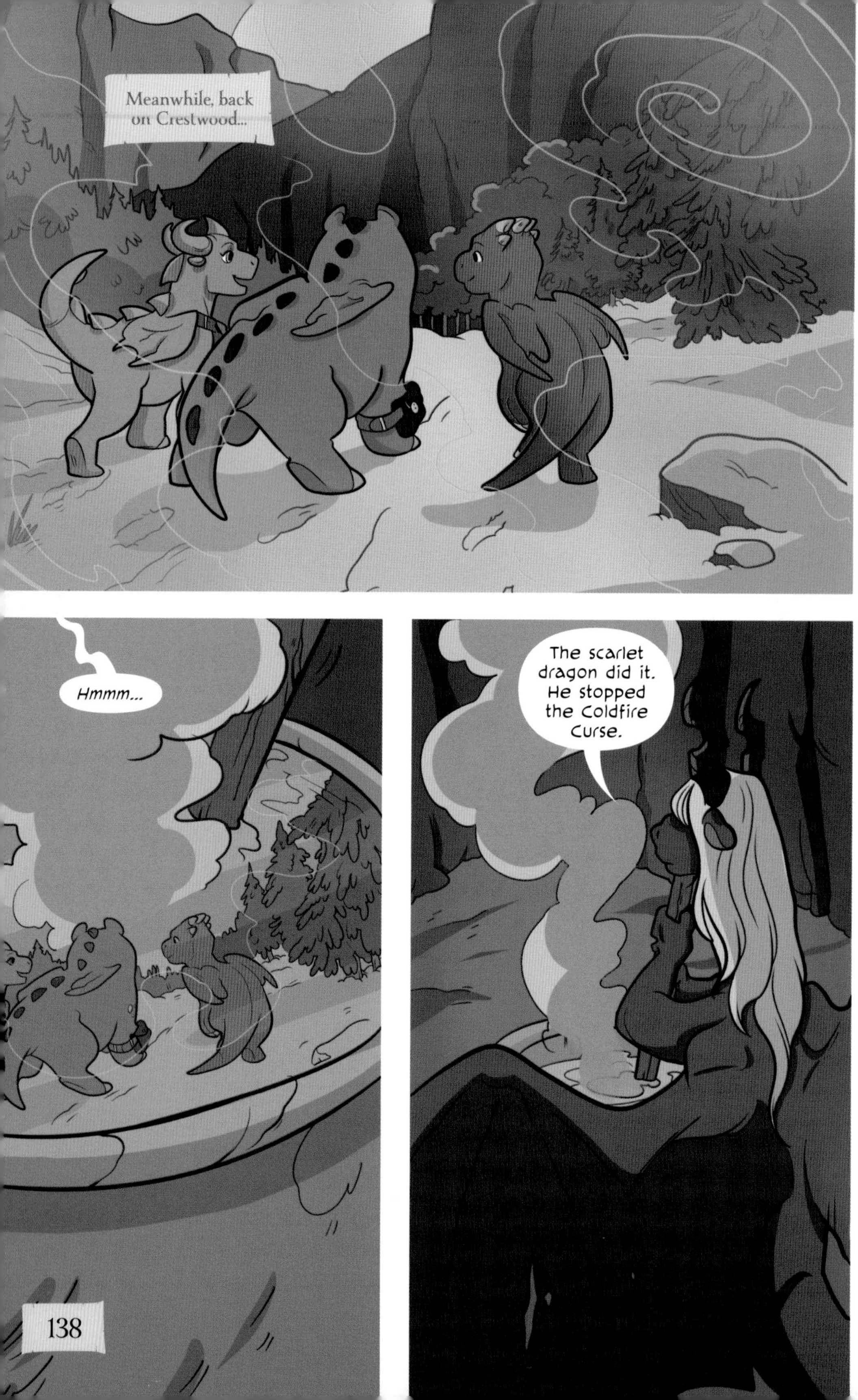
Meanwhile, back on Crestwood...
Hmmm...
The scarlet dragon did it. He stopped the Coldfire Curse.

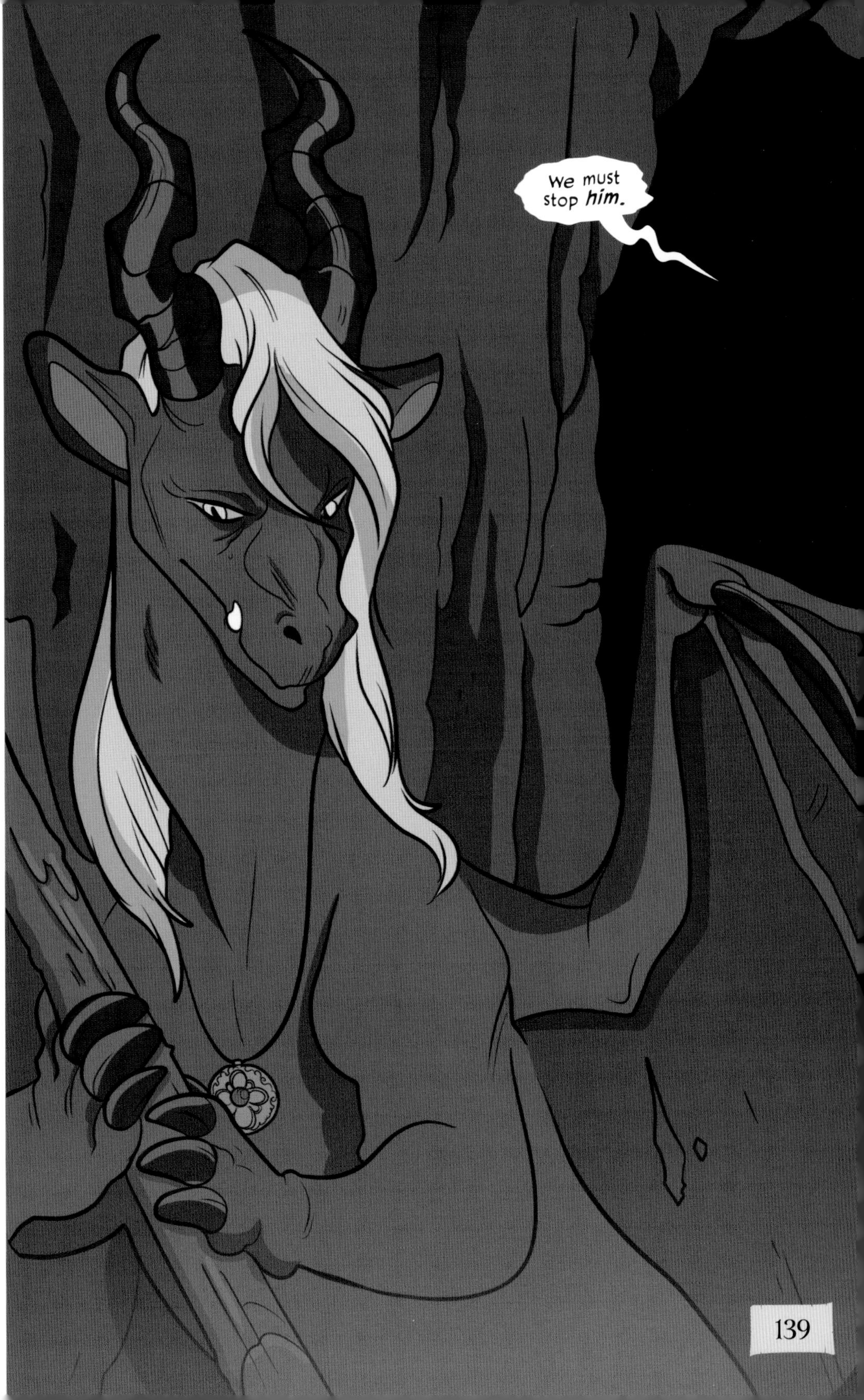
We must stop *him.*

What's in store for Ruskin and his friends next? Find out in . . .

Graphic Novel
DRAGON KINGDOM
of Wrenly
SHADOW HILLS

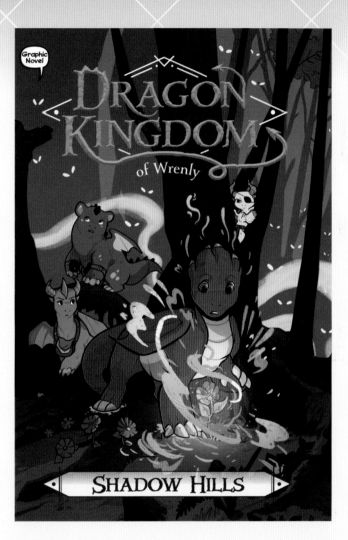

Turn the page for a sneak peek . . .

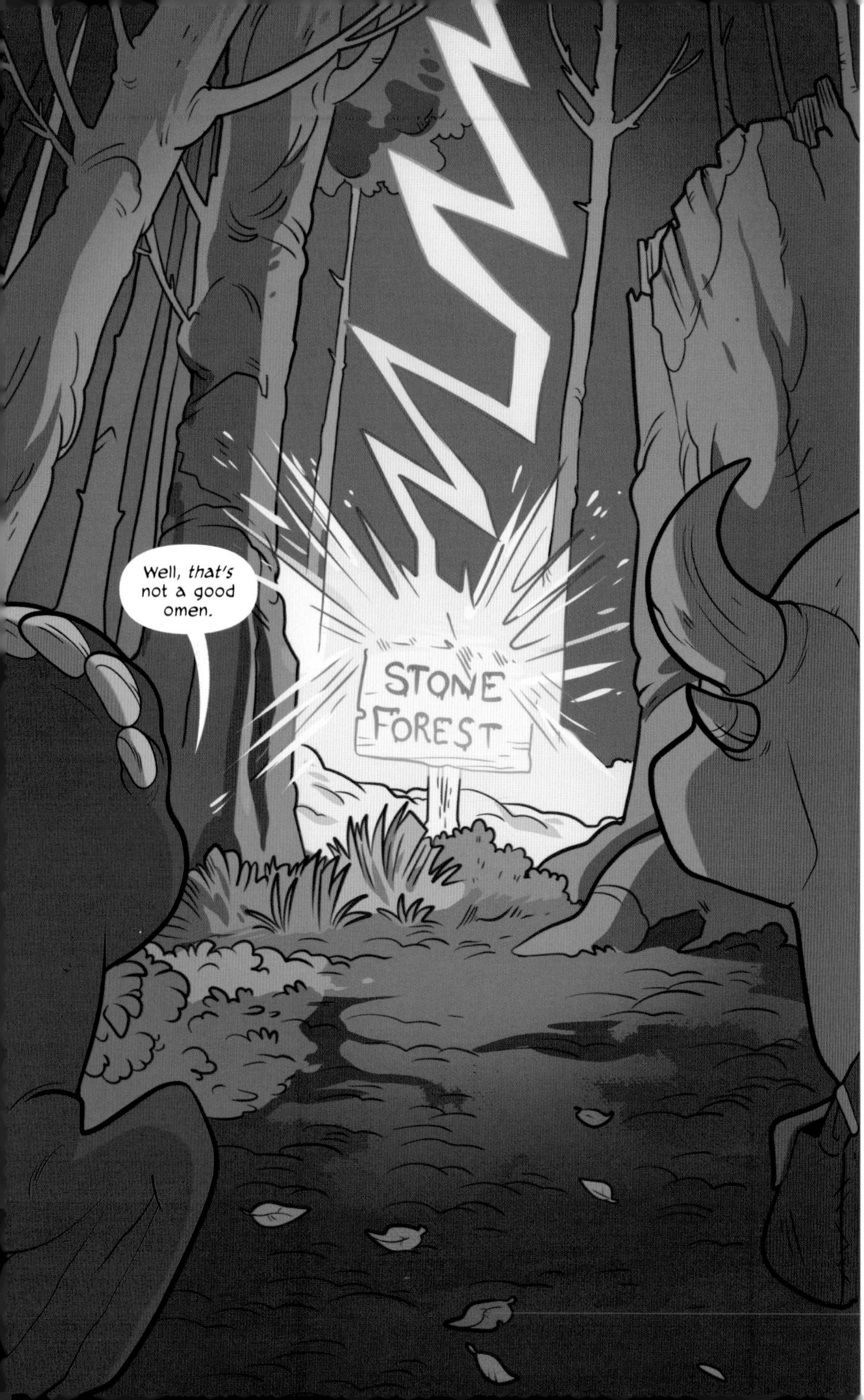
Well, *that's* not a good omen.
STONE FOREST

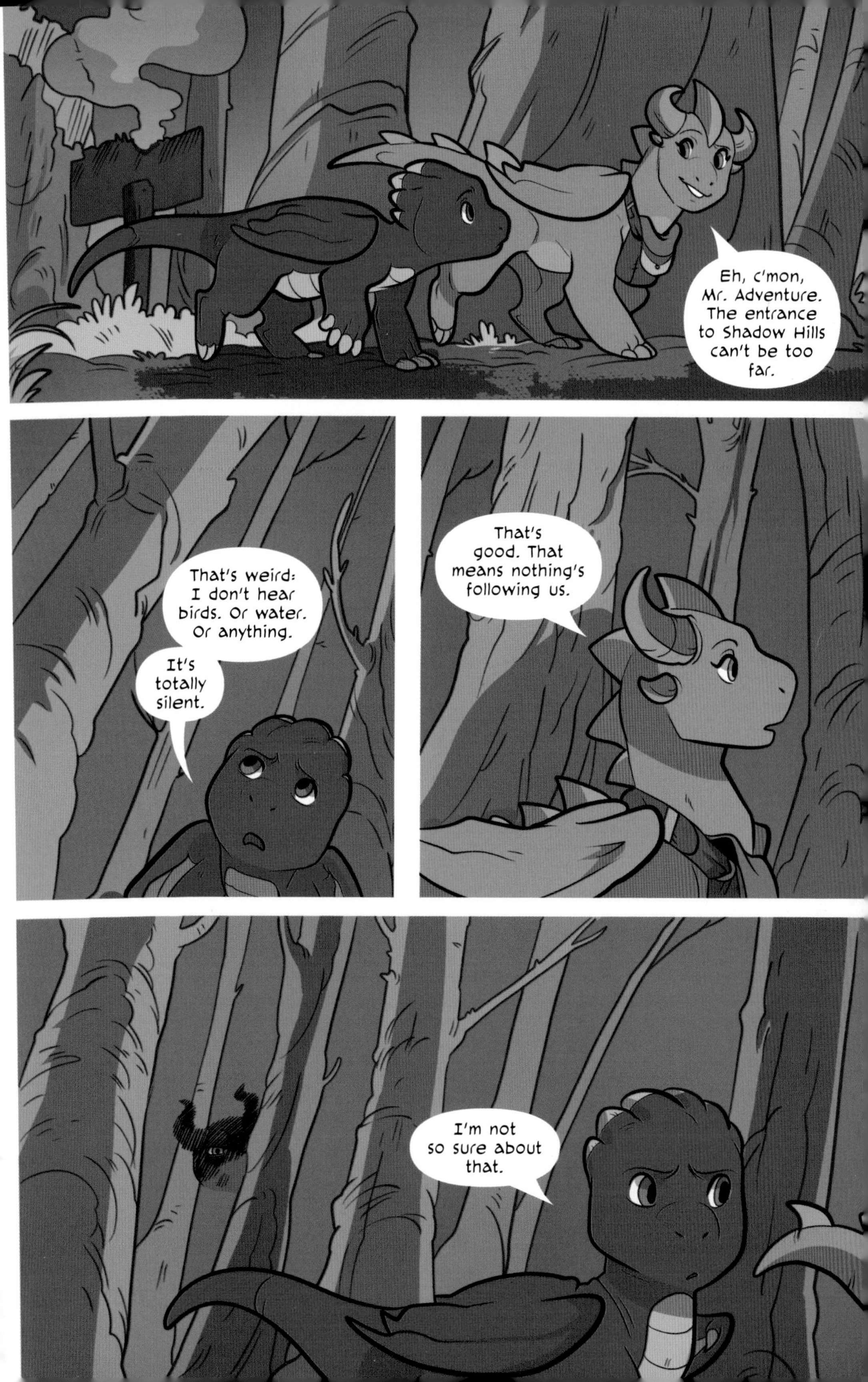

Eh, c'mon, Mr. Adventure. The entrance to Shadow Hills can't be too far.
That's weird: I don't hear birds. Or water. Or anything.
It's totally silent.
That's good. That means nothing's following us.
I'm not so sure about that.